D1607957

The Seraphim Kill

The Seraphim Kill

P. B. Shaw

Walker and Company
New York

First published in the United States of America in 1994
by Walker Publishing Company, Inc.

Published simultaneously in Canada by Thomas Allen & Son
Canada, Limited, Markham, Ontario

Library of Congress Cataloging in-Publication Data
Shaw, P. B.
The seraphim kill / P. B. Shaw.
p.   cm.
ISBN 0-8027-3181-3
I. Title.
PS3569.H38424S47   1994
813'.54—dc20   94-37915
CIP

Printed in the United States of America
2 4 6 8 10 9 7 5 3 1

$\triangledown$

1

SHADID GARBER'S PLUMP body strained against his solemn, lawyer-in-the-courtroom suit. He bounced and jiggled behind Monk Smith's long strides with the tenacity of a midge glued to a horse's rump.

The church they were inspecting had been hollow and vacant for almost three years, since its parishioners had outgrown and discarded it. Thick crimson carpets had been rolled up and stored away, and sound echoed from marble floors and bounced around vast, empty spaces in a way that made the usually urbane Monk nervous. He suppressed a compulsion to whisper.

"I'm not sure . . ." He made an equivocal gesture with an elegant, well-cared-for hand. "It's larger than I thought."

He was lying, of course. He had never wanted anything so much in his life. Built in the late 1800s from the plans of a local architect who had once been to England, the church was bastardized Victorian Gothic. It had turrets and niches, plaster frescoes, pilasters and parterres. A vaulted ceiling rose over their heads. Lavish carved cherry wood paneled the walls and traced peaked arches surrounding windows colorful as roses in blowsy full bloom. The whole was somewhat kitschy and, to Monk, totally charming.

Shadid laughed. "You want it. Don't ever play poker with me, Monk. I can read you like the morning paper."

"Perhaps. If I take the place I must have a long-term lease. And Shadid—at half the figure you quoted. This building will cost a fortune to renovate for my purposes."

"Jeeesus . . ." The lawyer turned to face a radiant stained glass window of Christ Arisen and laughed nervously. "You're stealing money out of my pocket, you know that? When I bought this"—he made an ineffectual gesture, struggled without success for a definition, then continued bravely—"I was sure some other church group would snap it up right away, considering the location . . . how long *have* we had it, Beth?"

Beth Farraday, Garber's law partner, seemed not to hear. She reached out and trailed fingers across the back of a pew. Her normally keen eyes seemed out of focus.

Garber broke the awkward silence. "No matter. Hell, Monk, you've got me over a barrel. I need to do something. Buildings shouldn't stay empty. Damn miracle it hasn't been vandalized. You ought to be ashamed to make such an offer, but you've got a deal."

Now Beth spoke, her voice subdued. "I went to church here a long time ago." She lifted her hand from the pew, inspected it, and brushed dust away. "I was fourteen when my parents died in a plane crash, Monk. I lived with an aunt after that—we were here every time they opened the doors. My brother Kent, too."

Garber grinned up at his junior partner. She topped his five-foot-six frame by at least five inches. "Kent? I bet he hasn't set foot in a church since he's been old enough to tell you and your aunt to mind your own business."

Beth gave him a cool look. "Why do you say that?"

"Hell, I didn't mean anything. Medical students are all atheists, aren't they?"

She shrugged and turned away.

When he talked to Beth, the bombastic little lawyer changed from caricature into human being. Monk thought about what he knew of them.

Garber had hired her as a receptionist when she was eighteen, an orphan with a twelve-year-old brother. In no time she was his personal assistant. Then she vanished, to rejoin the firm five years later as a full partner.

Monk worked with Beth in a local theater company; they had become friendly over several seasons. She told him Garber had not only financed her schooling, he'd paid her salary during the five years. No hanky-panky—just the understanding she'd come back to the firm when she finished. Monk supposed even the most confirmed sons of bitches were afflicted with odd pockets of decency. They said even Hitler liked dogs.

Beth touched his shoulder. "Still with us on Planet Earth, Monk?"

"Sorry." He raised a hand to indicate a circle of stained glass windows. "I was just wondering about these. Do they remain in the building?"

Garber pointed to the stained-glass Christ behind the altar. "I've sold that one. It'll go as soon as I find someone smart enough to take it out. The rest stay."

Monk was relieved. "The rest" were smaller and much less militantly religious, mostly flowers and animals with an occasional scripture quotation scrolled across. Nothing to interfere with his purposes.

"So—when do you want to sign the lease?"

Monk took a deep breath. What the hell. Nothing ventured . . .

"I'll need the whole property—grounds and parsonage included."

Garber waved an expansive hand. "That's understood. Beth'll have the papers ready tomorrow." He sighed. "I should have had better sense than to buy a thing like this."

"You bought it because it was cheap and you thought you were getting away with something," Beth said affectionately. "Now get out of here; you're due in court at one-thirty. Monk will give me a ride to the office."

At mention of the hallowed halls of justice, Shadid straightened his tie and buttoned his coat. "I'm off, then." He waggled a finger at Monk. "You needn't think you'll talk my partner out of any extras. She's tougher than I am."

Later, walking to the car, Beth pointed out a handsome

old brick apartment building across the alley. "We'll soon be neighbors if you lease, Monk. Shadid bought that, too. We're renovating to move the firm there."

The words were friendly, but Monk thought her voice seemed cool.

An old woman came out of the apartment building as they watched. At first he thought she was pulling an obstinate dog, but when the creature finally appeared he saw a large, battered tomcat wearing a red harness. He nodded at the pair. "What happens to them? Are you and Garber tossing old ladies and kitties into the street?"

Beth laughed. Perhaps he had imagined the coolness.

"Everyone moved without a whimper—except Miss Maude Mae Haslip, there, who calls herself 'a spinster lady.' She won't budge. I'm beginning to like the old bat. I told Shadid we should let her stay. Good public relations, and we can spare the room."

They watched as the tomcat, his dignity insulted by leash and harness, stalked behind his mistress with a filthy look on his face. As woman and cat progressed, several elderly people paused in their own walks to visit. They cast furtive glances toward Monk and Beth.

Monk knew they made a striking couple—never mind that he was twenty years older, and his feelings toward her definitely platonic. He was a tall, well-built man with a pleasantly rugged face; and she, almost equally tall, a slim woman with brilliant gray eyes and thick, shiny brown hair pulled with severe elegance into a single French braid.

No admiration showed in the closed, watching faces.

"Natives don't seem too friendly."

Beth shook her head as she climbed into the passenger seat of his old Bentley. "That's just the beginning. Wait till they find out what you're going to do with their neighborhood church."

"If the neighborhood was so proud of that building, why did they desert it and build themselves a modern megalith two miles away?"

Beth's chuckle had a weary note. "Not fair, and you know it. Many of the people around here aren't of that denomination, and probably haven't even been inside the doors. But it's 'their' church just the same. A fixture on the landscape."

Monk absently muttered something that sounded like "Yes, well . . ." He felt uneasy. Beth had a point. Just how much resentment would there be, when people saw the church reincarnated?

2

AT FIRST THE Seraphim's clientele ran the same as any trendy new nightclub; but over a period of time it inexorably became a gay hangout. The straights who came were there to gawk and gossip.

What could Monk have done differently? He wondered about it months later, at five-thirty on a Friday evening, while checking stock with his bartender-cum-bouncer, Frannie Da Sorta.

"We're low on vodka. And we'd better have a gallon of light rum. We can't wait for a delivery; send Ned to the liquor store when he gets here." Monk rubbed his forehead. "I've got a bad feeling about this shindig tonight, Frannie. I wish it were over."

The old prizefighter shook his bald, knobby head. His eyes, slitted almost closed by scar tissue from too many right jabs, looked sad. "How come you're doing this drag queen deal, boss? It ain't your kind of scene."

Monk nodded. "You're right. Somebody thought it up on Archie's birthday, a couple of weeks ago. We had a party at the parsonage. Champagne flowed a bit too freely."

"I wish you'd quit calling your digs 'the parsonage,' boss. Don't sound right. It's—it's—" Frannie fumbled for the word.

"Sacrilegious? But it *was* a parsonage. Anyway, someone suggested a drag party, and the whole damn bunch went wild. I heaved buckets of cold water at the idea, but it was like trying to put out the Chicago fire with a water pistol."

"Archie wanted you to do it."

Monk pulled at his earlobe and made a face. "Yeah."

"Archie's got no business sense—he don't know what's fitting in a place like this. You should have told him no."

"Of course I should. But you know how sick Archie's been. Goddamn mononucleosis, and everyone in the goddamn city thinks he has AIDS. Do you know what he did? Tacked an affidavit from his doctor on the door, one night."

"You still shoulda told him no."

Monk picked up a towel and polished an imaginary spot on the mirror behind the bar. "Frannie, I've been afraid he might commit suicide. That was the first time in six months he's been excited about anything. I couldn't shoot him down."

"He comin' over?"

Monk threw the towel on the floor. "No," he said bleakly. "He's run a high fever the last couple of days. Flu, the doctor said. With mono, your whole system gets run down."

Frannie reached over and touched Monk's arm. "Hell, boss. We'll get through this. In a few hours it'll be over with. Right?"

Monk nodded, but apprehension made a tight fist in his stomach. He couldn't afford trouble. The High Bluff Historical Homeowners' Society, slavering with fury about this "desecrated" church, watched for a chance to close down the Seraphim with the rapacity of a chicken hawk after a tasty pullet.

He grinned at Frannie. "One good thing. The weather's supposed to turn to pure shit in the next couple of hours. Maybe nobody'll come."

How wrong could you get? Four hours later, as if the wind and sleet had added a fillip of derring-do, the place was jammed with undulating, flamboyant bodies. Monk was raking in money, but that didn't help the apprehension that gnawed his gut.

The crowd was nearing capacity. Very soon he would have

to begin turning people away. Please God they wouldn't start a brawl in the parking lot.

Please God. Hah. As if he'd listen.

Monk moved toward the door as three men he recognized entered. They'd been around before—well dressed, discreetly behaved. This time two of them looked the same as usual. They snagged an out-of-the-way table and settled back to watch, their faces supercilious masks.

The third was the one who worried Monk. He was wearing an evening dress.

A man in his position should know better. If he were recognized by the wrong people his career would be shot to hell, and the Seraphim could go down in flames with him, Monk thought bitterly.

Maybe he could reason with the other two, get them to take their buddy home.

He started toward their table but was swept up in a wave of boisterous friends. He lost sight of the third man. Later he saw him again, talking quietly with someone in a corner. Monk looked at his watch. In an hour he could close. Possibly everything would be all right, after all.

$\triangledown$

3

MAUDE MAE HASLIP sat bolt upright in bed and clutched her chest.

"My glory, cat, what a god-awful howl. You want to give a body a fit?"

Once her heart stopped trying to leap out of her chest and she calmed a mite, Maude Mae figured out what possessed Duke. Outside, wind howled like a soul in purgatory. Sleet flung itself against the windows and walls of her apartment, noisy as she remembered Pa's old twelve-gauge when he blasted off at a ferret in the henhouse

Wily and scarred veteran of alley warfare he might be, but Duke cut up like a puling kitten when it stormed. He went daft. Maude Mae cooed soothing nonsense and reached to pull his rangy orange body against her breast, but she was too slow. He leaped from the bed with an outraged yowl.

Resigned to the chase, she switched on her bedside lamp and reached for slippers and robe. Out from the warmth of a down comforter her thin body flinched. She scuttled after the big cat.

"Come back here, you miserable feline, you mangy bag of fur. It's only sleet." The coax in her voice made love-words of insults.

Duke ignored her. With small, battered ears flattened against his head, he dashed from window to window, intent on finding the intruder.

House slippers flapping, Maude Mae trailed. It *was* a nasty storm. She wanted back in her bed.

"You're an old cat, Duke, and I'm an old woman. Now stop that foolishness and come here."

Duke ignored her. Up, down, up, down; then in a north window overlooking the alley, he stopped. The outraged howl became a chattered hiss as he crouched on the sill.

Maude Mae sank gratefully into an adjacent chair and began to stroke his bristling back.

"You *are* an old fool, if you think I'll fall for that. I won't look." Her tone was more bravado than conviction.

The apartment she had occupied for almost fifty years was no longer the safe, neighborly haven it had been—not since that law firm gobbled it up, paid tenants to leave, and began tearing everything to thunder to make their blasted offices.

Maude Mae had held out. She had her lease, and she was going to stay until they dragged her out feetfirst.

To be fair, that girl lawyer in charge of the project seemed to have come around to her side.

"All right, Miss Haslip. I'll try to persuade Mr. Garber to let you stay. Just you and Duke keep a low profile. Can you manage that?"

Hunh. Whatever a low profile was.

When the workmen left at night the building creaked and crackled with emptiness. Lately Maude Mae had resorted to patent medicine sleeping pills and a shot of Scotch before she went to bed. Even that didn't always work.

But tonight she was really groggy. She scrunched up her eyes and rubbed them with the back of one fist as she reached to scoop the cat out of the window.

Duke was an immovable lump. He dug claws into the soft wood of the sill.

"Not one damn thing in that alley but garbage cans, you old villain. I won't look."

She did, though. With a hand that vexed her by not being quite steady, she pushed back the lace curtain and peered into the sleet.

A car was parked against the dark mass of fence, trees, and building across the alley. Incredibly, two people were standing outside it, visible in the dim glow of a security light.

Maude Mae clicked her tongue and turned away. Signs were posted all along that alley, and they were clear. No one was allowed to park there. *No one.* But ever since that big duded-up man—some said he looked just like the fella who played the vampire in "Dark Shadows"—ever since he bought High Bluff Presbyterian and all those goings-on started up over there . . .

Above the noise of the sleet she heard a cry. She lifted the curtain again, and saw one of the figures sink to the ground. It was a slow-motion thing, unreal, as if someone stuck a nail into an inner tube and all the air oozed out.

The other human shape bent briefly over the still shadow on the ground, then disappeared into the car, whose cold engine came to life with a cough of protest. The car nosed out of the alley and disappeared.

Maude Mae watched the shape on the pavement for a long time. It didn't move. Finally she fetched her glasses.

It was a person, all right. A woman in a long, pale dress, lying on her back. Must have passed out, Maude Mae figured. She'd freeze, is what she'd do; unconscious in that hellacious sleet. Reckon why her friend—or husband—would leave her like that?

"Maybe it isn't real," she told Duke.

The cat, who had calmed as soon as he saw his alarm taken seriously, now washed his belly, hind leg waving in the air.

"Listen, Duke. A prank is what that is down there. One of those big dolls. Life-size, they are. I've seen 'em at the shopping mall."

Duke, who had started on another section of mottled yellow fur, stopped and focused a green-eyed glare at Maude Mae.

"Oh, drat you, I know I'm talking nonsense. Jokes like that're only done where there's a bunch of people to fool, not in an alley on a night that's plumb ripe for Satan's mischief. With all the goings-on in that heathern place across the alley—anything could happen. Down there's a human being, Duke, and it's my duty to call the police."

Still she hesitated, pacing the room.

"They'll think I'm a crazy old biddy, seeing spooks in shadows. All right, all right, I gotta do it. If there's any life in that thing down there, it'll be froze to a puddin' in an hour."

She picked up the phone and dialed 911.

$\triangledown$

4

"WOMAN DOWN IN the alley between Eighteenth and Nineteenth on North Jefferson Boulevard, west side."

The call, issued from Communications at 0135, was a welcome diversion to rookie patrol officer Joanne Lindstrom. She keyed her mike.

"Twenty-four Alpha, Fifth and Montana. On our way."

"Twenty-four Alpha. There's an ambulance en route." Communications gave her the time and incident number. Joanne jotted them down and accelerated, taking care not to skid on the ice. Before her cruiser reached the end of the block she heard her shift lieutenant report on the same call. He was farther from the scene; Joanne knew that she and her FTO would arrive first.

Her field training officer, Master Patrolman Jed Duckett, sat beside her, a two-hundred-twenty-pound lump of righteous disapproval. Duckett's bitch against women officers was infamous. This was her first night to ride with him. Things had not gone well.

The shift had been slow and deadly dull, as they often were in nasty weather. Duckett hadn't helped. No small talk, no police gossip, nothing but stony silence. She'd been ready to jump out of her skin by the time they caught a call.

Her mind kept replaying the incident, as if she could make it come out different. Drunk adolescent boy, filthy and shoeless, had built himself a healthy bonfire under a low-hanging viaduct. Joanne was at the stage in her training when the FTO rode as an observer only, except in emergencies.

She approached the boy alone, desperately conscious of the omnipotent Duckett. Two steps out of the car she realized she hadn't asked for a fire truck to handle the blaze.

Then there was the boy. Alone, and for whatever reason shelterless in this vicious weather, he was dressed in a ragged shirt and jeans so tattered and filthy they were almost unrecognizable. Joanne felt pity.

He watched her, smiling foolishly, his dark head bobbing to some internal tune. When she drew near he stood and held out his hands.

"Hey, officer, I'm cool—"

Fatal sympathy made her careless. Suddenly he lunged. She fell hard on her back, the boy on top of her.

Tripped out as he was, it had been easy to dislodge him and pin his arms before Duckett, galvanized out of the warm car, arrived to help, but there was scant satisfaction in that.

She glanced at him now, knowing his fingers fairly twitched to write up the incident. Ass. Good luck catching me out like that again, you sexist bastard.

The cruiser's headlights picked up the woman's body as soon as Joanne nosed it into the alley. EMS was already there. As she watched, two figures carrying equipment backed carefully out of the area.

"They're following protocol." Duckett amazed her by remarking on someone's actions with approval. "There was a time we had a shitload of problems with those people. Fouled up crime scenes like you wouldn't believe." He sneezed and blew his nose.

"You got a dead'n on your hands," he continued, commenting on the obvious. The EMS techs were packing to leave.

Not sure what to make of this deluge of conversation, Joanne shrugged into her yellow slicker, got out of the car, and walked carefully toward the white-rimmed figure. The sleet had lessened, but her shoes crunched in an inch of grainy ice.

One of the emergency crew, a slim girl who had thrown

dress code to the winds and was enveloped in what looked like something snatched off her grandma's feather bed, spoke.

"We ran a tape on her. Nothing. She's all yours."

Joanne knelt beside the body. She remembered from her training that sometimes, exposed to cold weather, people survived with wounds that ought to be fatal. This woman hadn't been lucky.

Sleet filmed the face. The eyes were caked. There was a vicious, vertical slash from beneath the nose to the bottom of the chin, severing both upper and lower lips. Ice covering that area was stained, as though someone had run amok with a tube of hideous brown-red lipstick. What had obviously been a lavish and expensive blond wig was now soaked and bedraggled. It had slipped, allowing a few strands of colorless hair to escape onto the forehead.

Joanne stood for an overall view. The woman was dressed in a long, pale silk gown. It was torn at the chest, where ice had fused with blood to form a dark corselet. A fur coat was bunched under her. A beaded evening purse lay several feet from the right shoulder. Hands, bony and capable looking, clutched at her ravaged chest.

Another set of lights rounded the corner and crossed those of Joanne's cruiser. Backing carefully away from the corpse, she joined Duckett, who was greeting the shift lieutenant.

"Lieutenant Grimes?" Joanne broke in. "She's dead, sir. EMS just left. Appears to be a homicide. Her dress is torn, and there's blood all over her upper torso."

"All right—Lindstrom, is it? Get tape from the trunk of my car and secure the scene."

He turned to Duckett. "Jed, will you notify homicide, the ME, and the tech people while I have a look?"

Joanne pulled the trunk release on Grimes's car, removed the yellow spool, and began to play out tape. Inside the other car, she could see Duckett on the mobile phone.

She felt eager and giddy, like a race horse at the starting gate. Her first homicide. So this is what it was like, this burst of adrenaline, the half-guilty exhilaration. Warm, sweet blood flowing in her veins, while someone else lay dead and mutilated. She had never felt more alive.

She heard a crunch of tires and looked up. Two men got out of a gray Crown Victoria. Joanne felt a stab of disappointment. After all, this wasn't her body, her case. She guessed that from this point on she would be the lowest of the low, ignored or given some dull, mindless job.

The homicide detectives had arrived.

$\triangledown$

5

DETECTIVE LIEUTENANT ABE Rainfinch had been called out of bed in the middle of the night, into a hell of a storm, to view a corpse.

Nothing could have suited him better.

He was on call and April wasn't, so they'd been at his house. A few months earlier leaving a warm fire, a soft bed, and April Morgen would have been intolerable.

Things had changed.

Rainfinch set a thermal cup precariously on the dash and guided his car down the long drive. He lived less than a mile from the crime scene, but he wouldn't break any speed records getting there. He took a sip of coffee, thick and hot as a lava flow, and thought about April.

She still drugged his senses—skin that glowed in the dark like white phosphorus, satin hair the color of taffy, the clean, subtle fragrance that enveloped her—so sexy, so damn beautiful.

Stop that.

Why the hell did she have to be a cop? He'd told her how he felt about that from the beginning.

"The day I graduated from the academy and hit the streets, I promised myself never to date a woman officer. It's too complicated. This is a dangerous, treacherous, mean damn job. I don't need to worry about a woman I love getting beat up, or stabbed, or shot."

She didn't flinch. "Then stay away from me. I'm a cop. I love it. I'm going to be one for at least the next twenty years."

He'd been with the department eight years when they got acquainted. She'd just been promoted to detective and drawn Special Projects, the undercover branch, as her first assignment. Abe had been in Projects two years.

A gulp of coffee brought him back to the present. It had a bite like battery acid. He made a face and drank it down, seeking the jolt of caffeine.

His thoughts strayed again. He and April had worked together, shared a few close calls, and the inevitable happened. Danger, the ultimate aphrodisiac.

They'd had the sense to keep their relationship secret. Abe had "formal" dates with TV newswoman Melina Moriarty; April went out with Frank Homer, an assistant DA. Things rocked along in shaky parity until Rainfinch was promoted and transferred to Homicide-Robbery. Two months later April drew Homicide, directly under his supervision.

Everything went to hell.

April was from a cop family. Her dad was chief of detectives in St. Louis. She'd cut her teeth on war stories. Rainfinch, on the other hand, was the son of a symphony conductor. Which made him damn self-conscious about giving her orders.

Like a lot of other times, that had provoked tonight's fight.

"Abe, why can't you tell me I've screwed up without being such an ass? You don't treat the men that way."

"Bullshit. You wear your feelings on your shoulder." He knew she didn't.

"That's a crock. You sound like you're talking to the village idiot—"

Rainfinch remembered getting right in her face, yelling at her. "Stop whining. You want to be treated like a man, act like one, Jane Wayne, tough girl cop."

He braked for a red light; the rear end of the car shimmied like a two-bit stripper. Tonight the thermometer had dipped into the teens, but the balmy weather of the past few days had warmed the ground enough to turn the bottom layer of ice into a broken, treacherous mass. Lieutenant Abe

Rainfinch decided to put his problems with Detective April Morgen on hold and tend to business.

At the crime scene, sleet had subsided to a sullen mutter. The mouth of the alley was blocked by black-and-whites, a detective cruiser, and the medical examiner's green Ford. Rainfinch parked.

A little red Japanese car pulled up and slid to a stop, slinging a fan of ice. Melvin Crib, obnoxious motormouth from KSIR Radio, jumped out. "Lieutenant," he bleated, breaking into a skidding run.

From inside the yellow tape enclosure Rainfinch pointed a finger. "You, Melvin. Back off. Stay clear of the barrier. I won't talk to you yet."

As he joined his homicide detectives, the black technical investigations van pulled in.

Lou Curran and Danny Bent had caught the call. They stood like stage figures illuminated by the cruiser headlights, their faces emerging wraithlike from the steam of their breaths.

Danny was young, clever, and quick-witted, with a strong Cherokee-Choctaw face. Lou, slat-thin, with homely, pinched-together features and sparse gray hair, was in his late forties. He affected a sour cynicism that fooled no one who knew him.

"How did you guys get here so fast?" Rainfinch asked.

"When *I'm* on call, I shave, shower, and lay out nice, fresh clothes before I hit the sack," Danny answered. He jerked a thumb at Curran. "The old buzzard there never bathes or shaves. He puts on a clean shirt once a month. He's always ready."

Lou muttered a retort, but Rainfinch could tell his heart wasn't in it. Then the three of them stood silent, staring toward the corpse.

"Bitch of a night," Lou said.

More silence. It would not be articulated, but Rainfinch knew they shared the same anger. A living creature shouldn't die like that, torn and mutilated in an alley. Ice, ripping at your eyeballs, gouging your cheeks, filling your mouth . . .

Lou turned to Danny. "Okay, Boy Wonder." His voice was loud, as if he'd lost the trick of modulation. "Show the lieutenant your casebook."

Danny shrugged. "Not much in it, yet."

"Never mind. Who was the first officer on the scene?" Rainfinch asked.

Lou jerked a thumb. "Over there. Her name's Lindstrom—Jed Duckett's riding with her. She looks like a Girl Scout; these damn rookies get younger every year."

Rainfinch grinned. "Duckett, huh? She must be having a swell time. Has she started the crime scene log?"

"Yeah. She was tickled as a hound pup with a soup bone when I asked her to do it. This is her first homicide."

"Can you remember your first, Lou?" Danny asked.

"Hell, yes. That's something you don't forget, no matter how long you're a cop."

As Rainfinch walked away he heard Curran say, "Your turn to lead, Boy Wonder. Get some writing in the casebook to show your cousin, there."

Curran knew better, but some people did believe he and Danny were kin. Many of those, the ones who didn't know his very British father, thought Rainfinch was an Indian name. Actually, his Cherokee blood came through his mother, Julia Charbonnet.

Carefully he approached the broken object that in its destruction had become a center of passionate attention. He followed tracks already made. Except for a narrow passageway, the gray carpet of ice around the body was undisturbed.

Medical Examiner Arthur Deethe stood. A slight, bearded man with wolfish incisors, Deethe always moved with an air of apprehension, as if anticipating another of the countless bad jokes about his surname. He had almost given up protesting *"Deethe,* not death."

"Hello, Lieutenant." He gestured at the corpse. "Pretty mess. Well carved. Best I've seen since the tattooed biker in miniskirt and handcuffs. By the way, it *is* a man."

"A man—" Rainfinch broke off and glanced to his left at the Gothic form of the church building behind its iron fence and trees. "I don't know why I'm surprised. Except that she—he—looks respectable."

Deethe shrugged. "An old queen with good taste. Hasn't been here long. I understand you've got an eyewitness."

"I didn't know that. Came over to look at the body and see what you had to say before I got details from Curran and Bent."

"Don't get excited," the ME warned. He gestured toward the one lighted window in a building across the alley. "Old lady up there. Curran couldn't get much out of her."

"Don't sound so pleased about it."

Deethe laughed, his incisors gleaming. "You love whodunits."

"Who spread that rumor? It's too early to expect a mystery, anyway. Fifty people may have seen him in a row with his lover."

Rainfinch walked back to the detectives, who were talking with the patrol supervisor. He joined them and greeted Lieutenant Bill Grimes. He knew Bill well; they'd ridden together in patrol during their rookie days.

"Things are not what they seem, gentlemen. We've got a carved-up old queen in society dowager's clothing," Rainfinch told them.

Curran simpered and repeated "society dowager" under his breath in a finicking voice. Rainfinch ignored him.

As they discussed the case, crime scene people quietly went about their business. Lights were set up, photographs taken, a grid search begun. He saw WROX-TV's mobile news van pull up. The crew tumbled out. Their rookie stood guard to keep the newsies behind her yellow barrier. They questioned her briefly, then a tall, shapely figure emerged from the van and spotted Rainfinch. She beamed a thousand-watt smile and waved. He lifted two fingers in a gesture that was half greeting, half warning.

"Moriarty the Magnificent," said Danny Bent with feeling.

Rainfinch's mind was on something else. So far they had no ID on the body.

Oklahoma City was small enough that any experienced cop knew the flagrant party queens. Even though there was facial mutilation, the detectives agreed none of them had ever handled this one before—at least not in drag.

The clothes worried him. Too expensive. The dark fur coat was stained and bedraggled, but blatantly the real thing. And the dress looked as if it had come from the Salon Room at Miss Ballard's. Nothing tarty; this lady would have been right at home in the blue-haired widows' section, Sunday afternoon at the symphony.

Money. Scandal, sensation, media nipping at the department's heels. Not a favorite Rainfinch scenario.

He spoke to a technician. "If you're through photographing, let me see that purse."

"Sure, Lieutenant. Come inside the van, why don't you? It's a helluva lot warmer, and the coffeepot's full."

The black van was set up to be an emergency command post. It had its own generator to supply portable lights. Cases, boxes, and bags held all sorts of esoteric equipment. Plastered on the inside walls were irreverent posters and cryptic messages, interspersed with a few genuine pieces of pertinent information.

Rainfinch and the detectives crowded around a countertop. He stripped off bulky leather gloves, flexed his fingers, and pulled on a pair of thin plastic ones.

The men watched with the intent curiosity of coyotes transfixed at a rabbit hole as he opened the queen's purse and retrieved a wallet. Cold fingers awkward, he found a driver's license in a windowed insert. Carter Hall. Age fifty-six.

Behind that was a compartment containing business cards. Rainfinch extracted one and read, then tilted the small piece of cardboard so Curran and Bent could see.

"God a'mighty," Curran breathed. "The effing chief legal

counsel to the effing governor. Ain't this a purty deal."

Rainfinch returned the wallet to the purse, then pulled out a key ring with six keys. Two of them had plastic heads that let you know you were in the presence of a Mercedes owner. He dropped them back into the purse, which he then encased in a plastic bag, and sealed the top. He reached for the telephone as an evidence technician tagged and marked the bag. "I'll call Major Adamson."

"How about Chief Jurgen?" Danny Bent asked.

Lou Curran laughed. "Don't fret, Boy Wonder. Adamson'll handle that. Better him than us."

$\triangledown$

6

CLOTHES AND SHOES landed in a heap on a tousled bed in one of the Washington Vista Hotel's less opulent rooms. At six on a dreary Saturday morning Susan Elias, press secretary to Governor Max Sanden, was preparing to leave the National Governor's Conference.

In her high-pressure job, Susan often felt like a bundle of nerves held together by caffeine and flimflam. Now the shell of competence had been blasted to hell by an early telephone call that set her packing like a crazed thing for a sudden flight home. Her ears roared. Her chest felt as if King Kong were sitting on it.

She'd been excited about the conference—her first time at the National. A lot was at stake. Everyone knew her boss was a hot property. Young and bushy-tailed, Sanden was being compared to John F. Kennedy in his early years. But then, what bright young politico wasn't?

Max and his staff were putting out feelers: a vice-presidential nod in the upcoming election? Maybe an all-out run for the roses? Who knew?

Heady stuff for a press secretary not yet thirty years old. The governor liked her work. So did chief of staff Robert Friar.

"Did it seem too good to be true, Susan, love?" She muttered, stuffing a rolled-up mass of skirts, blouses, and underwear into a smart leather bag. "Well, that's because it was. 'Small-town reporter becomes press secretary to president before she's forty.' Damn that miserable ass, Hall. I hope he's roasting in hell right now."

She stuffed a hairbrush and makeup case into the bulging bag and answered a knock on the door. Orange juice was delivered by a waiter with a smile so mechanical Susan considered he might be an android. She stuffed a tip into his hand, signed the ticket, and pushed him out. The juice went down in one long gulp.

Dressed and packed, her bag following docilely on rollers, she descended to meet Friar.

He'd sounded like a bad movie version of a secret agent over the phone. "C. H. has been stabbed to death outside the Seraphim. In an evening gown."

"What? Robert, is this some kind of joke? Who the hell is C. H.?" She had peered nearsightedly at the bedside clock. "It's five-thirty. You've been drinking all night, haven't you?"

"Wake up and listen to me, Elias. Think about home. The Seraphim. *C.H. Think* about it."

Susan had felt the electric fist hit her diaphragm. "C-Carter—"

"Don't say anything. You've got to get back there and handle it. I can't leave."

"What the hell do you mean, handle it?"

He'd given her the flight time and said he'd meet her in the lobby. She could ask questions on the way to Washington National.

Susan had been on staff three years. She was hired as assistant press secretary. Four months ago, when Kevin Garrison left to hang out his shingle as a political consultant, she took his place. "Piece of cake," she told herself. "I write better than Garrison, and I can handle the slavering wolves as well as he did."

And she had. The legislature was out of session, not due back until January fifteenth. Most days the capitol press room was empty. Boy, would the honeymoon be over now. She felt like a hiker clinging to the side of a volcano as it began to erupt.

"Welcome back, ladies and gentlemen of the media. I'm sure you're all too polite to mention a slight embarrassment—our top legal eagle murdered while wearing drag. Could happen to anyone. Terrible tragedy. No one in this group is gauche enough to dwell on it, I'm sure."

She rubbed the back of her neck, where a tension headache throbbed. Waiting for the elevator, she burrowed in her purse for aspirin.

So nice of Carter to call everyone's attention to his aberration this way. If he had to get himself murdered, why couldn't he have had the decency to do it in the privacy of his own home?

Oh, Elias, that's cold.

But damn it, damn it, homosexuals in government were political hot potatoes—at least in Susan's part of the country, where "Bible Belt" and Moral Majority" were statements of fact, not dirty words.

Maybe it was good she'd been in Washington. Hall hated her, everyone knew it. She had no idea why. Did he think she was after one of his lovers? God knew—and Susan didn't really give a damn. Most of the time she was able to avoid him.

"At least they can't accuse me of doing him in," she muttered. Not that it wouldn't have been a pleasure.

In the limousine, Robert Friar gave her hug and a pep talk. His hazel eyes were somber behind round spectacles. The thick, rather long brown hair was totally awry.

There was something very sexy about Robert, and she was more than a little infatuated. Not handsome, he was brilliant and witty. Few people realized that beneath his low-key manner lay a very high-pressure man.

Robert had recently divorced. In the last few months he and Susan had begun to date. Nothing hot and physical, just public functions or an occasional movie. They were both career-oriented, she told herself. Neither had time for a heavy relationship.

Robert was a workaholic. Rumor had it that's why his wife, a demanding postdebutante, finally called it quits.

But Susan had to admit that even his fast embrace in the

limo flustered her. She tried to tune in on what he was saying.

"—need to contain the damage as much as possible. I haven't told the Big Max yet. He needs what sleep he can get."

"He knew—Robert, he had to know Carter was gay."

"We never discussed it. Carter and his family were heavy financial supporters in the first campaign. Before your time or mine, love."

"Oh, yes. The great, untouchable Hall family. His grand-father was a senator, and blah, blah, blah."

Robert looked attentive. "You two never got along, did you?"

"It wasn't a matter of getting along. He loathed me. Don't stare like that. Remember, I was *here*."

He laughed. "Even if you hadn't been, I can't picture you lurking in an alley to carve him up."

"Don't be too sure. At times the idea would have recom-mended itself. Oh, damn. I'm sorry. Tasteless crack. Rob-ert—what about the press? Has anything leaked?"

"Police Chief Jurgen says not. He'll try to hold off on a public identification until Big Max and I get home and hammer out some kind of a statement."

Susan nodded. "Okay, good. What do you expect me to do?"

"For now, deal with the cops. Jurgen says his detectives need to talk with someone on staff right away. After the governor and I get back, we'll circle the wagons." Robert shook back his hair and hunched his shoulders in a shrug.

Susan felt a pang of sympathy. She was, after all, only a spokesman. Big Max and Robert would have to call the shots.

The cab pulled to a stop in front of American Airlines. Robert squeezed her arm and gave her a fast peck on the cheek. "Keep us posted. See you later."

7

"SO LOU, YOU talked to the old lady who saw the killing. What do we have?" Chief Jurgen stood abruptly and walked toward the sliding glass doors that led to a balcony outside his office.

It was ten o'clock Saturday morning. Besides Jurgen, the group consisted of Rainfinch, Curran, Bent, Chief of Detectives Adamson, and Public Information Officer Clifford Stamps.

Rainfinch looked at Stamps through narrowed lids. He was bandbox neat. A small-boned man with hair and eyes the color of dried grass, he passed for the department's resident pseudoyuppy. Rainfinch thought he was an ass.

Stamps constantly yapped about his influence in high political circles. He assailed the social ladder with the zeal of a fundamentalist preacher in an opium den. Now he interrupted as Curran tried to explain that, so far, they didn't have very damn much.

"This is a bombshell," Stamps ranted. "It's got to be contained. I promised Robert Friar, Sanden's chief of staff—why wasn't I called to the scene, Rainfinch? How the hell can I deal with the press and the governor's office when I don't know what's going on?"

As a captain, Stamps outranked Rainfinch. In the chain of command, however, he had no authority over the detectives. Rainfinch answered, not trying too hard to hold down sarcasm.

"If the old queen had been wearing a sign around his neck

saying he was Sanden's legal counsel we'd have called you right away. Everyone knows you're just like that"— he crossed his fingers—"with the governor."

"Rainfinch, you—"

"Cut it out." Chief Jurgen turned away from the balcony. He was a tall, well-built man who worked out regularly at the police academy gym. Intelligent and able, he had risen to the top with only moderate use of the political infighting that always pervaded the upper ranks. "Stamps, hold it a minute. You can have your say later. Right now I want to talk to Adamson and Rainfinch."

Stamps grabbed a pitcher and poured himself a glass of water with an exasperated sigh. He drank it off and began a staccato pencil barrage on the table.

You're pushing it, Rainfinch thought.

Jurgen turned to the detectives. "I want an incident room set up immediately. Mark, what help will you need to staff?"

Major Mark Adamson glanced at Rainfinch. "Clerical people. I'll shift three or four detectives from Projects and Burglary, if necessary. Abe, I know your captain's on vacation—how's Homicide fixed? Is there another team who can help work this deal?"

"Well—we're busy as hell—as you know. There's Morgen, I guess."

"April Morgen? Who's her partner?"

"Mitchelson. He's off for three weeks."

"Okay, let's get going. You figure out manpower later," Jurgen said. "I want the tech and forensics people to understand this case has priority. Mark, Abe, we'll get you some clericals from Patrol. Activate the room, get your phone system going. Are the computers set up? Okay, get it done." He turned to Rainfinch. "What's your first move?"

"I have an appointment with Sanden's press secretary in two hours. She's flying in from Washington. Sanden and several of his top people are there for a governors' conference."

Jurgen grunted. "Too bad they didn't take the fruit fly with them."

Stamps couldn't contain himself. "I'm going along if you interview Susan Elias. I know her, you don't. And something else, Rainfinch. Who the hell has what information, at this point? You say Moriarty and her crew were at the scene, and that idiot Melvin Crib, from KSIR. How close a look did they get? Did they see it was a fag in drag? How the devil can I be expected to deal with these people if—"

"They didn't see anything but a distant view of a dress-clad figure killed during a sleet storm. But knowing Moriarty—she'll get suspicious fast if we stonewall her. And Stamps, you are *not* going with me to interview Susan Elias."

"The hell I'm not—"

"Rainfinch is right," Jurgen cut in. "You can talk to her later, Stamps, if you have to. But don't do or say anything to compromise the investigation. You got that?"

"What about the rest of the press? How do you expect me to hold them off?" Stamps didn't bother to hide his fury at the reprimand.

Jurgen brushed him off impatiently. "So far, all they know is we have a body. Nothing connects it to the governor's office."

"Word's already out around the department that an old queen in drag got offed. Rumors'll start about the rest. They always do," Stamps said.

"When that happens we'll deal with it—and God help any cop I catch running off at the mouth. Stamps, I want this understood. No media statements without my authorization. I want to know what you say before you say it." He looked around. "That cover everything? Okay, let's get busy."

The three detectives and their major formed a small knot as they left the room. Jurgen called out to Rainfinch. "Abe? Find out when the governor gets back. Tell Susan Elias we'll try to hold the media off until he's on the scene, but we can't guarantee anything."

Rainfinch lifted a hand in acknowledgment. "Yes, sir."

* * *

When Abe Rainfinch was in the third grade, Miss Wilding took her class on a field trip to the state capitol. Vaulted ceilings, marble steps and corridors, and an awed peek at the houses of the legislature in session had been major excitement for eight-year-olds. Now, wearing the cloak of cynicism that is as fundamental to a cop as the air he breathes, he still felt echoes of that childhood excitement as he circled the massive south steps to use the modest working entrance.

It was Saturday and state offices were closed, but tourists, tour guides, and a smattering of workaholics kept the place from being deserted. On the second floor, where a set of heavy bullet-proof glass doors separated the governor and his staff from pedestrian bustle, it appeared to be business as usual. Rainfinch remembered he'd heard that Sanden worked eighteen hours, six days a week. His people did the same, or they didn't last long.

The receptionist's desk was an island in a wide, thickly carpeted corridor. Offices opened off either side. He nodded a greeting toward the first door on the left, where he knew security people were manning video screens. A head appeared. One of the plainclothes state troopers, whom Rainfinch had seen around, said "Hey, Lieutenant, who let you in?" then abruptly disappeared.

Rainfinch introduced himself to the receptionist, a glorious black girl with a voice like spun honey.

"Miss Elias is expecting you, Lieutenant. I've already buzzed her assistant. Will you sit?" She indicated a clutch of silken chairs that stood in aloof splendor against the wall.

"No, thanks." Rainfinch pretended to study the portraits of past governors that lined the area. He was impressed with the young woman's composure. No gushing, no "Isn't it awful?" No tears, either.

A tall, thin girl shot through a set of double glass doors to his right. She had long, shiny, pale brown hair, and her smile showed braces on her teeth. "Mr.—Lieutenant Rainfinch?"

She stuck out her hand. I'm Cal—Calla Magee. Assistant press secretary. Susan's in her office. Come with me?"

She led him back the way she'd come, through a small conference room. On the far side, another door led into a narrow passage. They walked by open offices, passed through cubbyholes filled with file cabinets. Rainfinch realized he was being exposed to the bones of the governor's office, the private-access areas where staff could move about without entering the public arena of that vast central corridor.

The press secretary wasn't what he expected. He'd pictured one of those tall, attenuated jobs, with a brash manner and a Calvin Klein suit. Her voice would drip arrogance— after all, she was dealing with a dumb cop, wasn't she?

Here was a small, slim young woman, with an Orphan Annie crop of brown curls. She had a wide brow and a soft, expressive mouth. Her brown eyes were round, magnified behind dark-rimmed glasses. To be sure, she wore a navy pinstripe suit, with a white silk shirt and a heavy gold chain at the neck. The fit was perfect, revealing a well-curved figure beneath. Regulation attire for the successful career woman—but on Susan Elias it looked like a costume that wasn't quite comfortable.

She stood when Calla Magee ushered him in. "Lieutenant Rainfinch? Are you—you must be kin to—"

Rainfinch didn't let her finish. "Martin Rainfinch is my father. I'm the member of the family with no talent."

A scarlet flush moved up her cheeks as she reached out to shake his hand. "I'm sorry. I guess you get that question a lot. It's just—such an uncommon name. The maestro is a great friend of Governor Sanden's."

Her handshake was firm, but he felt a slight tremor when he touched her, like laying his hand on the flank of a skittish horse. "I know," he said dryly. "He mentions the governor frequently. 'Big Max,' I think his friends call him?"

Susan's laugh skated on the edge of hysteria. She controlled it quickly. "That's awful. Sounds like a gangster."

"Ms. Elias, I know you left your conference and flew in from Washington this morning. I appreciate what a shock you've had. There must be many things for you to attend to."

Another nervous laugh. "I'm sure you're right, but I'm damned if I know what they are—other than talk to the police—to you, that is."

Before he could comment she left her seat as if she'd been fired from a catapult. "Coffee. Do you need it as badly as I do? I'll just get some—it's right down the hall. Black?"

Rainfinch nodded and she disappeared, stirring the air with the scent of a faintly nostalgic perfume.

He looked around with a cop's intent curiosity. The office was small, but it did have an outside window; one of the full-length, arched ones that looked so impressive from outside. The walls were painted soft yellow and decorated with thumb-tacked photos of political events, most with whimsical, handwritten captions.

Her computer occupied a table just behind the desk; she could reach it by reversing her chair. Papers, press releases, and files crowded every flat surface, including a good portion of the floor. The marble windowsill supported three fat, smug plants with shiny leaves.

It was tiny, crowded but pleasant, obviously not a place to entertain members of the press. She must use one of the small conference rooms for that. He wondered why she had allowed him to penetrate her inner sanctum. Was it strategy—"Look, I'm laying all my cards on the table"?

She reappeared, carrying steaming mugs emblazoned with the blue-and-gold state seal. Rainfinch, who was sensitive to such things, hadn't heard her approach. He began to appreciate why the marble floors were cloaked in thick, sound-muffling carpet throughout the governor's offices.

He suspected there were people working all around him. Some, beyond partitions, were probably not ten feet away. Yet he couldn't shake off a sense of solemn, almost majestic stillness.

Susan gulped coffee, made a face, and took the initiative,

searching his face with a level stare. "What do you want to know, Lieutenant?"

He delayed answering long enough to create tension. He was in control of this exchange, not she.

"How long has Carter Hall worked for the governor?"

"Since Sanden was elected to his first term. Before, during that campaign—I guess he was unpaid staff." She picked up a file folder and offered it. "These are photocopies of everything pertinent in his personnel file. I thought it might help."

"Everything pertinent?"

She shrugged. "Everything, really. I don't know why I qualified it."

Rainfinch thumbed through the folder, then put it in his briefcase. "I'm sure you must have known Carter Hall well. Tell me about him." He was surprised to see a deep flush spread across her face.

"I, of course I know—knew—him. I mean, the staff isn't that large, we all know each other. But Carter and I didn't work together, or socialize. . . ." She stumbled into silence.

Rainfinch couldn't keep from grinning. "I didn't suppose you frequented the Seraphim. You must know the people closest to him. I need to talk with them. What about family?"

"That's in the personnel folder."

"I'd rather hear it from you."

If she was irritated, she didn't let it show. "His parents are alive. They're old; people say they're very reclusive. He was married and divorced, a long time ago."

Rainfinch followed a hunch. "You weren't his friend, and yet you're terribly upset. How come?"

"Wouldn't you be? How would you like it if one of your top police brass was killed outside a fag bar in a dress?"

Not bloody likely, Rainfinch thought, but he had to give her the point. "That's the only reason?"

"Yes . . . no." She sighed. "I might as well tell you, someone will. Carter and I loathed each other—or at least he loathed me. Wouldn't even speak. If you find out why, I'd love to know, because I haven't a clue."

"Well, if you were in Washington all last night, you don't need to worry."

"I *was*—I'm *not* worried. It's just . . . awkward."

"Okay. Why don't you give me the names of his buddies and arrange for me to meet with them. Also how friendly—or unfriendly—were his relationships with other staff members? Was he feuding with anyone else besides you?"

"We *weren't*—Lieutenant, can't that wait? The governor will be back tomorrow, and our chief of staff, Robert Friar. They can help you a lot more than I. What I'm mainly concerned about is the publicity—"

"I understand that. We'll be as discreet as possible. Murder investigations can't wait for absent governors, though. Chief Jurgen is sympathetic, but you must realize the whole powder keg will explode sooner or later."

She ran restless fingers through her hair in what seemed a habitual gesture. The curls became wilder, if that were possible. "Even the fact he was wearing a dress? Oh, of course it will. But for God's sake, give us time to work out damage control."

"It isn't really up to me—how are you going to manage that?" Rainfinch's voice was bemused.

"Damned if I know. It's so unfair—Governor Sanden doesn't quiz people about their sexual preferences before he hires them. He doesn't care, as long as they do their jobs."

"Can a political figure afford to be that broad-minded?"

Her small laugh was devoid of mirth. "He could until this happened. I'm not sure how well Carter's lifestyle—or death style—will go down with Uncle John and Aunt Minnie."

"Who are Uncle John and Aunt Minnie?"

"It's just a saying. Part of the lore of the capitol. A rural senator used to complain that 'Uncle John and Aunt Minnie' wouldn't be pleased with some piece of legislation when he had to go home and explain it. The phrase stuck."

Rainfinch nodded, and drained the last of his coffee. No

one understood the jargon that built up around a profession better than a cop.

She gestured at his cup. "More?"

Rainfinch felt a prickle of warning. In an ingenuous way, Susan Elias was an extremely appealing woman. He reminded himself that she was a press secretary, and would circle him in a minute if it suited her.

"No, thanks. I'd like to see Hall's office."

She picked up the change in his manner. Setting aside her own cup, she stood, all business. "Come with me. I'll introduce you to Nell White, Carter's secretary. They're—" she shook her head impatiently. "I'm sorry, were, good friends. She'll show you the office. And she can tell you a lot more about his personal life than I can."

As they walked down the hall Rainfinch asked one more question. "Governor Sanden's a bachelor, isn't he?"

Elias pulled up short and gave him a furious look, then abruptly grinned and shook her head. "You bastard."

Rainfinch laughed in spite of himself. "From what I hear, there are hordes of women who can bear witness to his sexual preference."

"Ordinarily I'd dispute that remark, but under the circumstances—"

Nell White was in her forties, with brown, close-cropped hair and a firm handshake. She wore no makeup, which was fortunate, since her eyes were red and puffy and her cheeks still runneled with tears. Here, Rainfinch thought, was someone who mourned the dead man.

He sat in the tiny reception area that was her office and tried to put her at ease. It was difficult; she was hostile and defensive.

"Carter was brilliant. I can't imagine anyone—but the world is full of vicious people. What has Susan been telling you about him?"

"Very little. Only that you knew him better than she." Rainfinch edited the truth. "She gave me copies of his personnel file." How much, he wondered, did Nell White know about the circumstances of her boss's death?

It didn't take long to find out. "Robert Friar called me from Washington. He said Carter was murdered." *Murdered* came out a choked strangle. She grabbed a tissue and angrily scrubbed her eyes. "Where? How? Do you have any idea who did it?"

"Sorry, I can't discuss that with you. Are you okay to answer a few questions? Then I'd like to see his office."

"What kind of questions? His office—I don't know. How could that help you? Nobody's allowed, when Carter's not there. You have to understand, we work with a lot of confidential papers and files. We can't have people rooting around."

Rainfinch nodded. "Cops have that problem, too. We'll work something out—I'm good at keeping secrets. Now. Miss Elias said you and Mr. Hall were friends. Who else on staff was close to him?"

Her chin came up. "Robert Friar—he's chief of staff—he admired Carter a lot. And Brendon Guiste, the governor's executive assistant—they'd known each other a long time. The others—" She made an expressive gesture. "In any office you have, sort of, allies—and people you don't like so well. It was that way with Carter. Lots of people were jealous of him."

"Okay." Rainfinch was jotting notes. "What about personal friends, outside the office?"

"I—do we have to talk about this now?" Her fingers gripped the edge of the desk as if it were her only hold on a wildly spinning universe. She shook her head. "I can't think—he was devoted to his mother and father. Aside from that, a lobbyist or two. There's Richard Henderson, over in the secretary of state's office, and—oh, I don't know. Ask Brendon, if you must."

Rainfinch didn't press her. She seemed more hostile by the minute, and he needed to avoid a confrontation before getting inside Hall's office. He wanted to see it, *now*. There was no guarantee he could get a search warrant quickly, and any delay would give her or someone else time to purge the place.

He changed the subject. "Where did he live? All the documents in his wallet listed the state capitol address."

"He has a house out on Blue Lake. Close to his parents."

"Did he live alone?"

"Yes," she answered defiantly. "Since he was divorced. That was years ago."

"His ex-wife—does she live around here? What's her name?"

"I have no idea. It happened so long ago. He never spoke of her."

Fresh tears filled her eyes. Her rough-skinned face was blotched with crimson spots.

Rainfinch felt compassion. As long as he'd been in the profession, he still had painful flashes of sorrow at the sight of naked grief. "Maybe his parents—"

"You're not going to—for God's sake, don't harass *them*. Mr. Hall is very feeble, and Mrs. Hall . . . they dote on Carter. He's taken such good care of them."

"We don't totally lack sensitivity, Ms. White." Rainfinch riffled through the personnel file. "One-eight-two-six Blue Lake Drive? That was Mr. Hall's address?"

"Yes." The answer was gruff with resentment.

"I'd like to see the office now. Is there a phone in there I can use?"

For an instant he thought she would refuse. Then she stood abruptly and opened the door behind her. Rainfinch followed.

"The phone's on the desk. Dial nine for outside." She took a position of stolid truculence beside the door, her arms folded.

Rainfinch wanted to look around the room without Hall's secretary hovering like an avenging angel. "Thank you, Ms. White. I won't be long." He sat in Hall's chair, picked up the phone, and turned his back.

It worked. He heard the door close.

He dialed a Homicide number. In a few moments Curran came on the line.

"Lou? I've got a home address. One-eight-two-six Blue Lake Drive. Rustle a search warrant and get out there fast as you can."

"Anyone have authority to give us permission for a search?"

"Apparently not. He lived alone, his secretary says. Can you run down an assistant DA to help with the affidavit?"

"I think so. Frank Homer, or maybe that good-lookin' Houghton gal. One of them ought to be around. What do we designate? Address books, letters that might contain threats, that kind of stuff?"

"Yeah. The DA'll know which district judge is on call."

"I'll try to locate Thomason. He doesn't nitpick bad as some."

"Good. I'll leave it to you. Did you get the incident room staffed yet?"

"It's activated. We'll have more clericals Monday; but for now we've got two computers going, the map's started, and the casebook. The phones are up, and we have two cops from Projects besides Danny, April, and me."

"Okay, good. Listen. Hall was divorced a long time ago, no kids. His parents are alive, their place is on Blue Lake, too. Secretary says they're pretty feeble. They've got to be notified, Lou. Apparently they're influential people. Better talk to Major Adamson, see how he wants to handle it."

"Gotcha. Anything else?"

"Not now. Get on that search warrant. If you need me, I've got my pager."

Rainfinch continued to hold the receiver against his ear after Curran disconnected. There was no telltale click. He walked quickly to the door and cracked it open. Carter Hall's secretary stood at an open file cabinet, several feet from her desk. As he watched she wiped her eyes with a tissue and blew her nose. Then she pushed the file drawer

shut and leaned over the cabinet, head cradled in her arms.
Her shoulders heaved with silent sobs.

She hadn't been eavesdropping then, but what about the
governor's security people, and the alert receptionist? He
cursed himself for not waiting to seek out a pay phone. It
had been a trade-off—security for time. He wanted someone
in that house at the first possible moment.

He began his search of the office. The first thing that
struck him was a complete absence of personal objects—
things that impress the personality of a man on the space
he occupies.

The walls displayed three or four innocuous prints and
one obviously posed picture of a smiling Hall with the
governor, dated the year Max Sanden had first been elected.
It was signed, "Thanks for everything. Couldn't have done
it without your help. Max."

There were no photographs on the desk; only neat stacks
of business mail, copies of house and senate bills, and
interoffice memos. He picked up the memos and riffled
through them. A good many were brief and handwritten, in
the same bold, cursive script he had seen on the posed
portrait. They were addressed to C.H. and signed merely
with a huge S. The rest were typed, with the "To–From" lines
properly filled out. None was remotely interesting.

He opened the desk drawers. Carter Hall had been pathologically neat, a count-the-paper-clips man. A single object
of interest turned up in the lap drawer, a matchbook with
the outline of a haloed figure above the words "The Seraphim." He opened it. Full of matches, but no cryptic
message. Pity. There would have been, in the movies. He
carefully replaced it.

No file cabinets in here. The handsome fruitwood credenza contained neat stacks of legal documents, many of
them made formal by the familiar blue-back cover Rainfinch
had often seen in the DA's office. They were headed with
titles like "House Bill 184" or "Senate Resolution 76." Some
were stamped "Enrolled" or "Enrolled and Engrossed."

Rainfinch shook his head and yawned. Boring. He completed his task with a quick search of an antique bookcase filled with heavy bound legal volumes, then sat again in the sumptuous leather desk chair. Except for the matchbook, he had found nothing that humanized Hall. Not even an invitation or a casual note from a friend.

"Careful bastard, weren't you?" That set him thinking. How could a man so obsessively neat suddenly throw caution to the winds and caper around a gay bar wearing an evening dress? Figure that out.

He leaned back. The damn chair didn't even squeak. What, he wondered, was Governor Sanden's attitude going to be? No matter how you cut it, Carter Hall's death was the ol' dead rat in the middle of the floor. You couldn't ignore it, and nobody wanted to pick it up.

He left Hall's office with a quiet thank you to Nell White. After a couple of false turns he found his way back to the central corridor, left the governor's wing, and found a bank of pay phones. He dialed Homicide again.

When Curran came on the line, Rainfinch said, "I've been thinking. We need to put out a limited statement to the media so people will start calling in if they have information. You heard Jurgen put a muzzle on Stamps—which is all to the good. But how about talking to Major Adamson, see if he'll run this by Jurgen? Adamson, or Stamps, if he must, says that someone was killed, the location, and approximate time. Standard disclaimer, 'Can't release identity of deceased pending notification of next of kin,' and so on. Then give out the phone number."

Rainfinch expressed his request as a question rather than an order; he respected Curran's opinion.

The line was silent for a couple of seconds. "Couldn't hurt anything," Curran said finally, thinking out loud. "No questions answered, because 'at this time it might jeopardize the investigation.' Hell, that won't do any damage. Adamson'll go for it, he knows we need to get the phones ringing. He can persuade Jurgen."

"Okay, get on it. You shouldn't have any trouble finding Adamson and Jurgen, even if it is Saturday. I expect they're staying close to the phone."

"You kidding? Adamson's been here all day. Jurgen calls every hour. And I fall over that mule's ass, Stamps, every time I turn around."

Rainfinch laughed. "You can fade it. Just remember to keep your sweet disposition."

Curran muttered something creatively vile, then added, "What are you up to?"

"I have the names of a couple of Hall's buddies who work here in the capitol. If they're around I'll question them. What's our status on the search warrant?"

"Bent has Jean Houghton from the DA's office in tow and is on his way out to Judge Thomason's house now."

"Good. What did Adamson do about notifying Hall's parents?"

"He sent April."

Rainfinch nodded. "Yeah. That's tough, but she can handle it better than anyone. Do we have word from the medical examiner yet?"

"No, but the major's talked to Deethe. He knows it's a hot potato. Maybe he'll expedite."

"Sure he will. Okay, I'll get back with you after I finish here."

Rainfinch returned to the governor's wing. The gorgeous receptionist, whose name was Ettalou Percival, rang Brendon Guiste's office. In a short time Guiste, a slight, handsome man, bustled in with an air of self-importance.

"Glad to meet you, Lieutenant. Come with me." His handshake was moist. He led Rainfinch all the way down the cavernous corridor, through a lavish, formal sitting area with a plaque by the door that read "The Blue Room," and into his own cubicle, a small, boxlike space sandwiched between Sanden's office and that of Robert Friar. Rainfinch figured it must have originally been designed for a secretary. Which led to the suspicion that Guiste himself was probably a glorified executive secretary.

"Terrible business. Dreadful—but I can't tell you how delighted—Susan Elias told me who you are. The maestro's son—I've heard him speak of you many times, of course."

That's a lie, Rainfinch thought.

"Such a tragic thing. I still can't believe it. Carter was"—he put a hand against his brow in an incredibly theatrical gesture—"a genius. I don't know what we'll do without him. I don't mind saying it's a sad commentary on what the world's coming to."

Rainfinch didn't like the man's voice. Even in sorrow, it had a sarcastic, snide quality that made everything he said sound like whispered smut.

"I just talked to Captain Stamps. Clifford's an old friend—"

Really? Rainfinch thought.

"—says you people are stonewalling the media until the governor and Robert Friar get back. I can tell you Max Sanden will appreciate that, Lieutenant Rainfinch. He's not a man who forgets a favor."

Okay. Enough smarm, Rainfinch decided. "You and Hall were close friends?" the question sounded abrupt. Guiste looked startled.

"Yes." He flushed. "And before you ask, I was with him last night. Early in the evening, that is. Look, Lieutenant, we went to that place as a gag. Lots of people do. Several of us had dinner at Greyfriar's Club, and a couple of drinks. Then someone said, 'Let's go to the Seraphim. They're having a drag night.' "

"Drag night?" Rainfinch deadpanned.

Guiste's face was now ugly purple. Rainfinch wondered suddenly if he might have heart trouble.

"We thought it would be campy, a blast. I didn't dress up, of course, and neither did Richard. But Carter—he loved a prank."

"Wait a minute, let me get this straight. You and Hall went to the Seraphim together? Directly after dinner at Greyfriar's Club? Who else was with you?" The thought of Carter Hall wearing a dress in the staid Greyfriar's was almost more than Rainfinch could bear with a straight face.

Guiste seemed to know what he was thinking. A pencil he had been fiddling with snapped. His mouth developed a tic.

"Of course not. We all went home after dinner. We had agreed to meet at the Seraphim at nine-thirty."

"Who is we?"

"Well—as it happened, the others chickened out. It ended up being just Carter, Richard Henderson, and me."

"Richard Henderson. Ms. White mentioned him. He works in the secretary of state's office?"

"That's right."

"So, the three of you met at the Seraphim. Then what?"

Guiste shook his head. "We all went together. And nothing happened, really. It was crowded. Richard and I were nervous. You know, even though it was just a prank, with our jobs—someone could have recognized us. You can't be too careful. We had a drink and watched the fun awhile. Then Richard and I decided to go home."

"What about Hall?"

Guiste lifted one hand in a helpless gesture. "He wouldn't leave. Of course, dressed up like that, there wasn't much chance of anyone spotting him. Even so . . . we finally gave up and left without him."

"How was he going to get home?"

"He said he'd catch a ride. He'd run into another friend."

"Who was it?"

"I don't know."

"Are you sure?"

"Of course I'm sure. I mean, he talked to lots of people. Richard and I just sat back at a corner table and watched, but Carter—he was very outgoing. Having a really good time."

"So you and Henderson went home? You took him to his house, then returned to yours? Or was he driving?"

Once again a wave of color surged across Guiste's face. "I drove. Richard was a little under the weather, so we went to my house. He bunked down there. In the spare room."

Rainfinch leaned forward in his chair as if to rise. Tension visibly drained from Guiste's face. It was obvious he believed the worst was over. Rainfinch could almost hear him thinking, "That wasn't so bad. I handled it."

"Thanks, Mr. Guiste. I'll get back with you. Try to remember if there are any details about the evening you haven't told me. Even small things might be helpful."

He stood, then delivered the punch. "We'll be talking to Mr. Henderson, of course." He pretended to check his notes. "Robert Friar—he's chief of staff? And the governor. I understand from Ms. Elias that Friar and Governor Sanden will be back from Washington and available tomorrow."

Guiste was a caricature of agitation. He almost crouched behind the desk. "Lieutenant—" He ran the back of his hand across his forehead, where heavy beads of sweat had gathered. "This is so damn difficult. I don't mean to sound unfeeling—with Carter dead, and all—but must Richard and I come into it?" His voice broke. He paused for control, and continued in a more normal tone. "We know nothing. Must you tell anyone we were there—Friar? The governor? What good would it do?"

"We won't go out of our way to spread the news, but homicide investigations can't be bent to protect people's sensibilities. By the way, I'll need the names of the others who had dinner with you at Greyfriar's Club."

Guiste slumped heavily in his chair. "What? But I already told you, only the three of us went on to the Seraphim."

"I need the names of the others, anyway."

Guiste's hands were folded on top of the desk. He stared at them as if they were alien manifestations. "All right. I'll make you a list."

"And Richard Henderson. Do you think he's in his office now?"

"I'm sure he isn't. He was traveling to the north part of the state this morning, to visit his brother."

"Does he know about Hall's death?"

It took Guiste several seconds to answer, which told

Rainfinch he was considering a lie. Finally he said, "Yes. I
called him."

"I see. When will he be back in the city?"

"First thing in the morning." A grievance was percolating
in Guiste's mind. "Lieutenant, you can hardly blame me for
telling him about Carter. We're all—were all friends."

"Of course. I can understand you might want to warn him."

"*Tell.* Not warn, Lieutenant. He had a right to know. After
all, we *were* with Carter, for a while."

"I see. And who else did you decide had a right to know?
Did you confide in any other members of the Greyfriar's
party?"

"No. I swear it. Richard's the only person I've told."

"Right. I don't suppose I need worry that you or Henderson will talk about this."

"Certainly not." Guiste managed to sound austere, as if
he were privy to a state secret.

"I'll take that list of names now. Everyone who was at
Greyfriar's Club with you, Henderson, and Hall."

Guiste pettishly snatched a notepad and pen. He scribbled
with an odd, jerky motion.

Suddenly Rainfinch tired of the game. Brendon Guiste
had been so sure of himself in the beginning, wrapped in the
panoply of the governor's office, holding up his alleged
friendship with Maestro Martin Rainfinch like a holy talis-
man. Now he was a broken man, slumped behind a desk
that was too big for him.

Leaving the office, he felt grim. If this killing didn't get
wrapped up fast and simple—fat chance of that—Guiste
wouldn't be the only one with his tail in a crack. Careers
would topple like chessmen off an overturned table; from
Max Sanden, the king piece, right down to Abe Rainfinch—a
battered knight.

He grinned. How goddamned poetic. Sometimes he surprised himself.

▽

8

ETTALOU PERCIVAL HAD abandoned her command post in the main hallway by the time Rainfinch finished with Guiste. The computer terminal had been neatly covered, her card files, pencils, and notepads stowed in drawers.

Lights in the corridor were dimmed, leaving a murky gloom that suited the impassive glares of past governors, imprisoned in their massive frames. A yellow rectangle spilling from the security office was the only sign of life.

As he left the governor's wing, heavy, bullet-proof glass doors swung shut behind him, and the lock engaged with an audible click. He took an ancient, irascible elevator down to the first floor and nodded to a janitor as he made his way to the side exit that led to the south parking lot.

It was five-forty-five when he stepped outside. The wind had subsided to occasional frigid gusts, and a fine, chill mist permeated the air. Lights in the parking lot came alive and splashed falsely cheery pools of yellow over icy asphalt as he walked toward his unmarked gray Ford.

Inside the cruiser, cold was a physical presence, mean and sullen. He pulled off a glove and dialed the incident room. Waiting through electronic buzzes and clicks, he looked back at the capitol building. Through the mist, bathed by floodlights, it looked as insubstantial as Kubla Khan's stately pleasure palace.

He felt a sense of isolation that wasn't entirely unpleasant. Where most would hurry toward warmth and company, some feral instinct made him relish being a part of night and cold and drizzle.

The detective who answered his call said that Lou, Danny, and April were out. Rainfinch's request for a limited press release on the killing had been granted. TV stations had already aired a brief statement giving location and approximate time of death without identifying the deceased, and asking anyone who might have information to call the incident-room number.

"Good. I'm going to grab a bite, then go by the Seraphim and talk to Monk Smith. Ask Curran to round up Bent and Morgen. I want them in my office between eight-thirty and nine this evening."

He stopped at Mary Lou's Homestyle Café and ordered a ham sandwich. A few minutes of flirting with Mary Lou, a pert and savvy redhead, improved his disposition. He felt considerably more human as he parked in front of the iron gates of the Seraphim grounds and turned down the visor that identified his Ford as a police vehicle. As if that were really necessary. Anyone who paid attention to such things was never fooled by an unmarked cruiser. Of course, the interesting array of vehicles used in Special Projects was a different matter.

Shrubs that in summer made the churchyard a cool haven now hulked and concealed as he approached steps that led to the Gothic entrance. The church seemed to have deliberately drawn them close, hiding the shame of its present existence. Like you'd caught the minister's daughter out whoring, and she'd veiled her face to cover the scarlet letter.

The doors were locked. He realized then that access to the Seraphim must be from the parking lot entrance at the side, under a maroon canvas canopy and a discreet sign. He banged on the door as a gesture, resigned to a wet, unpleasant walk, but as he turned to leave it cracked open against a heavy chain.

An authoritative voice said, "Please come around—" then broke off as Rainfinch turned and was recognized.

"Come in, Lieutenant," Monk Smith said. "Going to be another bitch of a night, isn't it?"

"Sweet Jesus, Monk, all you need is the sound track from a Dracula movie. This place must be jolly on Halloween."

"We did have quite a party. At times, though, I could do with less atmosphere."

He led the way through a dark vestibule and into the club. Rainfinch looked around. Someone had done a good remodeling job.

Inside, church gave way to castle, but the effect was subtle. Parti-colored silk pennants descended from the vaulted ceiling and made spots of red, green, and blue against paneled walls. Tapestries of medieval battles hung from balconies. The blatant had been shunned; there were no fake suits of armor, no papier-mâché shields or tin battle-axes.

Part of the area that had once been filled with pews was now a vast, polished oak dance floor, flanked on either side by twin mahogany bars. The pulpit area had become a bandstand, one section of which housed a throne and esoteric keyboards for a disc jockey. Tables fringed the perimeters like an encampment around a jousting arena. Upstairs in the balconies there must have been more tables; he could see a few pale faces floating above a brass railing.

Though it was scarcely past seven, Rainfinch estimated there were fifty or more people scattered about the room, talking with the self-conscious chatter of guests arrived too early for a party. Music was low, and only three or four couples clung to each other on the dance floor.

Monk read his thoughts. "An hour from now my Saturday-night band will be here. We'll max out on decibels, and that floor'll be packed." He nodded toward the choir loft. "See those girls? Airline stewardesses—three or four crews of them."

He motioned down a hallway behind the bandstand, then continued, his voice carrying a faint tinge of bitterness. "They have a hell of a good time. Drinks, plenty of men to dance with, and no one hits on them. Word's gotten out this is the place to come. We have groups almost every night."

They entered a room that might once have once been a parson's study. The gleaming oak floor was mostly covered by a Chinese rug in muted shades of gold and green. Soft yellow walls displayed a handsome collection of Renaissance-style drawings.

Monk took his place behind a large ebony desk, and Rainfinch sat in, or rather was engulfed by, one of a pair of black leather chairs that faced the desk. The soft padding made him realize he was very tired.

There were three closed-circuit television monitors on a credenza to Monk's left. One was trained on the front entrance where Rainfinch had come in; another showed a group passing under the canopy to enter from the parking lot. The third picture was from a camera placed high in the main room, displaying both bars and the dance floor.

"That's how you knew I was storming the street door. Are these sets monitored most of the time?"

Monk shrugged and shook his head. "As you see, this is my office. No one else uses it. When I'm in here, I glance at them now and then. I like to know what's going on."

"Are the cameras hooked up to a VCR? Are there any other cameras—one scanning the parking area?"

"No, and no. Why?"

"Have you a security force?"

Again Monk shook his leonine head. "Not really. We haven't felt the need, so far. Haven't had any real problems. Oh, the usual things—someone drinks too much, or sniffs coke in the rest room. I don't put up with dope—let that kind of thing get started, and you're in for real trouble.

"You remember Frannie Da Sorta," he continued, "the ex–prize fighter? He's my club manager. He doubles as a bouncer, if necessary." Monk grinned. "People don't mess with Frannie much. And I have a couple of bartenders I can count on, if push should come to shove."

Rainfinch nodded. "I can think of people I'd rather tangle with than Frannie—or you, for that matter."

The big man laughed. "I try to keep in shape." He leaned back in his chair. "So, Abe. Why all the questions? What can I do for you?"

Monk had earned the right to call Lieutenant Abe Rainfinch by his first name several years before, when Rainfinch worked undercover to infiltrate a neo-Nazi gang. Monk had been an intelligence source and collaborator—a gutsy, valuable ally. He had proved himself a man of integrity. Ruggedly handsome, he made no secret of his sexual preferences. Nor did he flaunt them. And he wasn't the type to play grabbie-feelie in a men's room.

An idle thought occurred to Rainfinch. "How the hell did you get stuck with a name like Monk?"

Monk laughed. "You don't think it suits me? It's one of those things that happens when you're a kid. Did you know I come from a theatrical family? Well, I was born a show-off—a real little wiseass. Monk for monkey, imitator. I hated it—but by the time I hit college it tickled my sense of humor. I was . . . a rather flamboyant character. So—Monk Smith. I liked the incongruity."

"And I'm Abraham Julian Rainfinch. *That's* incongruity for you." Rainfinch got down to business. "You heard there was a killing in your alley last night?"

"Of course—Lou Curran came around and talked to me. He never said who was killed—I got the impression it was a woman. And it's not *my* alley, Abe, thank you very much."

"You had a drag party here last night?"

"Yes." Comprehension dawned. Shock collapsed Monk's face into gray folds. "Oh, my God."

Rainfinch nodded confirmation. "You got it. One of your customers took a knife in the heart."

"Sweet Jesus. Who? Do you know who did it?"

Rainfinch took a deep breath. "Monk, there've been times when you've known things that would have gotten me a fast trip in a body bag, if you'd blabbed. Give me your word you'll keep your mouth shut until what I tell you comes out in the media."

"Of course."

"Did you know Carter Hall? Governor Sanden's chief legal honcho?"

"That son of a bitch! It was him? I damn near asked him to leave when he showed up in drag—but I couldn't think of an excuse. He wasn't making trouble."

"Too bad you didn't follow your hunch."

Monk rubbed his eyes wearily. "God, I wish I had, and told him never to come back. Someone like that—a public figure—they're nothing but trouble to a place like this."

"You've lived here most of your life, haven't you? Anyway, you've been in the city a long time. You must have known there'd be trouble when you opened a gay bar in a building that'd been a prominent church since statehood. Why did you do it?"

"Having a case of twenty-twenty hindsight, Abe?" Monk raised a palm in a defeated gesture. "I understand what you're saying. You know who Shadid Garber is?"

"Yes." Rainfinch was puzzled by the change of subject.

"He owns this building. I saw the For Lease sign, and had what I think is commonly called a brainstorm—I had to have the place."

Monk's fingers unconsciously pleated and unpleated a sheet of paper. "I told myself that since High Bluff Presbyterian had sold out and moved, it was just another building. And Abe, I opened a nightclub, not a gay bar. What you saw out there"—his massive shoulders drooped—"just happened."

Rainfinch shook his head. "I'm sorry—but even a night-club. This will never be just another building."

"I know that now. From the day we opened, the High Bluff Historical Homeowners' Society has been trying to close us down."

"Do you have a financial backer?"

Monk shook his head. "It's all my money—and Archie's. If we come a cropper on this, we're wiped out."

"Look, Monk, we don't know Hall's death had anything to do with the Seraphim. Chances are it didn't—just your tough luck he happened to be here in a dress the night someone decided to off him."

"Yeah. My tough luck. I have a long-term lease on this place at a pretty good price, so we went overboard remodeling. As I said, if it sinks, I'm ruined."

"It looks great, incidentally."

Monk brightened a little. "You like what we did? Archie's responsible. You've met him, haven't you?"

Rainfinch had met Monk Smith's lover—a handsome man about fifteen years Monk's junior. "Archie's a decorator, isn't he? I'd forgotten that."

"Yes, and a good one. That's another thing—maybe there's a curse on us. If I were superstitious . . . Archie got mononucleosis shortly before we opened. He had to give up his job. Word got around that he was sick—you can guess what that meant. Everybody's so terrified of AIDS. With good cause. Anyway, we felt like putting an ad in the paper stating that all he had was a stupid childhood disease."

Rainfinch was sympathetic, but he had a murder to solve. "That is rough. Listen—"

Monk stood. "We live in the old parsonage. It's just a few steps away. Archie'd love to see you, how about saying hello? He's been damn near suicidal—he's on the mend, now, though."

"I doubt he'd be thrilled to see me, considering the news I bring." Rainfinch looked at his watch. "Besides, I have a meeting in my office right away. Was Archie over for the party last night?"

"No. He'd planned to come—in fact, it was really his project. I'm not into drag. You know that."

"But he wasn't well enough to make it?"

"Right."

"About Carter Hall, Monk. Did you see him with anyone in particular—someone you recognized?"

Monk slumped back into his chair. "I *was* watching him. He arrived with those two supercilious stooges he buddies with. They were dressed straight and had sense enough to find a corner table, sit down, and keep a low profile. Not Hall, though. He came to party.

"Anyway, the two stooges left pretty early. I did see Hall with a younger guy—his face seemed familiar, but I can't give you a name. I got busy after that, and didn't see Hall leave."

"Will you talk to Frannie, and any other of your employees you trust to keep their mouths shut? If you learn anything, give me a call. This is my private line." He handed over a card.

"Okay. Sure, Abe."

"I'm on my way. I'll be back in touch. And give my regards to Archie, will you?"

"Sure." Monk stood again, and started for the door.

On the way out Rainfinch knew he was the subject of covert but intense speculation. Frannie Da Sorta nodded, with a smile that never reached his eyes.

Walking back to the car, his mind churned through thoughts of the murdered man, Monk Smith, the Seraphim—and the High Bluff Historical Homeowner's Society. Might be something interesting there, since they were so eager to close Monk down. One unbalanced weirdo—he'd check into it.

Then he thought of the governor and his staff. So far he'd questioned only Susan Elias, Brendon Guiste, and Nell White. He wasn't particularly looking forward to a session with the governor and his top man, Friar, but it had to be done as soon as they came back from Washington.

What had Carter Hall really been? A twisted genius, a fool, an arrogant ass, or a man devoted to his fragile parents? A little of each, he supposed.

Rainfinch sighed.

Monk left the building through a private exit and walked slowly toward the parsonage.

It never occurred to him not to tell Archie about the murder. He didn't even consider whether he was technically breaking Rainfinch's confidence. He thought of his lover as an extension of himself. Archie might be a bit erratic in some people's books, but he was about as likely to betray Monk as to take up skydiving—without a parachute. In fact, the skydiving would be less dangerous, and Archie knew it.

As soon as he opened the cottage door plangent notes greeted him. Something sad, played on a balalaika. Archie had Ukrainian grandparents—when he was ill or unhappy he became the quintessential melancholy Russian.

Now he lay against pillows on the sofa, eyes closed. Monk tried to stifle a great rush of conflicting emotions—love, aggravation, concern. How long had it been since Archie's presence had brought a spontaneous surge of pure and shining joy? Monk wanted those days back.

It wasn't Archie's fault. Compressing his lips, Monk crossed the room and turned off the music. Archie's eyes opened, he began a protest.

"I was listening—"

"You don't need that mournful crap. No wonder you don't get better, wallowing . . ."

Archie swung his feet to the floor. He upturned the palms of his hands in an eloquent gesture. In an infinitely weary voice he said, "What do you want from me? Do you think I'm enjoying myself?"

Monk was instantly contrite. "I know how tired you are of being sick. But I'm right about that music, it sure as hell won't improve your mood."

Archie's mouth curved slightly. He shrugged.

Irritably, Monk shoved a stack of magazines off his favorite chair and sat. Archie had always handled housekeeping chores. Since he'd been ill the place looked like a dump, and more often than not their meals were carryout. But now was not the time to get involved in another argument about whether or not they should hire a housekeeper.

He took a deep breath. "We have a problem," he said. "It concerns the club."

$\triangledown$

9

RAINFINCH FOUND APRIL, Danny, and Lou in the incident room. April was at a computer terminal, her back to the door. Her hair, held away from her face by a wide yellow band, concealed her neck and shoulders in a profusion of curls like a Dresden milkmaid's.

Danny sat at a long, scarred table, making entries in the master book. Major Mark Adamson silently watched.

Lou stood at a window with another veteran detective. They conversed in low voices about something visible outside. Lou's face wore the look of combined malice and humor familiar to, and dreaded by, everyone who knew him.

Rainfinch joined them. He saw immediately what held their interest. A white Ford Thunderbird, nicely lit by street lamps, sawed impatiently back and forth between a black-and-white and an unmarked cruiser. It was a moot point whether the space was large enough for the car. As they watched its right rear tire mounted the curb.

Lou turned. "Major, your wife's outside." His voice was butter, his eyes innocent.

Adamson joined them at the window, looked down. "That's not my wife," he stated firmly.

"I believe it is, sir. That's your car, isn't it? Thought I caught a glimpse of her inside," Lou insisted blandly.

As the four men watched, the Thunderbird's right front tire joined the rear astride the curb. A blond emerged from the driver's side, shut the door with a determined thwack and headed toward the station's front entrance.

All three detectives stared at Adamson. Lines of humor formed around his eyes. His mouth twitched. In a solemn voice he insisted, "That is *not* my wife," turned, and left the room.

Rainfinch knew Lou Curran and the major went back a long way, which gave him the nerve to bait a man the rest of them treated with healthy respect. Everyone knew Adamson was smart, quick-witted, and stood up for his troops, but when you got crosswise of him his temper was legendary.

"Keep that up and you'll find retirement papers on your desk some fine morning," Rainfinch told Curran. "Come back to my office." He raised his voice. "April. Danny. Let's go."

They trooped down the hall to the Homicide squad room, past crowded, littered gray metal desks, and into the small cubicle that belonged to him—except when he was gone and someone else commandeered it.

Lou had snagged the coffeepot and a stack of Styrofoam cups. He poured, and set the pot beside the black-and-orange ceramic buzzard that every homicide cop's desk wore as a badge of honor.

Rainfinch took a swig and tried not to shudder visibly. Homicide coffee was something only the hardened could tolerate. He was never sure exactly what made it taste so foul. Sometimes his mind strayed to thoughts of rat droppings, roaches, and floor sweep, but he tried not to dwell on it.

He briefed them on his talks at the capitol with Susan Elias, Brendon Guiste, and Nell White, the dead man's secretary. Then he described his visit with Monk Smith at the Seraphim. He finished with a question.

"What about Hall's house, Lou? Anything there?"

Curran shrugged. "Not so far—unless you count a closet full of dresses, high heels, and silk teddies. I left Len Porter out there, he's still looking around.

"That bastard was pathologically neat. I've never seen anything like it." He settled back in his chair, reached in his pocket for a battered pack of cigarettes, caught the glares, and put it back with a sigh.

"Hell of a beautiful place," he continued. "You know how

wooded that area is—the house fits right in. Stone and shingle, with the backside all glass, facing the lake. Inside it looks just the way it must have when the decorator walked out the door. Most impersonal home I've ever seen."

Rainfinch nodded. "His office was the same way. House didn't look like anybody'd been sharing it with him, I suppose?"

"Hell, no. Not even a dirty sheet on a bed. We did pull some linens, shirts, and shorts out of a hamper in the laundry. Which I bagged, labeled, and took to the lab."

Rainfinch nodded. He knew the reason for Lou's personal attention to dirty laundry. In itself it might not be important, but this *was* an important case. The fewer people involved in the chain of evidence, the less likely some dipshit defense attorney would be able to obfuscate the issue. "You mean four different officers handled this pair of shorts before they went to the forensics lab? How many technicians had access to them? How can you tell us with any certainty the evidence hasn't been contaminated?"

So far he hadn't met April's eyes, but now he spoke to her. "You went out to the family. Tell us about it."

She didn't answer immediately. Her delicate face, normally pale, was so white the shadows under her eyes looked like grease paint. Abe felt a twinge of guilt. She must not have slept at all after their quarrel the night before. He'd only had a couple of hours' rest himself, but he'd been so absorbed in the case he was only now beginning to realize the depths of his own exhaustion.

"Their house is just beyond Carter's. Not close enough to cramp his style. They're both on wooded land, a couple of acres apiece, I'd guess." She closed her eyes in a long blink. Curran reached across and silently poured her another shot of coffee. She nodded thanks and drank.

"A housekeeper answered the door. I had to lean on her to get to see the senior Halls at all." She sighed. "They were so damned fragile."

That must have made three of you, Rainfinch thought.

"The housekeeper took me to a small sitting room. Mama came in first, then Papa, accompanied by a male nurse. I told them as gently as I could," she said defensively.

Nobody spoke. After a gulp of coffee April continued. "They were shattered. I was afraid one of them might have a stroke and die on the spot."

"Did you have a chance to ask about their son's acquaintances? Friends or foes?" Rainfinch asked, as carefully as possible.

"No. I got out of there as fast as I could and left the nurse and housekeeper to cope."

"You'll have to go back. Set up an appointment—wait. Better find out from the nurse who their physician is. See if he wants to be there when we talk to them. Ordinarily I'd fight a sack of wildcats before I'd involve somebody's officious doctor, but if they're as infirm as you say—"

"Can't we leave them alone? Those poor old people don't know come-here from sic 'em about their only child, Abe. Except he was good to Mommy and Daddy."

"Nevertheless—"

She sighed. "All right."

Rainfinch turned to Danny Bent. "What have you been up to? Were you with Lou?"

Although Danny hadn't slept any more than the rest of them, he seemed fresh and clear-eyed. The French cuffs of his white shirt gleamed, his suit vest was neatly buttoned. His only concession to long hours was an unbuttoned collar and loosened tie.

He shook his head. "I went out to the crime scene. Checked with the guys doing house-to-house. So far, not a damn thing. The building where our old lady witness lives is empty, except for her. It's being converted into law offices. Across the street are shops, all closed at the time of the killing, of course. We're running down owners, in case someone worked late.

"No sign of the murder weapon. We're checking dumpsters within a mile radius."

Rainfinch nodded. "I'll be surprised if we find anything. The killer took off in his car. No one pursued, he had no reason to believe anyone saw him. He could get rid of the knife at leisure, or not at all.

"And speaking of that, I want it impressed on everybody— no one's to know we have an eyewitness. If that ass Stamps finds out, I'll beat the person who let it slip to a bloody pulp. Lou, you told the old lady to keep her mouth shut, I'm sure."

"Yes, but the cat paid more attention to me than she did. I couldn't figure whether he was gonna spray my pants or bite my leg."

Danny grinned evilly. "It's that gamey aroma you always have about you, Lou. Poor cat couldn't resist it."

"You better not go over there, Lover Boy. Damn perverted feline'll go berserk over that sweet-smellin' stuff you wear, and breed your leg."

Rainfinch felt as if his brain had gotten disconnected. All he could come up with was a mental image of himself climbing between warm, clean flannel sheets. Alone.

He sneaked a look at April. Usually she got a kick out of Lou and Danny and their continual lip, but now she looked like a casualty, one of the walking wounded. Did she expect something out of him? he wondered. An attempt to smooth things over? He yawned and closed his eyes. God, he hoped not.

The sound of her voice made him jump. "Abe, you're asleep in your chair, and I'm falling out of mine. Can everybody please go home now?"

He was off the hook, at least for the moment. "Good idea. Let's get out of here."

"We coming in, in the morning?" Danny asked.

"What's the matter, got a hot date?" from Lou.

"Yeah, with my bed. Boss?"

"Everybody keep their pager handy—wait a minute." Rainfinch pulled a piece of paper out of his inside coat pocket. "Danny, got a project for you. These are the names of the men who were at dinner with Hall, Guiste, and

Henderson at Greyfriar's Club. Run them down and interview them, will you? Diplomatically."

"Why him, Lieutenant? How come I get old ladies and cats, and he gets the big shots? I'd handle 'em like silk—suave's my middle name."

"Right. When Stamps executes his coup d'etat and takes the chief's job, I'm recommending you for public information officer. Now, if nobody else wants to be a wiseass, let's get out of here."

Abe maneuvered his Ford between the narrow sandstone posts of the porte cochere, killed the engine, and sat, staring at the side door of his house with a familiar mixture of affection and despair. He lived in the Charbonnet Mansion, according to a small brass plaque the city historical commission had insisted on placing by the curb.

His great-grandfather, a Cherokee horse and mule trader gone rich and at least nominally respectable, had built it in 1901. Designed by an architect from London, as an old newspaper story boasted, the house was constructed of brick and chiseled red native stone in a style Abe thought of as Addams Family Victorian. It sat back from the street, with a copper-roofed three-story tower facing the corner.

It had been a great place to play when Abe and his sister were kids. Nooks, crannies, an enclosed "secret" staircase built for servants in a more lavish and less egalitarian time. And there had been the third-floor ballroom—you could skid for yards across the mahogany floor in your sock feet.

Rainfinch sighed. Not anymore, you couldn't. There were a dozen receptacles in varying sizes across that once splendid floor, put there to catch drips that filtered through broken tiles on the roof.

The mansion now belonged, in all its failing splendor, to Detective Lieutenant Abe Rainfinch.

The roof leaked badly. Tiles needed to be removed, broken ones discarded, the underroofing replaced and tarred, and the tiles reset. Handpainted canvas walls in the gold sitting room were in bad need of restoration after a plumbing leak. And the plumbing—and wiring—nightmares. Not to menton magnificent old draperies, hangings, tapestries, all in need of expert repair.

He sighed. Got out of the car. Walked inside.

The state historical society was drooling to buy it. "We'll use it like they do Gracie Mansion in New York," someone had babbled.

Goddamnit, this was his home. He couldn't afford to live here, but he didn't want to leave.

He flipped on lights and walked to the second floor and the two rooms he used most—the master bedroom and its adjacent sitting room.

The light on his answering machine was flashing its silent scream. He flipped it on and began shedding clothes.

There were five or six messages from Melina Moriarty, escalating in frustration. Then his sister's voice, urgent. It seemed to him Julianna had learned to talk like a native New Yorker in the five years she'd been there—her voice had lost the soft, lazy inflection of Oklahoma.

"Abe, I'm calling—it's Saturday morning, eight o'clock. Where the hell are you? Mama's had a stroke. It's serious. She's been killing herself over that damn concert tour—she just collapsed. Only fifty-four years old, Abe. It isn't fair." The voice disintegrated into harsh sobs.

"I can't deal with this alone. You've got to come—and Daddy. This divorce foolishness of theirs . . . well, surely they'll come to their senses now. If she lives." More sobs.

"Oh, Abe. Phone as soon as you can. Get Daddy—kidnap him if you have to. And get the hell up here."

With great deliberation Abe hung up his slacks and coat, put his underwear in the dirty clothes hamper, and turned the ancient brass shower head on full blast. He stepped inside the claw-footed tub, closed his eyes, and offered his face to the beat of steamy water.

After several minutes he toweled dry and wrapped himself in the old terry robe that had been his mother's Christmas gift, back in the days when the house had still been full of music, laughter, and Rainfinches.

He dialed Julianna's number, got her machine, and left a message that he'd call again in the morning. He went to bed, thankful his exhaustion was so great that his mind and body would shut down immediately despite decay, sickness, death, or murder.

Consciousness came instantly, then moments of agonizing disorientation; heart thudding, blood pounding, hand already on the 9mm under his pillow. Something wrong, some noise—it took him a few seconds to identify it—something that sounded like dirt clods being heaved against his bedroom window. He grabbed the robe, padded over barefoot, and looked out.

"I know you're up there. Abe, you son of a bitch, let me in!"

He opened the window, then ducked as another clod hit the screen. "Shut up, Moriarty. You want to get me lynched? What the hell is your problem?"

"Get down here and let me in. Unless you want the whole neighborhood to hear what I have to say."

"I'm coming. Will you for God's sake put a lid on it?"

She was there when he opened the door, one finger jammed against the bell for good measure. Even furious, which he was, he couldn't help thinking she was one hell of a gorgeous woman.

Her hair was a red-brown shade that made him think of oak leaves and acorns. She stood damn near tall as he was and got right in his face, the pupils of her ale-colored eyes enormous.

"Why the hell didn't you return my calls?"

Abe pulled her inside and shut the door. "It was late. I was tired. What's on your mind that couldn't wait until tomorrow?"

She grinned, momentarily sidetracked. "You have anything on under that robe?"

"Never mind that. Go on up, I'll get beer."

She leered. "The bedroom?"

"No, goddamnit, the sitting room. You know where I mean."

Carrying a cold six-pack of Mexican beer, Rainfinch detoured through his bedroom and pulled on jeans and a sweatshirt. Moriarty was not a woman who could safely be given a psychological advantage.

She sat on his mother's favorite Empire sofa, boots off, wiggling her sock-clad toes.

He handed her a beer. "Don't be so formal, Moriarty. Try to get comfortable."

She drank off a healthy swig of cold Dos Equis, then her generous, warm-lipped mouth curved into a grin. "You're such a romantic son of a bitch, Abe."

"Cut the compliments. It's two o'clock in the morning. What the hell are you here for?"

"That's right, sweet-talk me. Works every time."

"Moriarty—"

She held up a hand. "All right." Her face was serious now, all business. "Abe, I've got a hot tip on that killing last night."

"You mean the woman in the alley?"

"Woman, my sweet ass. I have good information your victim was Carter Hall, one of Governor Sanden's top people, in drag. I want you to confirm or deny."

"I'm not about to do that. Don't push me, Moriarty. In the first place, you know that kind of information has to come through the PIO."

"Stamps? That jerk."

"I realize you love the guy, but try to contain yourself. He is the police department's official source of press information."

"Any idiot can tell he's been muzzled—I see your fine Comanche hand in it."

"Cherokee. And my father wouldn't thank you for that."

"Yes he would, I've talked to him. He thinks you're a study in atavism—your mother's ancestors, of course. If he could force you to call yourself Charbonnet, he'd do it. Don't get me off the subject. I want confirmation or denial."

"How about the governor's office? Why don't you ask them?"

"Sanden's out of town, as I'm sure you know. So is Robert Friar, his number one. Susan Elias won't return my calls. Which says something in itself—she's an all-right gal who doesn't duck the press unless there's good reason. Someone answered the phone at Hall's house, but it sure as hell wasn't him. I think it was a cop. I tried the Hall seniors. Housekeeper wouldn't let me talk to either of them and wouldn't comment. I could swear she was crying."

"Melina, be reasonable. *If* what you say were true, you must know I couldn't confirm it. Hold off for one more day, okay? I promise no one will have official word of the identity of the deceased before you."

Moriarty began pulling on her boots. "Not good enough, Abe. I'm gonna go with what I have."

Rainfinch rubbed his eyes and stood. "Suit yourself, I'm too damn tired to argue. But remember, if you're wrong, you'll catch hell. You're making some pretty sensational accusations. Your station could get its corporate butt sued, and you'd be such a pariah you couldn't get a job in Dog-Trot, Wyoming."

Moriarty laughed. "No pain, no gain. I live on the edge, man. I'm going with it."

$\triangledown$

10

JULIANNA DID NOT take the news well. It was eight-thirty in the morning, New York time, when Abe called again and caught her home from the hospital for a shower and a brief rest.

He tried to explain why he couldn't leave, why the Hall case was so important. Her words came back through the wire, tired and bitter. "She's your mother, for God's sake. If you needed her, nothing would prevent—" and "I don't care if the Prince of Wales was dismembered while wearing a tutu—" and the worst, gut-wrenching, undeniable, "I can't handle this alone. She could die, Abe."

"You said the doctor told you she was stabilized—"

"What the hell do doctors know? You're the precious only son, the damned light of her life. I'm supposed to tell her you won't come because of that shit job of yours?"

Julianna knew better than anyone, he thought, how to gut-punch. No visible marks, just internal bleeding.

Not fair. She had a right to be mad.

His mother was made of strong stuff, he assured himself after Julianna hung up on him. She would be all right. And she would understand. She was the only member of the family who hadn't given a performance worthy of Olivier playing Hamlet when he'd announced he was going to become a cop.

Julia'd understand if her mind was working properly. A stroke—no, don't speculate about that. *She would be all right.*

As a parting shot Julianna told him she'd given up her chance to tour Italy and France with the *musica antiqua* ensemble she belonged to—*her* career was on hold while she cared for their mother.

Rainfinch had promised a try at persuading the maestro to join his daughter at his ex-wife's bedside. That idea would be met with about as much enthusiasm as asking Mother Teresa to drop in at a bikers' convention, he figured.

He tried to put a better face on it. Mightn't the great man go for love of Julianna, the talented child, his pride and joy?

Not a chance. He was proud of Julianna; she reflected well on him—an affirmation of his musical genius. But Abe Rainfinch believed Martin was incapable of love. Martin had always viewed his son's lack of musical genius as a willful act of defiance. His wife's demand for a divorce three years ago had been an inconvenience, an embarrassment, nothing more emotionally shattering than that.

Rainfinch had a sudden flash of intuition. Maybe Julianna perceived more than he'd given her credit for. Which was why, subconsciously, she hadn't risked calling their father herself. Better to run the black sheep out front.

Well, he couldn't blame her for that.

The phone rang while he was shaving. It was Susan Elias.

"The governor and Robert Friar are on their way home in the state plane. ETA is about an hour from now. They'll freshen up and sleep a couple of hours. Can you be at the governor's mansion at two this afternoon, for a conference? I've already talked with your chief and Major Adamson, they're coming."

"Did the major know you were going to call me?"

"Yes, I told him. He agreed you should be there."

"Okay—who else will sit in?"

"The governor, Robert Friar, and me. Come to the north gate of the mansion grounds, security will be expecting you."

"Wait a minute. I want to be sure I have this straight. You mean your friend Clifford Stamps isn't invited?"

"My friend—I don't know what you're talking about. He's

public information officer for the police department, isn't
he? What gave you the idea we were friends?"

"He did. Will he be there?"

"No, of course not. You guys handle your own media
people; that's not our business."

"Good enough. I'll see you later."

Before he finished dressing, Rainfinch called Major Adamson for confirmation.

"You knew they were going to include me, sir?"

"Yes. After all, you're in charge of the investigation. I
might say, it was very astute of somebody not to leave you
out."

Rainfinch chuckled. "I may be flattered, but I'm not
disarmed. See you later, Major."

Maestro Martin Rainfinch lived in a fashionable condominium he had purchased after his wife divorced him. Stopping
at the pretentious stone guardpost to identify himself and
be allowed in—or not—Abe Rainfinch tried to ward off a
mixture of defeat, futility, and that damned sense of free-
floating guilt his father had managed to instill in him at an
early age. He wasn't one of the chosen.

It wasn't that he didn't like music. He loved to hear, feel,
absorb, the magnificent sounds that had been a part of his
life since the day he was born. And he still played the violin,
but never in front of his father, who had made it clear his
abilities were mediocre. From Martin's point of view, that he
had been an outstanding athlete who was usually on the
dean's honor roll, that he was popular with his classmates,
and that he had gone to college on double scholarships,
athletic and scholastic, meant nothing.

The condominium was another point of friction. When
Julia left for New York City to pursue her long-delayed
musical career, she had deeded the house to her son. For her,
it had been a symbolic burning of bridges.

The maestro loved his wife's family home; it suited his
sense of grandeur. Abe had never doubted he would continue

to live there—had been astounded when his father huffily insisted on moving out. The whole deal had in some subtle way left Abe in the wrong.

He pulled to a stop in the parking area nearest Martin's door. As he rang the bell, a bit of childhood doggerel popped into his mind. *Pardon me for living, but the graveyard's full.*

Martin answered the door wearing, incredibly, razor-creased slacks, a striped silk smoking jacket, and an ascot. Where the hell did he get clothes like that?

"Come in, Abe. Why am I honored by this visit?" Martin looked at his watch. "You know the orchestra has a performance this afternoon at two."

Perfect. Genius afflicted by rudeness of cretin son.

"I won't take up much of your time. Julianna called last night. Mother's had a stroke. She's in pretty bad shape."

Martin's handsome face revealed nothing but irritation. He frowned. "That's too bad, of course." A shrug. "It's the strain of trying to become a performer at her age, after so many years of scarcely playing at all—at least not seriously."

"Fifty-four's not old—you're older than she is."

"Chronologically, yes, but I've never let up. As an orchestra conductor and composer I'm just approaching my prime. An out-of-practice woman pianist, who never possessed anything but modest talent—"

Abe's hands, inside his pockets, balled into fists. "I didn't come here to argue with you. The point is, Julianna's left holding the bag, physically and emotionally. She needs someone, and I can't leave."

"*You* can't leave. I realize it's nothing to you, but the orchestra's winter season is in full swing. *I* certainly can't be expected to forsake my job and rush to the bedside of a wife who left me for no reason at all three years ago."

The wave of livid fury that overwhelmed Rainfinch frightened him. He turned his back and walked to a window.

"You have an able second in command. I've heard Contrera conduct. And it's not for Mother you'd be going. Julianna needs you."

"I agree Julianna needs somebody. It seems to me that a very junior police official is far more expendable than I."

"I told you—"

"I haven't lost the ability to hear and retain information. It might interest you that I know all about this big case of yours." Martin looked as if he smelled something distasteful. "Carter Hall, murdered while wearing female attire. The governor is understandably distressed."

"He called you about it? Why?"

"You know we're close friends. When they found out my son was involved in the investigation—"

"They? Who is *they*?"

"What I'm trying to do, if you'll leave off interrogating me, is give a friendly warning. Now you have a perfect excuse to drop this affair like the hot potato it is. This is a no-win situation for you, Abe. The powers that be in the governor's office will not thank you for poking into their affairs."

"You're warning me off? They thought they could get to me through you? My God!"

"Don't be an ass. No one's trying to bribe or threaten you, this is just compassionate, father-to-son advice."

"Okay. You're not going to New York, then?"

"Certainly not."

"Will you call Julianna and tell her yourself?"

"I see no need to do that. *She* didn't see fit to telephone *me*, after all."

"Then there's nothing left to say. I won't keep you any longer."

Martin turned away with a stiff nod.

Rainfinch left. He managed with tremendous effort not to slam the door.

With almost two hours before he was expected at the governor's mansion, Rainfinch found himself automatically heading downtown to the police station. Although it was Sunday, someone would be manning the incident-room phone.

He hadn't specifically asked Lou, April, and Danny to

work today. He knew them well enough, though, to figure they'd be out beating the bushes, trying to scare up some kind of lead. In spite of the fact they wouldn't get paid for it. Since the oil boom busted, the city was in a funds squeeze; orders had come from on high: no more overtime. Of course, good detectives worked anytime they needed to, they just didn't get paid for it.

A black-and-white had commandeered his space in the underground lot. Rainfinch pulled into the Police Cars Only area out front. Inside the main doors he came face to face with the sound, fury, and color of a wonderful brawl.

Lindstrom, the female rookie who had been first officer at the Hall scene, was attempting to cuff a drunken rich bitch, whom Rainfinch recognized as the now eloquently profane wife of a prominent attorney.

Duckett, Lindstrom's FTO, was standing well back from the action. He caught Rainfinch's eye and winked. Two officers behind the high front desk wore ear-to-ear grins. So did a couple of tall booted and helmeted motor jocks.

The lawyer's fair lady had apparently not been home after a Saturday night celebration. She wore an electric blue thigh-length sequined dress, stained down the front with a substance best not identified. Her bottle-black tresses, once marvelously coiffed, now resembled a magpie's nest. Her eyes were smeared pools of iridescent blue and black shadow.

As her audience watched, fascinated, she pulled an arm free, snatched one of her spike-heeled shoes, and aimed a vicious swipe at Lindstrom's forehead. Lindstrom ducked, but the heel plowed a nasty red furrow.

Rainfinch suppressed an urge to help. The rookie needed to handle this on her own.

In fact, the wound seemed to be all she needed. "Okay, bitch," she snarled. "You wanna play rough?" She caught the shoe-baring arm and twisted it viciously behind the woman's back. The pump hit the floor. A wail of pain was followed by a hiccup and a screeched threat. "You'll pay for his. My husband'll have your dykey little ass—"

Lindstrom gave the arm another jerk and snapped on the cuffs. "I *am not a dyke*," she roared, giving the woman a shove. Then, realizing she'd been stung into a dumb retort, she blushed to match the red streak on her forehead.

She shoved her prisoner onto the jail elevator. Duckett followed, trying without much success not to smirk.

Lindstrom was coming along nicely, Rainfinch thought. She had the makings of a damn fine cop.

Upstairs, walking through the silent and empty homicide squad room, he was surprised to see a light in his office. Clifford Stamps sat at his desk, going through a stack of papers.

"What the hell do you think you're doing?"

Surprised, Stamps was not repentant. "Damn it, Rainfinch. You startled me." He made no move to vacate.

"I asked what the hell you're doing at my desk."

Stamps's fastidiously groomed features pulled into a frown. "You don't work undercover anymore, Lieutenant. Besides, I'm a cop too, remember?"

Rainfinch pushed the office door shut behind him.

"Stamps—"

The PIO stood and backed away, perhaps a little faster than he had intended. "I was looking for your copy of a memo I sent around—the chief asked me to make a couple of changes—but since you're here, I want to talk to you about the Hall case."

Partially victorious, Rainfinch dropped into his chair and glanced down at field notes and a report from Lou Curran pertaining to Hall's death, now in disarray, in front of him. He sighed. What the hell, why not another confrontation? It was turning out to be that kind of day.

"Let me tell you something, Stamps. If I catch you rifling my desk again, or hear of it happening, or even suspect you might have, I'm going to do something to you. You won't know where, or when or how—and you'll never be able to prove I did it. But I will."

He could tell from Stamps's face he'd drawn blood. The

PIO, a charter member of what street cops called the empty holster gang, was pathologically suspicious of anybody who had worked in Projects. Everyone knew that was where crazies lived and bred, like the cockroaches that shared their basement quarters. Now Stamps was livid. One side of his face appeared to be paralyzed. A vein that stretched from his left temple and across the forehead, where it disappeared into the hairline, popped out and began to pulsate.

This was a well-noted phenomenon, watched for throughout the ranks and the subject of much humor. Each occurrence was lovingly charted and gloated over. Trouble was, Rainfinch thought regretfully, it was better to have a witness. Individual sightings of the engorged purple mass were not discounted, but they carried limited clout.

"Y-you—you're as bad as—" Stamps fought for control. "You'll go too far, one of these days," he continued in a more normal voice.

"I know. When you're chief, all us wackos'll be out of a job. No more scruffy narcs, no intelligence officers, no more snitches, just good, clean cops who get their street information from Sunday school deacons."

Watching Stamps struggle for a retort, Rainfinch suddenly tired of the game. "What do you want? I have a meeting to attend."

That did it. The PIO was off like a runaway fire horse. "You're not—you're going to that meeting at the governor's mansion? Rainfinch, it's imperative I sit in on that. I've got to be kept briefed. Surely you must understand—"

"Why are you telling me? Talk to Major Adamson or the chief. You know I don't have any control over who is or isn't involved."

Stamps's shoulders were rigid with indignation. "Mark Adamson's worse than you. And I've dialed Chief Jurgen all morning—something must be wrong with his pager. He isn't at home, and I haven't heard from him. Rainfinch, I'm asking you to talk to Adamson. I can't handle the press unless I know what's going on."

As if he'd been conjured, Major Adamson appeared at Rainfinch's door. "Abe, I thought I saw you come in here. Are you ready?" He spotted Stamps and nodded curtly. "Clifford."

Dead silence. Two pairs of eyes steadily regarded the PIO.

His stuffing melted. "I was just leaving. Rainfinch, think about what I said. I'll be in my office."

Adamson sat. "What the hell was that all about?"

"Stamps wants to go with us. Governor's throwing a party, and forgot to invite his buddy, Cliffy Stamps."

Adamson grunted. "Some party."

"You have to get inside Stamps's head, Major."

"God forbid. But speaking of the governor, Abe, I need to ask you about something." Adamson looked uncomfortable.

What the hell, Rainfinch wondered. "Sir?"

"I've heard from several sources that your father is a good friend of Governor Sanden's. Is that going to be a problem during the investigation?"

Rainfinch controlled his ire. Who had put that flea in the major's ear? "Absolutely not. My father and I don't get along well, to be honest with you. I rarely see him, and I certainly don't run in his crowd. I've never even met Max Sanden."

"Good enough, Abe. I had to ask—but your answer's a relief." He looked at his watch. "Shall we go?"

▽

11

THE YOUNG STATE trooper who stopped them at the entrance to the mansion grounds was all spit and polish. He checked identification.

"The governor's expecting you, gentlemen. You can park in the drive and go right in the front entrance."

Tripped from inside the guard shack, iron gates swung open. The home of the governor of the state loomed before them, a cold, amorphous mass of pale stone that tour pamphlets called "Dutch Colonial."

"I've always wondered why we elect a man to the highest office in the state, then force him to live in that god-awful place. We must be a bunch of sadists," the chief said.

Rainfinch and Adamson laughed.

"It reminds me of one of those old black-and-white prison films with Jimmy Cagney. It's where the warden lives—you know, the guy who runs around with a blacksnake whip, beating prisoners into submission," Adamson said.

"Abe," he continued, "You live in a damn palace. Not fitting for a police lieutenant. Why don't you do the governor a favor, and donate it to the state? Think of the tax write-off, and besides it'd keep Internal Affairs off your rear."

"If they'd show me where to get the money to fix the roof and plaster the cracks, I'd be obliged," Rainfinch said, laughing along with the others.

Inside, the mansion seemed more livable. They were ushered into a small study, where bright wallpaper, golden pecan woodwork, and a well-tended wood fire tried to make

you forget the grim exterior. Max Sanden himself came
forward to greet them.

Rainfinch was impressed in spite of himself. Sanden's
handshake was firm. He was tall and muscular, with thick,
unruly brown hair and bright blue eyes that had a look of
good humor about them even now.

Susan Elias and Robert Friar stood behind him. Sanden
quickly handled introductions and got down to business.

"I don't mind telling you this is one hell of a shock. Carter
Hall was an old friend, an adviser from the beginning of my
political career. I had no idea—but that's neither here nor
there. His parents—I'm going out to see them this evening—

"Sorry. I'm rambling. Chief, I want to thank the police
department for its discretion in handling this matter up to
now."

"We've been lucky as hell. We've muzzled our officers, but
Major Adamson and Lieutenant Rainfinch tell me some of
the media people are already smelling a rat—sorry, that's an
unfortunate way of putting it." Jurgen laughed nervously.

Robert Friar leaned forward. A lock of hair fell across his
forehead. "We've got to keep the circumstances of Carter's
death away from the media. We can't have—"

"That's impossible," Rainfinch cut in. He had taken an
instant dislike to the governor's chief of staff. Which, of
course, had nothing to do with the fact that Susan Elias was
looking at Friar as if she'd like to smooth back his hair and
pat his hand.

"You can't keep facts surrounding the murder of a member
of the governor's staff a secret," he continued. "There were
radio and television reporters at the crime scene. They saw
the body was dressed as a woman. Once they find out about
Hall—it won't take a genius to put two and two together. In
fact, one TV newswoman already has."

Adamson looked startled at the vehemence of his lieutenant's statement, but had begun to back him up when
Friar interrupted. He ignored both Rainfinch and Adamson,
and spoke directly to the chief.

"We expect you to keep a lid on this. Handle it. There's no excuse—"

"Back off, Robert." The governor's voice was angry. He turned to Susan Elias. "Schedule a press conference for nine in the morning. I'll make a statement." He looked around the room. "Lieutenant Rainfinch is right. It's useless trying to sweep a thing like this under the rug. I'm just grateful for the chance to lay it out myself, in my own words. And then hope to hell you guys find the killer, before my whole staff is crucified."

The meeting went on with a quick summary of the investigation to date by Major Adamson and an establishment of communication lines between the governor's office and the police department.

Rainfinch made a game of staring at the governor's chief of staff, who refused to meet his glance. He resolved to find out everything there was to know about Robert Friar. Pity he'd been in Washington at the time of the murder—but then, maybe he hadn't. No harm checking airline schedules.

The cops were leaving when Susan Elias approached Rainfinch. "Lieutenant." She blushed furiously. "Could I have a word with you?"

"I'm driving the chief and Major Adamson back to the station, Miss Elias. May I get in touch with you later?"

Mark Adamson grinned evilly and waved him off. "Chief Jurgen and I can find the way back downtown by ourselves. He's all yours, Miss Elias."

This was interesting, Rainfinch thought. He didn't flatter himself that Elias's reasons for appropriating him were personal. What was she up to?

The cops were gone. Robert Friar peered into the hall, then closed the door to the study. He propped himself restlessly against the mantel beside the fireplace. "We've got to get Jurgen to call in the State Bureau of Investigations. That way we can control—"

"Don't be stupid, Robert. That would stink to heaven. In

the first place, I *don't* control them, and in the second, it's
not their jurisdiction. So your idea would give us the
appearance of hiding something without any benefits at all."

Friar perched on the edge of a chair. "Sir, you could lean
on OSBI. Most of the board members are your appointees. I
think it's a mistake not to—"

"Forget trying to manipulate the investigation. Let me tell
you what I expect from you."

Friar was startled. Among his top staff, Max Sanden's style
of command was normally low-key and good-natured. Now
there was a tone to his voice and a steely look in his eye that
told Friar he'd better shut up fast.

"I want to know who among my staffers besides Carter
Hall was involved in this kind of behavior—gay bars, cross-
dressing. I don't give a big rat's ass about anyone's sexual
preference, but by God, when aberrations are flaunted in
public, it becomes my business. Our salaries are paid by
taxpayers; they have a right to expect dignity from their
governor and his employees."

Aren't we sanctimonious, thought Friar. "You're right,
sir," he said.

Sanden, who was trying to cut down on smoke inhalation,
picked up a pipe and began stuffing tobacco into the bowl.
He lit a match, stuck it into the bowl, and inhaled. The thing
flared up like a torch. Sanden cursed and began poking at
the tobacco with a metal tamper. "I'll never get the hang of
this."

Friar, who usually found this procedure hilarious, didn't
smile. "If I'd had any idea—" he began.

Sanden put the pipe aside. "That's a point, Robert. Why
weren't you aware of something as potentially explosive as
this? I count on you to know what's happening on my staff,
it's your job. Carter must have been close to a breakdown,
to behave like that in public. Didn't you have any inkling?"

Goddamn Hall. If he weren't dead, I'd kill him. "He'd been
a little—surly lately, said he was putting in too many hours.

Hell, who doesn't? You can't expect me to have anticipated—"

Sanden made an impatient gesture. "All right—it's done. But if there's anything else nasty finning its way around under the surface of my staff, I want it fished out. Any sensational revelations, we'll make them ourselves. You get on top of things, and keep me informed. And Robert—cooperate with the police department in every way. Do you understand?"

Friar's face felt like a mask made of hot pitch. He was so furious he thought it must show. He turned away. "I apologize, governor. We worked so hard preparing for the Washington deal—there could have—must have been things happening around here I should have noticed, and didn't. It won't happen again."

"Okay. This is a bitch, Robert, but we'll get through it." Sanden's voice had regained most of its good humor. "Find out about Carter's funeral arrangements, and have Ettalou order flowers. Now, let's get to work on my statement to the press. Where's Susan?"

"I sent her off for a private talk with Lieutenant Rainfinch. You realize, sir, he's Martin Rainfinch's son? After Clifford Stamps told me who was on the case, I took the liberty of calling the maestro. We should have some clout, there."

Sanden looked skeptical. "I'm not sure it was a good idea to call Martin. Until today I'd never met, or even heard of the son—they can't be very close. And Lieutenant Rainfinch didn't seem especially friendly."

Friar grinned. "That's why I sicced Susan on him. The maestro probably hasn't had time for a fatherly chat, yet. Incidentally, Cliff Stamps isn't too impressed with Rainfinch junior."

"Stamps—the PIO for the police department? He's the one who keeps sniffing around for a job, isn't he?"

"He wouldn't say no, if we offered him a goodie."

Sanden shook his head. "No goodies. Not even a hint. Is that clear?"

Friar sighed. It was very difficult, sometimes, to work for a man who could be so naive about the ways of government. "Yes, sir," he said.

At least, not that you'll find out about.

Susan was working hard not to feel exploited. Because if she was, Robert Friar was the exploiter, and she didn't want to cast him in that role. He wasn't—couldn't be—cruel enough to stake her out as bait to Rainfinch, like tethering a lamb at the tiger's water hole.

She was driving the white Mustang convertible she'd bought in an excess of glee over her promotion to press secretary. Abe Rainfinch sat next to her, stiff as a marine cadet during inspection.

You could try a little, Lieutenant, she thought. Make conversation. Say something trivial.

More silence. Without conscious volition she had headed for the Solon Club, a favorite hangout of legislators and other state house types. Now, pulling into the parking lot, she wondered if it was a good idea. Oh, damn, of course it wasn't a good idea. She was bound to see people she knew. How could they talk freely? And how the hell would she introduce her stone-faced escort?

She looked at him. "Is this okay? Maybe someplace else would be—?"

His face broke into a grin that was pure wickedness. "This is fine. I've never been here, but I've heard about it. It'll be an experience to see our lawmakers cavorting in their natural habitat."

"Swell. We aim to entertain. And I'm sure you believe the stories about how half the legislation that reaches the senate floor is proposed and debated in advance right here in the Solon Club."

"I'm not sure. Do you?"

"No. Well, maybe. What difference does it make? I expect most of the momentous decisions in the history of mankind were made over tavern tables by men stuffed with food and half sloshed. Lubrication of the brain is a wondrous thing, Lieutenant."

"That's a fine piece of cynicism, Miss Elias. Now that you've flayed the honor of my sex, may I remind you of something? It was you who filched me from the company of my superiors and brought me here. Do you mind if I ask why?"

Susan's throat felt lumpy. Her nerves were stretched like high-tension wires, and she was making a fool of herself. "I'm sorry if I sound irritable . . . Abe. It's just—I'm worried. Shabby of me to take that out on you. May we go in and have a drink?" She tried a smile. "My brain could do with a little of that lubrication I was so sarcastic about."

She led him to a table beside a glass wall that looked out over the city. The Solon Club was built on the crown of a steep cliff. Although it was only five o'clock, the winter afternoon was dark. Streetlights had come on; headlamps from cars snaked their way in and out like lasers at a rock concert. Other, vari-colored lights glimmered from businesses and homes. A desultory snowfall was in progress. The town laid out below seemed warm, snug, and sleepy.

When a waiter came to the table Susan was greeted as an old friend. After they ordered she nodded a quick hello to people at a couple of nearby tables. When drinks came they chatted aimlessly, as if a truce had been set out and the terms agreed upon. For a few minutes she allowed herself the fantasy that she was simply a young woman on a date, not a governor's staffer on assignment to pry information out of a smart, tough cop. She looked at him, wondering how to start.

"Abe—"

"Yes?" He turned from the window. Something in her tone had warned him. The spark was gone, leaving his eyes black, flat, opaque. It was a strong face, the Indian blood apparent in heavy black brows, skin with a dark glow that didn't depend on sunlamps or days at the beach, and a strength and definition of bone structure she had grown up to recognize as uniquely Cherokee.

The hell with Robert Friar. She wasn't cut out to be a spy. "Abe, what if I told you I didn't have any great mission in kidnapping you? What if I just felt like it?"

She was rewarded by a smile of sudden, piercing sweetness. "If that's the case, I'll drink to your impulse."

Half a dozen hours later a very thoughtful Abe Rainfinch climbed the stairs to his bedroom. It might be rude to question an evening out initiated by a woman who was witty and damn sexy, but it had been years since he'd been naive enough to buy her explanation that she'd carried him off on a sudden madcap impulse.

It was cold in the bedroom. He stripped fast and slid his naked gooseflesh between covers, ignoring for the moment the frantic flashes of red light from his answering machine.

▽

12

RAINFINCH FORAGED IN the pantry until he found a stale cinnamon roll. He sat at the scarred kitchen table, which had been there since the beginning of time, and began to chew. It seemed fitting; stale pastry went well with his early-morning attack of guilt and inadequacy. If he got to feeling much worse, he might as well shop for a hair shirt.

There had been no message from his sister Julianna on the recorder. She wasn't home when he telephoned. He thought about trying to reach her at the hospital, but his mother was still in the intensive care unit. He knew Julianna would be floating around like a disembodied soul, waiting for the five-minute visits allowed each hour.

Julianna was vivid in his mind. Her straight dark hair, the color of blackstrap molasses, framing the clever, intelligent face. Her hands, long-fingered, with short nails immaculately buffed, always seemed to be in motion. His sister possessed a kind of concentrated, passionate energy that had always awed him. He pictured her now, pacing like some exotic animal testing the boundaries of its cage.

And here he sat.

The kitchen was the only room on the first floor of the Charbonnet Mansion that Abe Rainfinch used, now that he was alone. Formal dining room, green sitting room, music room—where the gleaming grand piano his mother loved, the one José Iturbi had once played, sat mute—and the French parlor, its walls handpainted in Gainsborough-type scenes, now were occupied only by ghosts of voices and laughter from bygone parties.

But the kitchen was different. A battered gas steam radiator hissed and rattled comfortably between the original iron cook stove and a modern version, all black enamel and stainless steel. The walls were papered in a yellow-and-white print. There were no cabinets, only an old pie safe, a sink and a venerable refrigerator. A huge pantry that had long ago lost its door held pots, pans, dishes, canned goods.

The whole area seemed perpetually perfumed by scents of fresh bread, ginger cookies, roasting meat. It had been some time since the kitchen bustled with preparation of such goodies, but Rainfinch could still smell them.

In the end, while he waited for coffee to brew, he talked to Julianna's sterile machine. After the beep he admitted he hadn't been able to persuade Martin to go to his ex-wife's bedside, and ended with "Please, Julianna, call tonight. If she isn't better maybe I can—" *beep again and you're finished, buster, like it or not. Only ninety seconds to spill your guts.*

His own recorder had contained a flurry of messages. Five, escalating in ire and verbal abuse, signed off with "Brenda Starr, girl reporter." Moriarty. Three calls from Clifford Stamps, in which he reminded Rainfinch that he was, after all, the spokesman for the department, and should be kept aware of how the Hall case progressed. One from Brendon Guiste, saying that Richard Henderson would not be back in town until Thursday, but leaving a phone number where he could be reached. Guiste was careful to inform Rainfinch that he was "Brendon Guiste, calling from the governor's office." Rainfinch smiled.

Four calls were from miscellaneous television and newspaper reporters savvy enough to circle Clifford Stamps. Which elicited another smile.

Giving up on the cinnamon roll, he threw it in the trash and poured himself a large glass of orange juice, which he carried to the kitchen window.

Across an expanse of winter-killed lawn he could see his next-door neighbor, a retired admiral with gouty legs. Admiral Vincent was the proud possessor of what had to be the fastest mechanized wheelchair in the entire nation. He delighted in terrorizing store clerks, small children, dogs, and above all, unsuspecting motorists.

As Rainfinch watched, the admiral lurked behind a tree near his drive until he saw a car coming. His timing was perfect. At the last possible moment his chair shot into the street. Tires locked; the car swung into a half circle. The admiral turned, yelled, and brandished a walking stick. The driver, reduced to a bundle of quivering nerves, emerged from his car on rubbery legs.

"Are you all right?" he called after the disappearing figure.

With a last brandish of his stick, the admiral shouted, "Watch what you're doing, pea-brain. Serve you right if you'd killed me."

The motorist seemed to ponder this remarkable statement. Then with a shake of his head, he returned to his car, made a shaky U-turn, and headed back the way he had come. At a speed of roughly fifteen miles per hour.

Rainfinch refilled his orange-juice glass, pulled on a jacket, and walked outside. As he had expected, the admiral came putting back home.

Rainfinch intercepted him. The old man stopped, cackling.

"You see that, Abe? I'll teach the sons of bitches not to use this street for a racetrack."

"Admiral, there are still patches of ice on the pavement. You were taking a hell of a chance. Besides, he had the right-of-way. I should give you a ticket."

Admiral Vincent looked smug. "Can't scare me with that kind of threat, boy. I have enough sense to know you haven't owned a ticket book since you were a pup in uniform. You probably don't even know how to fill one out anymore."

Rainfinch laughed. "Don't provoke me, Admiral. I might torpedo you."

The old man's thoughts had moved to other things.

"What do you hear from your mother, Abe? She still in New York? I miss her. Special girl, Julia always was. When she was little she used to—but you've heard my stories a million times. How's she doing up north? Do you think she'll ever come back here to live?"

Rainfinch hesitated. He didn't want to tell this crotchety, kind old man that the little girl he remembered, now a middle-aged woman, was in a hospital fighting for her life.

"She's doing fine, sir. She and my sister share an apartment. Mom's working on her music full-time. She wants to go on concert tours."

"Good for her. Always was a talented girl. Never could understand why she married that pretentious creampuff."

"You mean my father, sir?"

Vincent laughed. "Don't take that tone with me, Abe. You don't get along with that trumped-up bandleader any better than I do."

Rainfinch recognized defeat. He withdrew from the field, saying, "Please be a little more careful. I can't afford to lose a friend, I don't have that many."

The old man's voice pursued him. " . . . need a wife, boy, and kids of your own. Shouldn't be living in that big place by yourself."

Inside, Rainfinch projected a face looking out at him through the kitchen window. He couldn't tell if it was April, or Susan Elias, or, God forbid, Moriarty. But the morning wasn't a total loss. A visit with the admiral always made him feel better.

Calla Magee, the governor's assistant press secretary, dropped a bulgy, fragrant paper sack on her boss's desk. She stretched, yawned prodigiously, and sank into a chair. Susan Elias thought she looked like a swooning flower, long petals of hair loose and drifting. Her multicolored skirt swirled and settled in ripples around her.

"What is *happening*?" Robert Friar and the governor blew in a few minutes ago. Robert looked like he'd been eating green persimmons, and Big Max had that weight-of-the-world-upon-my-shoulders expression. So what gives?"

Susan opened the doughnut sack. "Umm, cinnamon sugar. Still warm. I'll get the coffee."

"*Susan,*" the plaintive voice followed.

She returned with the carafe and handed Calla her own cup, which proclaimed, "Live a Little—Correct Your Overbite."

In spite of her jokes, Calla was sensitive about the braces on her teeth. She'd confided to Susan that her parents hadn't been able to afford an orthodontist. Now she was making her own living, and intended to have the best smile money could buy. And if that meant having a mouth full of plastic and stainless steel for a while, well, she'd scowl and bear it.

"Susan Elias, sit down in that chair, eat your doughnut, and tell me what's happening."

Susan shrugged. "Carter Hall."

"Carter. Okay, he was murdered. In the interest of good taste I'll resist saying it couldn't have happened to a more deserving person. Anyway, his death doesn't gore anybody's ox around here. Or does it?" The familiar state-house expression sounded incongruous on her lips. Her eyes got huge. "Don't tell me they suspect one of us?"

"Maybe. I don't know. But there are circumstances—oh, Calla, in your worst nightmares you couldn't imagine."

"But you're going to tell me, because if you don't, I'll—" She hesitated, searching for a threat dire enough to get results. In final exasperation she flung up her arms and said, "Susan Elias, sometimes I could just flail you like Daddy did the ol' wild pecan back of the house. You're just as stingy with information as that tree was with nuts."

Susan grinned fleetingly at the mental image of Calla attacking her with a flail pole, then shrugged. "Big Max is going to make a statement in a few minutes, so it can't hurt to tell you. Besides, you *are* assistant press secretary." Susan took a deep breath. "Carter was found outside a gay bar, wearing drag."

Calla's lips moved, but no sound came out.

"Say something. Stop looking like you just swallowed a fly."

"He's going—the governor's going to *say* that?"

"Of course not, silly. I doubt he'll make any comment on Carter's costume. But some of our more resourceful media friends are already putting two and two together. WROX TV had Melina Moriarty and a crew at the homicide scene Friday night. I've been dodging calls from her all weekend."

Calla made a face. "Moriarty can be a pain in the butt. Sometimes I think she's got more people feeding her information than the CIA. Did you write Big Max's statement?"

Susan wiped cinnamon sugar from her mouth and shook her head. "Robert and Big Max did it themselves, after we met with the chief of police and a couple of detectives at the mansion yesterday. I was otherwise occupied."

Calla, picking up the irritation in Susan's voice, seized on the last sentence. "What do you mean, you were otherwise occupied?"

Susan and her assistant had a running joke about clichés—of which politicians and news reporters seemed inordinately fond. She held up an index finger for attention and solemnly pronounced, "It's a small world," then waited for Calla's moan. She continued, "The detective in charge of the case is Maestro Rainfinch's son."

Calla nodded impatiently. "I know. Or at least I guessed. Remember, I brought him back when he came to see you Saturday, the day after Carter's death. Rainfinch isn't a common name—they had to be relatives."

"That's right, I forgot you'd met him. Anyway, as the meeting broke up Robert took me aside and asked me to invite the Lieutenant out for one-on-one conversation. To see if I could learn anything about the investigation."

"You're kidding. What were you supposed to do, offer your gorgeous bod for information? Well, did it work?"

"It wasn't like that. Robert wouldn't—I didn't find out a damn thing." Susan lowered her voice. "I was embarrassed.

Abe Rainfinch was too smart to be taken in, and too nice a guy to be rude."

"He's gorgeous. If Robert decides to send in a first-string seductress"—she arched her shoulders and threw out her chest—"I'm available."

Susan laughed. "Get serious, Magee. You wouldn't do anything but blush and run."

"Okay then, seriously, I wonder why we've never seen him around. Maestro Rainfinch and Big Max are such buddies."

"My guess is father and son don't like each other much. I mentioned the maestro a couple of times and Abe got all flinty-eyed. He did talk about his mother—you knew she and the maestro were divorced? She lives in New York. Abe had her on his mind, told me she had a stroke a couple of days ago. He's worried.

"You know he's Cherokee, on his mother's side. She's a Charbonnet. Don't you think he has that Cherokee look—strong features and bold eyes?"

Calla gazed heavenward. "Oh, yes. A Charbonnet? As in Charbonnet Mansion?"

"That's where he lives. Alone."

"God—it's a museum. Or should be. Did he take you there? Did you frolic naked among the antiques?"

"Of course not. Don't be an ass."

"You *are* going to see him again, I hope?"

"How the hell can I avoid it? He's in charge of—"

Robert Friar came through the door. Susan broke off in mid-sentence, shocked by the look of him. A prime example of the walking wounded.

It wasn't like him to be unnerved. Robert thrived on trouble, controversy. She could remember the last campaign, his grin and wickedly gleeful command: "They wanna play rough? Grab a spade, troops, Sanden's Happy Band can shovel shit with the best of them."

Maybe now, though, the stakes were too high; with heady talk of the vice presidency, even a tantalizing distant chimera of the Oval Office. The chief of staff's face was pale and pinched, and it scared her. She greeted him quickly, thus alerting Calla, who had her back to the door.

"Elias, the governor wants all executive staff at the press conference," he said.

Calla spun around. "Executive staff. Does that include me?"

Friar examined her. "Not the way you're dressed. You look like yesterday's fruit salad." He turned to Susan. "Come on, Elias. We need to make sure the conference room is set up properly."

"That's *my* job," Calla said. "I've already taken care of it."

Susan saw her assistant's lips quiver as she slipped past Friar and fled down the hall.

"Why don't you run out and pull wings off a few butterflies, while you're at it. That was uncalled-for."

"You're right," he agreed instantly. "I'm on edge. Big Max and I were up all night. I'll find Calla and apologize, later. I promise."

When Susan didn't respond he threw an arm around her shoulders in a fraternal hug. "What's wrong? Mad at me for sending you off to work on tall, dark, and surly, yesterday?" Now came a ghost of that grin.

Robert always had the ability to make her insides feel like a mushy strawberry popsicle, but for once Susan didn't give in. "You put me in an impossible situation. Abe Rainfinch isn't stupid. He knew what I was up to, but was nice enough not to make me feel any shabbier than I already did."

Robert's left eyebrow went up. "*Abe* Rainfinch—not Lieutenant? Well, well. How nice was he? Should I be jealous?"

In spite of herself, Susan felt her lips curve.

"That's my girl." He sketched an X across his chest. "Promise, I won't ask you to fling your charms at any more stormtroopers." He gave her shoulders a final squeeze, then released her as voices approached.

Serious again, Susan pulled him aside as they neared the conference room. "What's the official stance, Robert? Will Big Max stonewall any nasty questions about how Carter died?"

He grimaced. "The official line goes this way: 'We're not at liberty to divulge any details at this time; to do so might jeopardize the homicide investigation. You'll have to take those inquiries to the police department.' "

Susan nodded. "Makes sense—but it won't satisfy them."

Robert shrugged. "When are they ever satisfied? Big Max'll have to rely on the 'heavenly blue eyes' and that 'insouciant charm' everyone babbles about."

Susan kept her own counsel. She knew most media people liked Max Sanden. He was quick-witted, disarming, and usually frank. But a story as juicy as Carter's death was bound to send the whole pack slavering after the gubernatorial jugular.

Friar seemed to echo her thoughts. "One taste of blood," he muttered. "That's all it takes to set them off."

$\triangledown$

13

BETH FARRADAY FINISHED the last bit of chicken salad on whole wheat and swept up the brightly colored travel folders scattered across her desk. They were dog-eared, some of them months old. "Garden Tour of the English Country-side," "Ireland on Thirty Dollars a Day," "See Historic Edinburgh in the Springtime. . . ."

She pulled off round, gold-rimmed reading glasses that were seriously out of style. She knew it because her brother kept nagging. "Where did you get those things, at a garage sale? They look straight out of the sixties."

That made her laugh. Because she had gotten them at a garage sale.

Beth leaned back until the chair creaked, and rubbed her eyes. Why bother with the travel-folder charade, why go through the motions of planning a vacation? She looked at file folders stacked on her desk, littering her credenza, spilling over onto the floor. Each wore at least one stick-on note, some half a dozen. "Beth, this guy's guilty as hell, but it's a first offense. I think we ought to plead on it." "Beth, I think we should stall for time, here. Work something up and file it in Judge Allen's court." "Beth . . . ," "Beth . . . ," "Beth . . ." She sighed. Sometimes she woke at night hearing Shadid call her name.

I owe him. She rocked her chair forward and pulled a file off the top of the stack. How many men would have done that? Paid my way through school, and not expected any-thing but hard work in return? He wouldn't even let me hold down a part-time job. "Study, Beth, study. I want you to be the best damn criminal lawyer in the state."

She knew what people said. "Pompous little shit," "ambulance chaser," "represents every whore and dope dealer in the county—at least if they've got money." And the most humiliating, "He's got to be getting in her britches. You can't tell me Shadid Garber suddenly turned philanthropist."

State v. *Sharmine Renee Crozier, aka Darlin' Sharmin'.* Beth read three pages of the file before she realized she hadn't the foggiest notion what it said. She shoved it aside. Hard to get worked up about Sharmine's civil rights being violated, when they threw her little candy ass in jail for indecent exposure.

Two things were eating at Beth that had nothing to do with the fact she was overworked. Hell, any good lawyer was overworked, and liked it that way.

Kent. Her brother, Dr. Kent Farraday. Unlike Beth, he'd worked at every odd job he could handle while he was in med school, and it had cost every cent she could spare, too. Now he was interning at Central City Hospital, and everyone said he had a brilliant future.

She grinned ruefully. Just what she'd always dreamed of, wasn't it? Only somehow, things had gone sour. Maybe she had come on too heavy as Big Sister Who Knows All. She couldn't help it, she'd been mother and father to him for so long. She and Kent had clung to each other after their parents died, forming a closed unit the relatives they lived with had never been able to penetrate.

She smiled again, this time with real pleasure, remembering the day he graduated from medical school. She'd given him the new car. Paid for. He'd been pleased as an eighteen-year-old.

The next day he announced he was moving into his own apartment. Not unreasonable. After all, he was a grown man. But like an idiot she had tried to insist he wait a couple more years, until he was ready to go into practice for himself.

She shook her head and fought a silly impulse to cry. Her

own fault. How could she have let a wall build between them? Criticizing his friends, his lifestyle.

She pushed up out of her chair and strode over to the window. No. She hadn't been wrong, she'd had to speak up. He could ruin a brilliant career if he weren't careful. But she'd done it the wrong way, sounding jealous and resentful instead of caring.

Outside, three forlorn sparrows were huddled on a frozen branch. Beth opened the window and scattered crumbs from her sandwich onto the sill. Almost before she could push the window shut, the sparrows were wrangling over the feast.

She walked back to her desk. She could mend this rift between herself and Kent. She could. But something must be done quickly, before it widened into a chasm.

She was distracted by the sound of Garber rumbling and roaring as he approached her office. Before he arrived Beth had arranged her face into a look of polite inquiry.

"What's up, Shadid?"

"Beth? Goddamn it, Beth, did you know some piece a scum got himself killed in the alley right by the Seraphim, Friday night? Monk Smith just called. The governor held a press conference a while ago, the goddamn fairy was one of his top aides. And that mother, that mother-blessed High Bluff neighborhood hysterical society is foaming at the mouth to put Monk out of business. Monk's a good tenant, and God knows who else we could get to rent the place. Especially now. You got to get over there and help him out."

It figured. After her brother the Seraphim, and the kind of place it had become, topped Beth's worry list.

"Come and sit down, Shadid. Catch your breath and tell me all about it."

$\triangledown$

14

MONK FELT HIS temper rising. Felt the angry flush of his face, the burn of acid in his stomach, the tension that ran from back of neck to knotted shoulder muscles. He circled the room, throwing magazines, clothes, an empty vodka bottle, even dirty dishes in a heap on the floor.

"*Archie,*" he bellowed. "Where the hell are you? This place looks like a bitch rabbit's den." He fanned a newspaper in a wide swath across the carved mahogany library table. Dust flew.

Archie stumbled from the bedroom hallway. He was shoeless and wore bikini briefs, exposing pale, spindly legs that had been tanned and shapely before he'd come down with the goddamned disease.

Monk watched as he struggled to find neck and armholes in a blue knit shirt. Finally his head emerged, revealing eyes that were startled as a fawn's. "What's wrong? What happened?"

"It's after one o'clock. You were still in bed, weren't you?"

"I, I, I—didn't sleep well. My, my fever w-was up again."

Archie had stammered badly as a child. He'd overcome it, except when he was especially tired or nervous. Monk remembered a time when he had found those occasional lapses immensely appealing. He closed his eyes, trying to summon patience, trying not to feel that their world was crashing around their shoulders while Archie slept.

"Governor Sanden held a press conference this morning, about Carter Hall's death. He didn't mention the Seraphim,

of course—he sidestepped all questions about circumstances, and lobbed the ball into Chief Jurgen's lap. Three
channels carried the conference live. Afterward hotshot
reporters were gushing enough rumors and speculation to
fuel half a dozen soap operas. And Frannie Da Sorta came
in a few minutes ago with news that the High Bluff people
have already hired a lawyer to force us out of business."

Archie collapsed into a chair and buried his head in his
hands. "V-vultures. What are we g-going to do?"

"Try getting dressed, and help me straighten up this
damned mess. Shadid Garber's partner, Beth Farraday, is on
her way over to discuss damage control. I'd as soon she didn't
see this—gerbil cage."

Archie's mouth twisted. "That's rather an unf-fortunate
f-figure of speech. But I see your point." His head drooped
like a child's. "I'm sorry, Monk. I-I've been so down. Can't
seem to p-pull out of it." He stood. "I'll get the sweeper."

"No time for that." Monk touched his shoulder. "Come on,
let's carry the junk out of here so she'll have a place to sit."

Archie brightened. "Yes, and I'll g-get the aerosol furniture
p-p-polish. A few spritzes and the p-place'll smell like we've
been cleaning for hours."

"Okay." Monk drew a deep breath. "Just don't open the
curtains, for God's sake."

"I'm worried about Morgen, Abe."

It was midafternoon. Lou Curran sprawled in front of
Rainfinch's desk. His lined face wore a scowl, which Rainfinch recognized as concern.

"Worried about her? In what way? You don't mean she's
not doing her job—April's a good cop."

Curran spat out the toothpick he'd been chewing. "Of
course she is. The best." He rocked back in his chair and
squinted.

Rainfinch thought he read accusation in the look. "So?"

"I'm just saying I think she's pushing herself too hard,
especially since her partner's been on leave. Have you taken

a good look at her lately? She's thin as a spook, and so damn pale someone's liable to stuff her in a body bag if she sits in one place too long."

"What are you suggesting I do about it, Lou? I won't pull her off the Hall case. That would be a slap in the face."

"Hell, of course I don't want you to do that. If she'd take a few days, rest—"

"You know she won't."

Curran leaned forward, elbows on the desk. "Then call Mitchelson in. I talked to him Friday, he's not doing anything with his days off but sittin' around the house feedin' his face and gettin' on Virgie's nerves. If he knew his partner needed him, he'd be back in a flash."

Rainfinch hesitated. He could justify calling Mitchelson, they were shorthanded. But would April smell a rat? "I'll talk to her," he said.

Lou nodded. "Good enough. See what you think. Hell, maybe I'm just tryin' to be everybody's pappy. From now on I'll mind my own business."

"The devil you will."

Rainfinch looked up as Danny Bent joined them.

"So the old man's in here, sucking up. It's three o'clock, Lieutenant, are you ready to meet? Morgen and I appropriated Patrol's conference room and a pot of coffee." Danny looked around the postage-stamp office. "But of course, if you'd rather we came here, to your own luxurious pad . . ."

Rainfinch stood. "You've been partnering with this old man too long; that was pure Curran sarcasm."

Lou beamed proudly at Danny. "Kid's shaping up, even if he is your cousin."

April was already in the conference room when the men arrived. They had a brief discussion of calls that had come into the incident room.

Danny shrugged. "Nothing but a bunch of wild hares, so far. Since Sanden's announcement all the crackpots and cretins are coming out of the woodwork, half of them demanding to talk to the chief."

"Never fails in a case like this, where prominent people are involved," Rainfinch said, wearily. "Lou, make sure all the calls are checked out, except for our regular nutcases. Danny, I don't suppose the neighborhood sweep came up with anything interesting?"

Danny shook his head. "No sign of a weapon. Lots of trees and shrubs in that area, but the chief gave us enough manpower to do a good job. One thing I did notice, though— skulls and swastikas sprayed on the backs of a couple of buildings."

Rainfinch looked up. "You're thinking neo-Nazis— skinheads? Have there been any rumblings in that area?"

"Not that I've heard of. Lou?"

"The little beasties have been unusually quiet lately, far as I know. Last time they cut up it was a long way from that neighborhood. Homosexuals are among their favorite targets, but we've never had a knifing. They usually just beat the shit out of someone."

Rainfinch turned back to Danny. "Check it out with Projects, will you? The intelligence guys may know something helpful. I don't suppose the house-to-house has turned up anything?"

"No." Danny grinned. "Hell, it was a 'dark and stormy night.' What do you expect?"

"What about the men who had dinner at Greyfriar's with Guiste, Henderson, and Hall? Have you had a chance to check them out?"

"I did. Couple of lobbyists, a state senator, and a highway engineer. They all went over to the senator's house after they left Greyfriar's, and engaged in some serious drinking. Best any of them remember, it was two-thirty or so before the gang broke up. That's corroborated by the senator's wife, who was one pissed-off lady. And if any of them are fags, it sure didn't show."

Lou leered and winked. "Bet the guy's wife was smooth as custard pie, before you left."

"Shut up, old man," Danny said, without rancor.

"Okay, listen," Rainfinch took the reins again. "We don't want to develop tunnel vision, be so obsessed with the homosexual angle that we neglect other areas. It's possible this could be a political killing."

April's laugh was incredulous. "Get serious. That kind of thing only happens in the movies."

"We don't know that, do we? I'm going to become a hell of a lot more familiar with Governor Sanden's people and the workings of his office. I don't trust that preppy chief of staff, even if he was in Washington the night Hall was killed. And he *was* there. I checked."

"What would his motive be?" April asked. "If Sanden goes down in flames, he'd have a lot to lose. If you're going to talk politics, what about the opposition party?"

"What opposition party? Sanden's got more bipartisan support than any politician since statehood."

"Hunh," April scoffed. "Let him stumble, and I bet we get a lesson in 'bipartisan.' "

"That's true," Lou agreed. "Even if you're Jesus H. Christ, you still don't win a statewide election without making enemies."

"You're right. And Lou, since you love politicians, how about checking on who has a grudge against Sanden, and is clever and twisted enough to get at him this way."

"Be a pleasure." Curran's smile reminded Rainfinch of a buzzard circling carrion.

"Okay, let's move on. Lou, do you think that old lady told you everything she knew? Is it possible she'll remember something else, now she's had time to calm down a bit?"

Curran rubbed the furrow between his eyes and lifted his shoulders. "Miz Maude Mae Haslip? Couldn't hurt to try. I don't think she likes me much. How about April making a run at her?"

"Good idea. April?"

"Okay. And I'm still trying to negotiate a second visit with Hall's parents. Their doctor—"

The conference-room phone rang. April, who was closest,

started violently, then laughed with embarrassment as she answered it. "Yes?" She nodded at Rainfinch and handed him the receiver. "For you."

He listened, said "I'll be right there," and stood. "That was Monk Smith. Did everyone know Shadid Garber owns the Seraphim building? His law partner is with Monk right now, and they're pushing the panic button. Seems the High Bluff Historical Homeowners' Society is ready to tar and feather Monk, not to mention close down his club. I'm going over to see if I can learn anything useful."

As he left the room the three detectives huddled again, bouncing ideas off one another. Rainfinch started down the hall, then turned and stuck his head back in the door. "April? Stay close this evening, will you? I want to talk to you later."

She looked up. "Yes, all right."

The expression on her face was remote and cool as January moonlight on a frozen pond. He couldn't read it.

$\triangledown$

15

IT WAS SIX o'clock when Rainfinch drove back to his office. The meeting with Monk and Beth Farraday had given him several things to think about.

He was impressed by Shadid Garber's law partner. She was a bright, classy lady; he couldn't figure out how she'd gotten involved with a sleazeball like Garber.

In a cop's book most criminal lawyers were scum. Rainfinch didn't feel guilty about this—it was a natural state of affairs, a simple equation. Cops put bad guys in jail. Criminal lawyers used every cheap trick, every obscure statute, to get them back on the street. And Shadid Garber was bottom of the dung barrel—he had the ethics of a hyena. So how had he gotten his fangs into Farraday?

Monk had outlined a history of problems with the High Bluff Historical Homeowners' Society, which interested Rainfinch. Its membership would be checked out. Maybe there was a psycho embedded in there who had chosen unilateral action.

Beth impressed Rainfinch again by volunteering to obtain a roster and fax him a copy first thing in the morning. She was already familiar with the leadership of the group and knew who their lawyer was.

Together they managed to calm Monk, who had embodied the "Patience hell, I'm going out and kill something" attitude when Rainfinch first arrived.

Then Beth left. Archie appeared from the kitchen with

three beers in pilsner glasses. Rainfinch regretfully shook his
head; this was a working visit.

Archie brought Rainfinch that old Southern cure-all, a
glass of iced tea. As they drank, Monk said he was no closer
to identifying the man he'd seen talking to Hall the night of
the murder.

Rainfinch looked at Monk, then Archie.

"He knows all about it, Abe."

So Monk Smith, whom Rainfinch knew to be a very
private person, trusted his lover. And yet there seemed to be
some kind of tension between them. He'd noticed that
Archie Keyes stammered slightly, a condition he hadn't
remembered from the few times he'd seen Archie in the past.

And speaking of tension, Rainfinch thought, I need to find
April.

That turned out to be easy. Back at headquarters, as he
exited the stairwell on the second floor, she came out of the
incident room.

He took her arm. "Just the woman I'm looking for. Let's
go—what the hell have you got all over you?"

"What the hell does it look like?" she said, brushing
furiously at the skirt of her navy suit. "Cat goddamn fur."
She sneezed and jerked a thumb at the door behind her. "Lou
and Danny are in there. Be back in a minute." She disappeared into the women's room.

Inside the incident room a heavyset, bored-looking burglary detective sat with a phone receiver propped between
shoulder and ear. He munched french fries as he listened,
now and then emitting a bored grunt. He wasn't taking
notes, so Rainfinch figured the caller wasn't a live one.

Danny Bent and Lou Curran were huddled in a corner of
the room with their case file. Rainfinch joined them, and in
a few sentences relayed his conversation with Monk Smith
and Beth Farraday.

"I hear Farraday's a sharp lawyer—way out of Garber's
league," Lou commented. "I got an old buddy in patrol; she
chopped him up in little pieces on the witness stand the

other day. And that ain't easy, he's been around the block a time or two."

Rainfinch nodded. "I'm not surprised. She impressed me. What have you two been up to?"

"I went over and rattled Dr. Death's cage," Danny began.

"Deethe," Rainfinch corrected, feeling he should take up for the beleaguered doctor.

Danny grinned, unrepentant. "In his profession? Not a chance. Besides, the ornery old devil likes it. He'd be disappointed if we called him anything else."

Come to think of it, Danny might be right. "So what did he say?"

"We'll get the official stuff tomorrow, but Death told me a few things off the record. Hall was stabbed three times in the left quadrant of the chest. Two blows were deflected by a rib and didn't do serious damage, but one entered the heart."

"Someone got lucky," Lou said. "Stabbin' a guy in the heart ain't nearly as easy as it sounds."

"Could you get the Doc to speculate on the kind of knife we're looking for?"

"Not a kitchen utensil. From the shape of the wound and bruising at the point of entry, he says it could have been a switchblade. But not to hold him to that."

Curran grinned. "Wile E. Coyote Deethe. What about blood work? Did the guy have AIDS?"

Danny shook his head. "Naw, he was clean. Careful or lucky, I guess. There were six different kinds of condoms in rainbow colors in a pocket of his fur coat."

Lou's eyebrows did a dance. "Is that a fact? You know, we didn't find condoms, or any of the other weird sex crap you might expect, in the guy's house. Suppose he might've had a love nest somewhere?"

Rainfinch nodded. "That's a good thought. Lou, since you brought it up, see what you can find out along that line. And that reminds me. Hall's keys—do we have them all accounted for?"

Lou shook his head. "Only six of the seven." He ticked them off on his fingers. "Two for the Mercedes, one house key, one to the governor's wing and one for his private office. Let's see—and a key to his parents' home."

"So that leaves one? Is it the type that might be a house or apartment key?"

"Yeah, could be."

The door opened. April was back. She pulled out a chair between Lou and Danny and sat. She sneezed. She glared at the men. "Just don't say anything."

"You mean about the fact you could build another cat with the fur your suit's wearing?" Rainfinch asked blandly.

"It won't brush off."

"Don't worry about it. We're probably the only ones who have noticed. Just don't get too close to me," Danny told her, moving his chair.

April pulled a yellow tuft off her sleeve and blew it in his direction. "Take that. Do you guys want to hear what I learned from Maude Mae, or would you rather sit around and make fun of me?"

She had their attention.

"I'm a cat lover. Duke recognized that right away. He vouched for me with Maude Mae, and she trusts anybody that cat likes."

"Do you want to get on with it?" Rainfinch asked.

"I'm coming to a point. I took her through the night of the murder, step by step. And she did remember more details. But not before I drank two cups of fur-laced tea."

Danny Bent groaned. "Okay, you suffered. We stipulate that you suffered. So what were the details, or do you need time to cough up a hairball?"

"First the killer. He was approximately the same height as the deceased. And he wore trousers and a jacket."

"So the killer wasn't in drag. Anything else?"

"Yes. The car was dark-colored, and streamlined. And it had wraparound taillights."

"All right!" Danny said. "That's something to go on."

"You don't think she might have made those things up, just to please you?" Rainfinch asked.

April shook her head. "I don't believe so. She's a sharp old gal."

"Okay, from now on you'll be our contact with her. Go around to Auto Theft, they'll know what models of cars fit that description. And they'll have pictures."

April nodded. "I'll get on it first thing in the morning. Now may I go home and take a hot bath?"

"Hell, no, you can't; no baths until we find out who stuck the governor's lad." Lou stood up and turned to Danny. "Come on, Boy Wonder, we got a date with an old buddy of mine who knows all there is to know about the political dirt in this state. If anyone's out to scalp Sanden, he can tell us who it is."

"Devil we do. The only date I have is with the new report clerk up the hall."

The two detectives headed out the door, still wrangling. "You mean the one that's got a wiggle to her ass like Gypsy Rose Lee?"

"Who the hell's Gypsy Rose Lee, old man?" Danny asked, as he disappeared.

"Come back here, smartass." Lou took off after him.

That left Rainfinch, April, and the burglary detective, who had finished off his french fries and shifted the phone to his other shoulder.

April picked up her notebook. She avoided Rainfinch's glance.

"I need to talk to you," he said. "Let's go by Bald Joe's and have a drink."

"Can't it wait?" Her voice was strained. "Look at me, for God's sake."

"It can't wait. Joe's is too dark for anybody to notice you're wearing a suit trimmed in cat fur."

"All right." She still wouldn't look at him. "I'll get my coat and meet you downstairs."

*   *   *

Bald Joe's was an insider place, a cop bar hidden in the depths of an area the chamber of commerce called Stock-yards City. Cowboys and old-timers called it Packing Town. In recent years a horse patrol had been reinstated in the area, whose thinly paved brick streets hadn't changed much from the days when the city's most notorious gambler and bawdy house operator had also been proprietor of a steak house, where the beat cop's rocking chair occupied a traditional place of honor by the front door.

Joe's was crowded when Rainfinch and April arrived. City cops, state and federal law enforcement types, sheriff's deputies, and prosecutors huddled around tables and sat on cowhide stools at the bar. There were also groupies: women who hung around hoping to leave with a cop, and the wannabe crowd, men who hovered on the fringes of law enforcement, bought drinks, and lived off reflected glory.

Once his eyes adjusted, Rainfinch saw friends, a couple of assistant DA's, who waved him toward their corner table. With an arm around April's waist, he guided her.

"I suppose you'd like for me to get up, so you can have the chair in the corner," the skinny bald man heckled Rainfinch.

"I'll take my chances. You probably have more enemies in here than I do."

It was a joke, and yet it wasn't. After you'd sent a few hundred people to prison, after you'd seen a lot of them back on the street, you got pretty damned nervous about some-body sneaking up on you. Rainfinch sat, but he turned his chair so he could see the door.

The DAs were waiting for a verdict in a rape case. They were restless; after a few minutes of shop talk with Rainfinch and April, they left.

People drifted by, stopped to chat, moved on. War stories were everywhere, tough humor—cop humor. The narcs sat off by themselves, scruffy and bearded or dressed like preppy drug dealers. One of the women, a tiny, wild-haired redhead, was telling about bringing down a house full of cocaine cowboys, where she had been working undercover for weeks.

"One of the neighbors who had come out to watch, a righteous guy in a silk robe, kept pounding on McNeil's back. 'You're letting one get away. That blowsy redheaded bitch, she's one of them.' "

"So did he arrest you?"

"Hell, yes. They were going to, anyway. Some of those rats are still running loose."

April grinned at Rainfinch. "For someone who wanted to talk, you sure picked a private place."

The unspoken question, of course, was, *Are you afraid to be alone with me?*

"You have a point. Want to leave?"

"No, let's get it over with. I'm assuming this is personal, not job-related—but it all gets jumbled together, doesn't it? What if I start? I don't want to see you anymore, Abe, except at work."

She had come to the same conclusion he had. He was off the hook. Why didn't he feel better about it? "April—"

She held up a hand, as if to ward off a blow. "Don't. I can't stand this anymore, it's gotten too complicated—all twisted up in work, and orders, and chain of command. I want out—I need out. And so do you, don't deny it."

Mary Lee, Bald Joe's wife and the best barmaid in the city, set two more rum and Cokes in front of them. April picked up her slice of lime and squeezed it, then took a long drink. She held up her glass. "A toast."

Uncertain, Rainfinch lifted his.

"Remember that war movie we liked, *Gardens of Stone?*" She clinked her drink against his. Even in the darkness of the bar, her eyes were very bright. "How did they say it? Something like this—'Here's to us, and those like us. Damn few left.' "

$\triangledown$

16

Robert Friar poured himself a generous slug of imported single malt Scotch. He couldn't pronounce the name of the variety, but he'd seen a bottle on the bar of one of the governor's jet-set supporters, and decided right away that's what he'd drink from then on. He inhaled the smoky fragrance, then shut his eyes and took a long swallow.

Usually he relished the nights he stayed in the governor's wing until long after everyone else was gone. In silence he could feel the essence of the place, almost hear the voices of men from other, rougher times—when governors and their chosen cohorts understood the license of political clout, and weren't afraid to use it.

Nothing happened in this part of the capitol that he didn't know about. Nobody's territory, no one's files were off limits. Robert had his own set of master keys, furnished by a young janitor who had his sights set on a better job. He'd get it, too. Robert believed in rewarding those who were useful. And properly respectful of Robert's power as chief of staff.

Not that the governor was a figurehead. Max Sanden was smart, Robert had to give him that—but entirely too damn righteous. Sanden was pathetically naive about the use of political muscle. He'd catch on, eventually, with the right guidance.

The trouble with Sanden was that he'd never had to scratch and claw for anything, never rooted in the muck for a prize like a pig sniffing out a truffle. It was easy to be idealistic if you got all the good stuff handed to you almost before you knew you wanted it.

Okay, this was only the state capitol. Maybe not even an important state, as national policy went. But you had to start somewhere—my God, look at Jimmy Carter. Georgia cracker, for Christ's sake. With Robert's brains and Sanden's charisma—-he hated the word, but that's what it was—they could have the presidency. Well, the vice presidency now—then the big one. Robert grinned. He was young, and so was Sanden. They could wait a few years for the top prize.

Unless . . . he took a slug of Scotch and savored the burn in his throat.

This Hall thing had to be contained. Isolated, like a filthy disease, and put behind them. He grinned ruefully, remembering John Dean's famous words to Richard Nixon. "Mr. President . . . a cancer growing on the presidency. . . ."

Dean had been a fool. A rag doll, played with and then trampled by the powerful. He grinned again. Not a bad thing, in itself. Now and then it was expedient to dangle a few effigies in front of the masses and then allow them to be hacked to pieces. The trick was to satisfy the blood lust of the rabble without being destroyed yourself.

And now and then it was expedient to cover one's own tracks.

The Scotch seared his throat again. *Goddamn Carter Hall to the deepest pit in hell.* How could a man who was so good at his job, who had money and social standing—the fool had been *born* with everything a man could want—how could he fucking screw up like that?

And why didn't I see it happening? The goddamned idiot was breaking apart right in front of my eyes, and I missed it.

That was the scary part. Robert had always been able to trust his instincts. He had a nose for trouble that had never failed in the past. Of all the rotten luck, one stumble and it could cost him everything.

Okay, no use brooding. He'd just have to cut his losses and go on. He could fix things. He could.

Susan Elias worried him. It had been a mistake to send her off with the maestro's son. Lieutenant Rainfinch was a different breed from his father. And Susan liked him, Robert could tell. The bitch.

He'd have to pay more attention to her, reel her back in. Easy enough, but the necessity irked him.

And Brendon Guiste. Brendon was an embarrassment, he'd have to go. There were things Brendon knew—but that wouldn't be a problem. The man was a whiner, a coward. Robert could convince him that keeping his mouth shut was the safest policy. If not—other measures could be taken.

He put the Scotch bottle in a bottom desk drawer and locked it, then walked to the window. His car seemed a long way off, a distant shadow in the dimly lit parking lot. He thought of calling capitol security to escort him, then decided against it. It wouldn't do for one of their officers to smell alcohol on the breath of the governor's chief of staff.

Every night at ten o'clock Maude Mae Haslip sat in her worn rocker, the one Mama had cosseted her in more years ago than she wanted to count, and watched the television news before she and Duke went to bed. Most times Duke curled up on the footstool and dozed until she turned off the lights and the TV and headed for their bedroom. He was there this evening, his head and one white-tipped paw across her ankle. He was snoring, his flank rising and falling with each breath.

Maude Mae reached down and stroked his belly. He stretched, flexed his claws.

She thought with a pang that Duke wasn't getting any younger. He might not like that red harness she insisted on, might dream about ranging free again in the alleys and among the garbage cans, but the truth was, he needed the pampering she gave him. Maude Mae was convinced that deep down he knew it, too.

She worked at a piece of dead grass that had become entangled in the long hair between his legs.

"We're a couple of tough old birds, Duke. We'll last a while, yet."

The cat's eyes slitted open. He purred.

The last car commercial ended, theme music for the late edition news swelled with the hard-driving beat that was supposed to convince you WROX's reporters buzzed around like flies on a dungheap, just so they could keep folks informed. If they were lucky, there'd be two or three juicy local scandals to dish up, voices solemn with the shock of it all.

Maude Mae loved it. And now she was a part of one of the best stories of all, an important witness to the killing of that fella who had worked for poor Governor Sanden. She could be famous, if the police hadn't made her promise not to say a word to anybody.

"Hush, Duke," she warned unnecessarily. "They're talking about *our* case."

Melina Moriarty was interviewing a member of the High Bluff Historical Homeowners' Society.

"Duke, that's Eugene Cook. Remember, he owns the flower shop up the street. 'High Bluffs Bower,' he calls it. Silly fool."

Eugene was mouthing off solemn as a preacher, while Moriarty squinted into a cold wind outside his shop and swiped at strands of hair that whipped across her face.

Maude Mae stirred restlessly in her chair, and almost elbowed her cup of hot lemon tea off the table.

"Silly fool," she repeated. "You don't know a thing, Eugene, you're just flappin' your jaws. Duke, wouldn't they be surprised if they knew what we'd seen? I guess that reporter'd want to talk to us, all right."

She had to laugh at the thought, at how excited everyone would be, if they only knew—

The night it happened, that dried-up old detective had warned her to keep her mouth shut. Warned her she and Duke might be in danger, if the killer knew she'd seen him. And now this afternoon, the pretty young thing, that April girl.

"Couldn't hardly credit she was a police officer, could you, Duke? Now there's a nice little'un. You thought so, too. Don't think I didn't notice you rollin' all over her lap like it was a bed of catnip."

Duke looked smug.

"You remember, she told us to keep our lips buttoned, just like that other officer did."

Duke sat on his haunches and stared at Maude Mae.

"Don't glare at me, you villain. I never told anyone except two or three of our closest friends. They promised not to breathe a word. If a body can't trust her friends, what's this world coming to?"

She turned off the set, tucked Duke under her arm, and headed for the bedroom. When she was all ready for bed, though, with Duke curled up on his own pillow, she walked back to the front door, checked the lock, and jerked at the chain bolt a couple of times.

"Man at the hardware store told me the solid slide-over bolts are safest, Duke. Maybe we ought to buy ourselves one. Bet we could talk one of those carpenters that's working downstairs on the lawyer's offices into puttin' it on the door."

She sighed as she slipped between the sheets and turned off the bedside lamp. "Seems like life gets so complicated, anymore, Duke." She chuckled. "Damn sight better than the alternative, though."

Rainfinch resisted the temptation to go up to the incident room when he took April back to her car. If they needed him, they'd call. The most important thing right now was to get in touch with Julianna and find out how Julia was.

What if she were dying?—if she died and he wasn't there, to tell her one more time how proud he was of her? How much she meant to him. She was a unique person, his mother.

The truth was, he could go to New York. He wasn't indispensable. He could explain the situation, ask for leave, and they'd give it to him. Twenty years from now the Hall case would be a dim memory, but his mother wouldn't. If he weren't there, and she . . .

As he unlocked the door he could hear his phone ringing. Twice, three times. He'd forgotten to activate the goddamned answering machine. Lunging up the stairs, he caught a toe in the worn oriental runner and sprawled across the second-floor landing. Stumbling into his bedroom, he snatched up the receiver and gasped hello in time to hear a click and the dial tone.

He turned on the lamp and punched out Julianna's number. The machine answered, aping Julianna's voice—finally, finally allowing him to say something.

"This is Abe. Phone me as soon as you get home. Please."

He called long distance information, got the number of the hospital. They had no Julia Rainfinch listed as a patient. After a moment of spiraling panic he thought to ask for Julia Charbonnet. Success.

She was still in intensive care. He told the nurse who he was and asked if she could page Julianna.

"I'm acquainted with your sister, Lieutenant Rainfinch. She told me you might call. She isn't here right now."

"I can't reach her at home."

"I'm sorry." Her tone dismissed him. The nurse had work to do.

"Please, can you tell me about my mother—how is she?"

The voice came back softer, more human. "She seems to be progressing well, Lieutenant. I wouldn't be surprised to see her in a private room, tomorrow. But I didn't tell you that—I'm not supposed to second-guess the physicians."

"Thanks. Thanks a lot."

He got up and walked to a small cubicle adjacent to what had once been his and Julianna's play room, and his mother's before that, and her father's. . . .

In the days of live-in servants, this smaller room had been

allotted to a nanny. Somewhere along the line it had been turned into an upstairs bar, with running water and a cabinet refrigerator.

Rainfinch reached into the fridge for a bottle of Dos Equis. Empty.

He walked downstairs into the frigid zone. Dim night-lights were on in the hallway. With the ease of familiarity he avoided pedestals holding Chinese vases, small, carved chairs, an iron-and-marble hall table that held an urn of eucalyptus branches.

The floors still creaked in the same places they had when he and Julianna were children. He smiled, remembering how they used to sneak downstairs on late-night kitchen raids. Hard as they tried, they never quite managed to avoid the noisy spots, and the old floor's protests had sounded like rifle shots to children on nefarious missions.

He remembered a time when their father had confronted them on their way back upstairs, each with a slab of cake in one hand and a glass of milk in the other. No spankings, but the lecture was worse. From the way he talked, Abe and Julianna figured their father had never in his life coveted a chunk of chocolate cake in the middle of the night.

Now, Abe retrieved a fresh six-pack from the big kitchen refrigerator and started back upstairs.

There were stories that his great-grandpa's ghost roamed the house. When the whole family had been there, a single elderly ghost wouldn't have had a chance, and the thought of running into him now never bothered Abe. He figured he and the old Cherokee horse trader would get along fine.

Back in his huge down-filled chair by the window, he felt bleak and lonesome. He thought of April, the nights she had been here with him. The feel, the taste of her. It had been good, once.

He sighed. It hadn't been enough. Something was missing—if that weren't so, they'd have found a way to work things out.

Maybe it was him, maybe he was looking for something

that didn't exist. An adolescent's dream of great and pure love—probably there wasn't such a thing. Probably there was only passion, followed by companionship, if you were lucky. And yet . . .

He thought of his parents. Had Julia ever been passionately in love with Martin?

Then, on some impulse he didn't understand, he telephoned his father.

"Hello?" The maestro's voice sounded irritated.

"It's me. Abe. I can't reach Julianna, she isn't at the hospital or at home. I thought you might have heard from her."

Martin sighed. "You must know there wasn't a symphony performance tonight. This is the only day in the week I can go to bed early. I was asleep."

"Sorry. *Have* you heard from Julianna? I'm anxious to know how Mother is."

"Your sister hasn't contacted me. Look, if Julia were worse, if she were in danger of dying, Julianna would get word to you. She's a very resourceful young woman."

"I know, but—"

"Now that you've gotten me up, I'm glad you phoned. About this Hall business—"

"It's just that, Dad. Business. I can't discuss the case with you."

"Don't be an ass. Abe, I won't have you embarrassing me, putting a strain on my friendship with the governor. It seems as if all your life, you've done whatever you could to—"

"I didn't kill Carter Hall. But I will investigate his murder, it's my job. I'm sorry if that inconveniences you."

"Why do I even try to reason with you? If you're so concerned about your mother, catch the first flight to New York and go hold her hand. You have the perfect excuse to get the hell out of this Hall thing gracefully. I'm not asking, I'm telling. Do it."

This attempt to exercise fatherly authority so astounded Rainfinch that by the time he formulated a response it was too late. Martin had prudently delivered his salvo and retreated from the field.

Rage, the old knee-jerk reaction, tensed his body like the recurrence of some childhood disease. With an effort of will he relaxed. Could parents always do that to you? When he was seventy and Martin was in his nineties, would they still be playing the same parts?

And speaking of outgrown roles, could he by any chance be clinging to the Hall case like a limpet on a rock just to make his father crazy?

He drained his beer and stretched. Too deep to ponder now.

$\triangledown$

17

DUTCHBOY SOLENT STOOD in front of the mirror Konnie had given him as a birthday present two months ago. A European antique, tall and haughty in its hinged frame with carved acanthus leaves bordering misty, silvered glass, it mocked him with thoughts of happier times. Dutchboy stroked the dark wood that curved so sinuously around his image, and abandoned himself to misery.

Tears flowed as he stripped naked and examined himself, feeling like some ghastly caricature of Snow White's step-mother, demanding lies from his reflection.

But the small flatteries of ancient glass weren't enough to hide the truth. In spite of exercise and a little discreet plastic surgery, his once-lithe image was gone. His skin looked like a badly fitted body stocking, with droops and sags at chest, stomach, knees. Fat billowed on his thighs; the calves of his legs seemed to be stuffed with bunches of grapes.

And his hair. He fluffed up the Dutch bob that had given him his nickname—it didn't seem long ago.

"Hey, Dutchboy," they'd called out. "Come go to the lake with us. Let's have a picnic!" Or "Dutchboy, there's a party at Noel's tonight. The cast from the new musical will be there—he said to be sure and let you know." Or "You lucky devil. Wish I'd been born with that elegant bod, and that wicked, golden hair."

Oh, he'd been something then, all right.

Now his beautiful, gleaming glory was sparse and

mostly white. Even hairspray and a monthly tint job didn't help much.

The apartment was cold. He pulled on a thick, wine-colored terry robe, a Christmas gift from Konnie—almost two years ago, that would be—and sat in his chair by the hearth. There was no fire, only gray ashes. It seemed fitting. Konnie was gone.

They hadn't even fought. Well, not really. Just that unpleasantness yesterday evening. It had been six o'clock. Outside skies were bleak and gray, but the fire had roared then, built up with fragrant piñon shipped from New Mexico. Dutchboy had sipped Courvoisier while he planned what they'd have for dinner. He'd held the great crystal snifter in both hands, swirling the liquid, savoring its fragrance. And wondered what the hell his young lover was doing.

Then Konnie had strolled by, dressed to go out, all in black leather with that stupid cap at a go-to-hell angle.

Dutchboy had handled it well. Tolerant smile, humor in voice.

"I thought we were staying in this evening?"

Konnie didn't look at him. "I won't be late. A few of the guys I used to work with at TrendScissors are getting together." He shrugged elaborately. "Nothing you'd enjoy. A flipping bore, really, but I promised to be there."

It was time for a little honesty. "Come over here and sit down, lad. I have something to say before you leave."

"Give me a break, I'm running late—"

"It's important. I won't take up much of your time."

So the youth perched reluctantly, wary as a teenage virgin invited to snuggle up with the neighborhood child molester.

Dutchboy smiled, shook his head. "My dear lad, you really haven't been as clever as you thought. I know you're seeing someone else. A little on the side, a young stud your own age, and the old man won't be any wiser, eh?"

"You're imagining things—"

Another head shake, a hand raised in an expressive

gesture. "We won't argue about this—tawdry little episode. Have your fling tonight, but I advise you to do some careful thinking. If you're not willing to cut the fooling around, to be totally faithful, I want you out."

"Oh, come on—"

"I said we won't discuss it. I think you enjoy the life I'm able to give you." Sophisticated chuckle. Dutchboy was a man of the world. "You're quite a beautiful lad, and we've had some good times. But the fact is, I have no patience with the kind of childish game you're playing. Now, go. I expect a decision tomorrow. And I'll hold you to it, one way or the other."

Dutchboy had sat up most of the night in the chair by the fire, with a volume of Renaissance poetry as a stage prop. He'd rehearsed.

"Waiting up for you? My dear boy, don't be absurd. This is the most wonderful book—a bit above your head, I'm afraid, but I could select some of the racier snippets and read them to you. That is, if you've decided to stay."

Of course he would decide to stay. Dutchboy knew his Konnie, didn't he?

But Konnie didn't come home at all. Early this morning Dutchboy had left the apartment, and not returned all day. Let the young fool wonder where *he* was, for a change.

Sometime while he was gone Konnie had been there, packed his belongings, and gone.

Water flowed from Dutchboy's eyes again. He dug at them angrily with his knuckles. Like a child. Like an impotent old man.

Self-pity was self-destruction. He would go out.

In his bedroom he carefully selected clothes—charcoal tweed jacket, black trousers, pale yellow shirt, gray suspenders, a rich russet silk tie. Black dress moccasins soft as glove leather, polished to a perfect, muted sheen.

He showered, shaved, and perfumed himself with the special cologne that was his trademark. Then he began to dress. Face flaming with humiliation even though no one

was there to see, he put on the thing he had recently bought.
The pantie girdle.

When he finished he examined himself in the mirror
again. Not bad, Not bad at all. Youth, muscle, and a flat
stomach weren't everything. There were such things as style,
wit, sophistication. Lots of people would say he'd been
casting his pearls before swine, allowing himself to become
so fond of an ill-bred youth like Konnie.

He would go the Seraphim. Monk Smith, an old acquaintance, would welcome him with the courtesy he craved
right now.

Dutchboy thought about Monk as he selected a topcoat.
It was damned unfair how time played favorites. There
couldn't be more than five or six years between them, yet
Monk was all clean-lined muscle, not a bulge or a sag
anywhere. One of those lucky bastards who got handsomer
in middle age. It was all in your genes, he'd read. Why the
hell hadn't his parents done better by him?

Dutchboy remembered he'd had a mad passion for Monk
once. Totally unrequited. He guessed he just wasn't the big
man's type.

He and Konnie had been at the Seraphim the night of the
murder—what? Three days ago? It seemed a lifetime. Friday.
The day he'd gotten the private detective's report on
Konnie's activities, and known for sure what he'd only
suspected before. He'd gotten pissed, made a bit of a bleary
ass of himself.

"But that was yesterday . . ." he sang jauntily.

He was beginning to feel lucky. He'd find someone new
and exciting tonight, he knew it. He was a good conversa-
tionalist, a gifted storyteller. Getting acquainted was never
a problem. And of course there was the unspoken, made
obvious by his expensive clothes and the roll of bills he liked
to flash. Dutchboy had inherited quite a tidy little income,
and was prepared to take good care of his lovers.

He had a flash of inspiration. It might be fun to hint at
something mysterious, some knowledge of Carter Hall's

killing he wasn't at liberty to talk about. Though not really friends, he and Carter had moved in concentric circles. They were close to the same age, and their families belonged to the same social set.

He stood in front of the mirror again, fully dressed, suave. Chuckled knowingly.

"Ah, poor old Carter," he told his imagined audience. "Got himself involved in some nasty doings, I'm afraid. The police will sort things out. I fancy I've been of some assistance, myself. Ahh—" index finger waggled, then pressed against lips—"mustn't say another word. I promised the officers."

If he met the right person, tonight . . . and he would. He began to feel stirrings of the old, reckless sense of fun. Yes, he would definitely have an adventure tonight. He might even fall in love.

Then let Konnie try to come back.

On Mondays the Seraphim closed at midnight, but it was one in the morning before the last straggler was out the door, the trash picked up, and the final bar glass washed and put away. Waiters and bartenders had gone, swooping out in a tidal wave of laughter and conversation, with the sudden energy of release.

Monk and Frannie Da Sorta, who never drank liquor while the club was open, were sharing a bottle of Kentucky bourbon. They sat at a small "house" table beside the bar.

Only night-lights were on. The sound system, kicked back to tolerable decibels, poured out the soothing melodies of Vivaldi's *Four Seasons*.

"We busted a record tonight, Boss. Monday, and we had to turn 'em away. Never seen anything like it."

Monk shook his head. "People never fail to amaze me. I thought the media binge on the Hall killing might hurt business, but it's just the opposite. I swear every one of our regulars showed up, plus a hell of a lot of new faces."

Frannie massaged the furrows between his eyes with a splayed thumb. "Kinda ugly, wasn't it? Hall was a shit, but

I heard say he came from a nice family. And the way he died—wearin' a dress, being carved up like that. No dignity. The crowd acted tonight . . . I dunno . . . like they'd come to see if the lions was gonna gobble up some more Christians. Made me want to puke."

Frannie's eyes were large and brilliant in the ruined face. For a fleeting moment Monk tried to imagine what he might have looked like when he was young, before flesh and bone and cartilage succumbed to years of merciless pounding.

"There was a whiff of Roman circus in the air, but I balk at the idea of Carter Hall as Christian martyr."

"I didn't mean that—" Frannie grinned. "Aw, hell, you know what I meant."

Monk stood, clapped Frannie on the shoulder, and carried his glass to the sink behind the bar. "I do. And I hate to leave good company, but I've got to get back to the parsonage. Archie made me promise to hurry home." With a sudden pang he thought about the solitary furnished rooms where Frannie slept. "Come over a while, why don't you? Archie's made something special for a late snack. He was fairly itching to tell me about it. And you know he's one hell of a good cook."

The old prize fighter stretched and yawned. "No thanks, Boss. I'm gonna stay and go over the work schedule. If business keeps up like this, some of the help are gonna have to put in extra hours."

"Okay. You could do that tomorrow, though."

"Sure I could." Frannie laughed self-consciously. "It's kinda nice, though, when nobody's here but me. When this place is dark and quiet, it's like—I dunno." He shrugged. "Peaceful."

Monk's grin was sardonic. "You mean, like a church?"

Frannie grinned back. "Now you mention it, yeah."

There was a private door to the outside in Monk's office. It opened onto a path that wound through a landscaped area and ended at the front door of the parsonage. The garden and house were separated from the parking lot by a white picket fence. In the last fine days of autumn Monk had caught several inflamed customers making profane use of this private bower, and he planned to have a businesslike six-foot iron partition fence built before warm weather came again.

As he left, Monk thought about Frannie. In the twenty-odd years since they'd met at the gym where Monk worked out and Frannie hung around, Monk had never known the old fighter to have a lover, woman or man. He had a few friends left over from his ring days. Occasionally he refereed Golden Gloves matches. He had his job. And that was it.

Monk had never picked up the faintest hint of what Frannie thought of his own lifestyle. If he disapproved he kept it to himself. The important thing was that Frannie was loyal as a bitch mastiff. And it was understood that whatever enterprise Monk Smith took on, there would always be a place for Frannie Da Sorta.

Monk wasn't dealing out charity. Frannie was surprisingly sharp for an old pug with an eighth-grade education. Monk often wondered what kind of man Frannie might have been, if he hadn't grown up the son of an alcoholic Packing Town barmaid and a long-haul trucker.

Monk locked the door behind him and stood still, letting his eyes adjust. It was a restless night, windy and crisp. The air had a clean and fragrant bite; the touch of it against his skin was good. The winter moon had set, leaving stars visible between ragged banners of cloud.

As always, Archie had left the porch light on at the parsonage. It beamed intermittently through tall cedars as they rippled and bowed to the wind. There was also a bare bulb above the church door, but the herringbone brick path twisted and jagged to the left, leaving its middle part dim and treacherous. Monk decided he needed to install a set of those black iron garden lamps on stakes.

One of these days I'll lose my footing and splinter something vital.

Thinking that, he stumbled and pitched forward.

His foot had caught on an obstruction that yielded, yet was solid. A son-of-a-bitching damn drunk, passed out after floundering around in the frozen garden, intent on God knew what.

Monk was tired. Fury seized him. He sprang to his feet and gave the figure a healthy kick.

"Get up and get out of here. Party's over."

No response. Some instinct made the nerves along his spine contract. He knelt for a closer look.

The drunk lay on his back with lower legs slung across the path. Head, shoulders, and torso were hidden by a tangle of barberry. Monk grabbed an arm and pulled. What he saw took him back to 'Nam, with the sick feeling that humanity was diseased and broken and nothing could fix it again.

Dutchboy Solent. Foolish Dutchboy, with his charming manners and his elegant clothes and his Ivy League education. And his fondness for disgusting young bullies.

Where the neck had been was a horrid jumble of blood and cut flesh. Monk could see stringy gobbets of things never meant to be exposed to the human eye. In shifting patterns of light through the restless trees, it seemed as if they moved, writhed, crawled.

Dutchboy's pants were unzipped and had fallen to his knees. Flesh, white and gleaming, ballooned over a rolled-down pantie girdle, which clung to his thighs like a giant rubber band. Where his genitals should have been was a dark, sticky mass. He stank of blood, feces, and urine.

Monk touched the head of his old acquaintance, whose eyes were open in a face that looked oddly calm and peaceful.

"Ah, God, Dutchboy. What have you gotten into, you stupid ass? You silly old queen."

When the paralysis of first shock receded, Monk began to think. The killer might not be far away. He loped toward the parsonage in long, uneven strides, his legs feeling like alien things.

Then he saw the debris. Plastic sacks, torn and gaping,

strewed paper, citrus rinds, coffee grounds. Archie must have been on his way to put household trash in the dumpster behind the club. Something had scared him so badly he'd tossed them and run.

Or maybe he'd thrown them at someone. In one corner, the monster who carved Dutchboy. In the other, Archie Keyes, invalid, armed with sacks of garbage.

Monk's gut cramped. He covered the remaining yards of path.

The door was open, but Archie hadn't reached it. He was sprawled across the front porch steps, one arm flung forward, reaching toward light, and warmth, and safety.

Monk gathered the slight figure and cradled it in his arms. "Archie?" he whispered tentatively.

For a moment Monk hoped. There was no mutilation, no blood immediately visible. Maybe he'd seen Dutchboy, felt sick, run for the house, and fainted. Or maybe it had nothing at all to do with the horror back on the path. Archie was still weak. Couldn't he have simply felt dizzy, dropped the trash sacks and headed back, then passed out on the steps?

Monk lifted his lover easily, carried him into the house and laid him on the green silk sofa. He tucked a needlepoint pillow beneath the gleaming blond head.

Archie's eyes were open. He wasn't breathing.

"Nooooo." He grabbed the fragile diaphragm, squeezed, released.

Blood gurgled out of Archie's mouth, obscene against his pale skin. Archie Keyes was dead.

Monk sat heavily on the floor, and thought he heard the music of balalaikas.

There were, of course, things he must do. But not just yet. Now he had to remember.

He'd lost patience, yelled—a dozen hours ago? Dirty dishes, dirty clothes, mess, muss, disorder—Monk wanted it understood he couldn't live like that.

As he sat on the floor, he could see the room fairly glowed

with cleanliness. No hasty pick-up job, no mere spritz of furniture polish in the air to fool the senses. The house was clean to the bone. Just what he had wanted.

Like a palsied old man, Monk pulled himself erect. He crossed the room, past the feast of pâté and imported crackers, and caviar with onions and cream cheese, and baked brie with fruit, and chilled champagne, into the hallway with its old-fashioned phone niche.

He dialed 911.

$\bigtriangledown$

18

IT WAS TUESDAY afternoon. Major Mark Adamson leaned across a desk whose outer perimeters held neat stacks of forms, memos, file folders, incidents to be reviewed, and six months' worth of FBI Association magazines he was going to read as soon as he got time. The inner core, just in front of him, bore a meltdown of urgent requests, most urgent requests, inquiries, gripes, and various other demands for immediate attention.

Lou Curran was talking. Rainfinch drank his diet cola and listened, thanking sweet heaven for the thousandth time that they had a major who'd come up through the ranks as a detective, instead of some trumped-up administrator with high-flown ideals and not the faintest notion of what it was like on the streets.

Their last chief had actually chewed out some of his deep-cover officers for picking up tips from pimps and dope dealers, prompting a tough old Projects sergeant to comment that he didn't know any Sunday school deacons who had the kind of information they needed.

The same old sergeant had also said, "Get crosswise with Adamson, and he can be meaner'n a skunk with the clap. But at least, by God, he's *our* varmint."

"—mutilation a lot worse than on Hall," Curran was saying. "Remember, Major, Hall just got a lick and a promise—couple of quick gashes across the face after he was stuck. Solent was done by having his throat cut, and then his privates were slashed to bits."

Adamson grinned. "Would you say the guy who did him was making a statement?"

"Oh, yeah," Curran agreed, "but what statement? 'I hate you because you're a stinkin' faggot,' or 'You belong to me, sucker, I'll fix it so you can't go out and get strange stuff any more'? Another thing, Major, Solent wasn't robbed. And he was carrying a roll of fifties and hundreds that would choke a whore."

"That's interesting. Wonder what kind of a person would pass up a deal like that, even if he killed for some other reason."

"Maybe the killer thought it was dirty money."

"We've checked on his love life," Rainfinch said. "Solent was an aging queen with plenty of cash who didn't bother to hide his proclivities. He had a live-in lover, a punk type named Konnie Kraft. Kraft walked out on him Sunday night and moved in with one of the heavy metal set, a local rock musician named Dirk Thunder."

Adamson shook his head. "You're making this up."

"Oh, no, Major." Curran took up the story. "And the two little shits were at the Seraphim last night. Kraft said they blew in around eleven, bought a drink, and saw Solent back in a corner putting the move on some young guy. Kraft was set to stay, but Thunder wanted to get the hell out before Solent saw them and raised hell. They left around eleven-fifteen, and went to a dive where some of Thunder's friends had a gig. We have corroboration on both ends. Unless something new turns up, looks like Kraft may be out of it."

Rainfinch laughed at Curran's doleful face. "Cheer up, Lou. It would make more sense if the old queen had done Kraft."

"Never met a little shit who needed it worse."

Now Adamson laughed. "Damn, Curran. How'd he get under your skin so bad? Make a grab at you?"

Curran ran a hand across his sparse hair and cranked out a sour chuckle. "No, but he sure seemed to like your cousin,

Abe. He was right disappointed when Danny Boy took off and left him with me and April Morgen."

"Did Kraft think he might be able to identify Solent's friend—the one he was sitting with?"

"He said not. His new boyfriend was in too big a rush to get him out of there," Rainfinch answered.

Adamson looked at his watch. "Okay, what else do we have? It's four-fifteen. Chief's going to talk to the media at five, we've been stalling them all day. I've got to brief him in fifteen minutes." He put on reading glasses and picked up a pen. "Deethe said the guys hadn't been dead long when Monk Smith found them?"

Rainfinch answered. "That's right. It was cold last night, that always makes it harder to pinpoint a time from physical evidence. But Monk had talked to Archie Keyes on the phone just before midnight. That's corroborated by the bartender who took the call—he knew Keyes and recognized his voice."

"What are the chances these killings aren't linked to Hall's?"

"There's always that possibility," Rainfinch said. "We can't rule it out. But on the whole, I think they're connected. Here's how I figure it. The killer was after Dutchboy Solent. He stalked him, got him out in the bushes with his pants down, and ripped him to pieces. Archie Keyes, Monk Smith's lover, came tripping up the path carrying trash to the dumpster, saw the killer putting on the fancy finishing touches, and ran for it. He made it as far as the porch steps before the killer shot him."

"Sweet Jesus," Adamson said. "A knife and a gun? This guy was carrying an arsenal—unless there could have been more than one killer?"

Curran shook his head. "Doesn't seem likely. The ground had thawed some, and that ol' brick path had enough dirt on it to give us some pretty good tracks. We found four sets of footprints—Solent's, Keyes's, Monk Smith's, and the killer's. And that's another point that helps us save Konnie

Kraft's gizzard. The unidentified footprints are nine and a half or ten narrow, and Kraft wears eleven and a half medium."

"Footprints. That's something," the major said.

"A hell of a lot more than on the first one," Rainfinch agreed. "Plus, we recovered a .32 slug from a wooden porch step, and after daylight this morning one of the guys doing the grid search found a .32 casing in the shrubbery just off the path."

"All right! I don't suppose our witness and her cat were on guard duty at the window again?"

To Rainfinch, Lou's voice and the major's began to merge and blur into an unintelligible drone. He stifled a terrible urge to yawn, and took a drink from his can of cola instead. It went down wrong. He gurgled, gasped, grabbed a handkerchief, and stuffed it against his face to avoid spewing. He saw Lou and the major watching him with the mild disapproval of two gentlemen regretting the antics of an uncouth lout. "Sorry," he whispered, and launched a fit of coughing.

"About the cat lady?" the major prompted.

Rainfinch, still gasping, looked at Curran. Curran was not about to take him off the hook. Between rumbling coughs Rainfinch said, "Her windows don't overlook the area where these two killings took place. Morgen interviewed her, asked if she heard anything. She said not; she and Duke slept through this one."

"Duke? Who's he?"

"The cat, sir."

"Of course. I knew that. How's the neighborhood canvass going?"

Rainfinch, still coughing into the handkerchief, glared at Lou Curran.

Curran relented. "Pretty well finished, Major. Morgen and Bent are out with a couple of uniforms, winding things up. No one admits to hearing shots. You know, Bluff Boulevard is lined with cute antique shops and stuff. Old houses and buildings converted into doctors' and lawyers' offices. A few months back Shadid Garber bought the apartment building where our old biddy lives. He's gonna move his dog-an'-pony show in there."

"Garber. Abe, didn't you tell me he owns the old church—the Seraphim building?"

"Right, Major. Monk Smith leases from him."

Adamson leered. "Gee, I hope these killings won't cause Shadid any problems. I'd hate that."

"We've all been losin' sleep about it," Curran agreed. "Anyway, on the street behind the church property there're those big ol' houses on large lots. The place directly adjacent to the Seraphim is vacant. In the others, no one heard a damn thing. Those people all had plenty to say, though, about how they'd like to see the Seraphim boarded up and Monk Smith tarred, feathered, and roasted over glowing coals."

"That reminds me," Adamson said. "What about that historical society?"

Rainfinch felt like maybe he could talk now without croaking. "We're checking out the membership. That'll take a few days."

Major Adamson had a new idea. "Abe—about Monk Smith, himself? I know he's been helpful to us on occasion, in the past. But how well do you know him? Is he capable of something like this? How did he and his lover get along?"

"We're not ruling anyone out at this point, Major. But Monk will be ruined, financially, if the Seraphim closes down. He's sunk every cent he had into it, and borrowed heavily. He told me that up front, and we checked on it. About Archie Keyes—they've been together several years. From what we've been told, it seems to have been one of the more stable homosexual relationships. Keyes used to be a very successful interior decorator. He's been ill with mononucleosis for the past year and couldn't work. The club employees agree on the fact that Monk's been worried sick and is totally devoted to him."

"Okay. Could there have been some kind of relationship

between Hall and Solent—or Archie Keyes?"

"Keyes, apparently not. But Solent—they knew each other. Solent and Konnie Kraft were in the bar the night Hall was killed. More important, Frannie Da Sorta, the club manager, says he heard Solent hinting around last night that he had some knowledge of the killing, and was 'helping the police.' "

"Solent got smashed out of his mind, last Friday night," Lou broke in. "Made an ass of himself. Da Sorta helped Kraft get him to their car, around midnight."

"So the poor old queen probably couldn't have known squat. Had he talked to any of our people—claimed to have information?"

Rainfinch shook his head. "No sir, not that we know of."

Adamson sighed, looked at his watch again. "Okay, we need to wind this up. Rainfinch—"

The office door burst open. Clifford Stamps appeared, clutching a leather-bound notebook, gold pen ready. "Rainfinch! Here you are. Goddamn it, why can't I ever find you? Chief's got a press conference in thirty minutes. I've been on the phone with Robert Friar in the governor's office. These new killings at the Seraphim—it's obvious we've got a fag-bashing nutcase on our hands. Friar told me Governor Sanden wants the chief to make it clear that, in light of last night's killings—well, that none of it has anything to do with the governor's office, or his staff. Carter Hall was just in the wrong place at the wrong time. Period."

"Over my dead body, he makes a statement like that," Rainfinch sputtered, and began coughing again.

Mark Adamson had risen during Stamps's speech. He walked around his desk and stood directly in front of the PIO. "Clifford, don't *ever* barge into my office that way, again. Goddamn it, didn't anyone ever teach you a closed door means knock, identify yourself, and ask goddamn permission to come in? Abe caught you going through *his desk*, the other day. One more incident, and I'll by God tell Rosie not to let you past the detective bureau reception room without a bell around your neck."

Stamps, outraged but outranked, began to stammer. "You don't understand—I want to make an official complaint—I can never find these guys when I need—as public information officer I'm entitled . . ." His words wound slower and slower.

"What'sa matter, Stamps? Pink battery bunny not on your side?" Curran asked.

"*What?*"

"Never mind that." Adamson's lips twitched. "The point is, Clifford, you don't just come bursting in here any time you want."

"If you like breathing." Rainfinch coughed.

"And about the press conference," Adamson continued, "I'm going to brief Chief Jurgen personally. I'm due up there right now. If you'll excuse us, Clifford, I want a few more words with Rainfinch and Curran."

Stamps gathered his tattered dignity and turned to leave. At the doorway he paused for a parting broadside. "The chief should think twice before he sets himself up against Governor Sanden."

"Give it a rest, Clifford," Adamson said, wearily. After the door closed, he picked up the phone and rang his secretary. "Marylou, I know you can't stop him, but at least—"

Marylou's retort was so loud Rainfinch could hear her through the door. "Major, if the little fart pulls that again, I'll kick him in the balls."

Earthy girl, Marylou.

"It would surprise the hell out of me if the governor ever heard of Clifford Stamps," Rainfinch said. "This interference comes straight from His Royal Highness, the chief of staff—Robert Friar. It's got his fingerprints all over it. He and Stamps could be joined at the hip and passed off for Siamese twins."

Adamson looked at his watch again. "I've got to get upstairs. God knows if I keep the chief waiting, Stamps'll find a way to get him cornered. I'll drill it into Jurgen's head

that we need to hold back as much information as possible.
And I guarantee he's not going to make any exculpatory
statements. Talk to you later."

After Adamson left, Rainfinch and Curran sat a moment
in satisfied silence. Killings, mutilations, were everyday
business. You either got used to them, or got out, or cracked
up. What kept you from cracking up was a sense of humor.
Never mind if it became warped at times.

Watching Clifford Stamps being chewed up and spit out
by Adamson was something to be savored. And there was no
question. Red face, throbbing vein in left temple. It had been
one of the better sightings of the Stamps Phenomenon.

Rainfinch and Curran grinned at each other.

Rainfinch coughed.

$\triangledown$

19

FOR THE FIRST time since that gut-wrenching telephone call while he was in Washington, Robert Friar felt in control of his world. In the best of times he liked to visualize himself with each of his fingers manipulating a dozen strings, maneuvering figures of his own creation in delicate, complicated scenarios with the virtuosity of a Japanese puppet master. Seldom did he lose control of his toys as he had in the past few days.

But the loss was only temporary. Now, he believed, the unruly had been disciplined. The play could recommence.

It was four-forty-five. He sailed past Meg, the governor's secretary, rapped twice on the door to the inner sanctum, and entered. His raps were perfunctory. Friar was sure of his welcome, no matter what Max Sanden was doing or who was with him. This chief of staff had prerogatives.

Sanden was seated behind his desk, signing letters. He looked up. "Robert? You seem pleased. What do you know that I don't?"

"Governor, I told you this morning we'd be off the hook. Now two more of 'the girls' got themselves dead in the backyard of Gay-guy's Heaven." He grinned. The devilish little-boy grin. "Bad luck for them, of course. Anyway, I've used the old carrot-and-whip ploy on Clifford Stamps, and he's going to persuade Chief Jurgen to say in his press conference—which will start in a few minutes—that it doesn't seem any of the killings could have had anything to

do with politics, or this office. They've got a serial killer on
their hands. That's obvious."

Sanden sighed. "I can't understand why you're so high
on that fellow Stamps. Robert, I talked to Jurgen himself
a few minutes ago. He won't make a statement like that.
He'd be a fool if he did. The public isn't entirely composed
of idiots, you know. It's not smart to give the impression
their public officials are holding hands and playing ring-
around-the-rosy."

Fury swept over Robert. What the hell did Sanden think
he was at, calling the chief of police? He was the governor,
for Christ's sake, and if he didn't terminally screw up he
could be vice president of the United States after the next
election. Compared to that, in Robert's book, a chief of police
was the same as a dogcatcher.

"Another thing. About you packing Susan Elias off with
Martin Rainfinch's son Sunday evening. Susan's not a
sugarplum, a goodie you can use to soften up the cop."

Robert's right hand curled into a fist. He curbed an
impulse to smash it into a wall. "I don't know what Susan
told you, Governor. I assure you—"

"Susan didn't tell me anything. I'm aware you have quite
a spy network, Robert, but it might surprise you to know I
have a few sources of my own."

A chill passed through Robert. The governor had never
spoken to him in that manner before. He sounded like a
general dressing down an incompetent aide-de-camp. They'd
always had a laid-back relationship, more like equals with a
single goal than boss and employee. In the past the governor
would have left the whole thing up to him, never questioned
his methods. Was Sanden losing faith?

Steady. He relaxed the fist, jammed his hands in his
pockets, and ambled over to a window. "If you think I've
used bad judgment, I'm sorry. It's just that I'm so eager to
nip this stupid affair in the bud, before it has a chance to
cause real damage."

"Robert, your methods—"

Robert threw up his arms in the universal sign of surrender and said, "You're right, as usual," in just the proper, rueful tone. "I stand corrected. It's nearly five. Want to turn on the TV, see what Jurgen does have to say?"

"I don't think so—yes?" He broke off and answered a knock on the door.

"Governor, it's me. Susan Elias."

Oh, swell. Perfect timing, Robert thought.

"Come in, Susan. We were just finishing up for the evening."

Robert watched her come through the door, face pale, a few freckles showing on the bridge of her nose. Her eyes seemed huge and round; her delicate features were framed, almost overpowered, by hair that looked like a mass of bronze paper ribbon someone had curled with the edge of the scissors.

"I'm sorry—Meg wasn't at her desk, so I knocked. I've been looking for Brendon Guiste. Do either of you know where he is? I gave him a ride to work. He'd called and said he had a flat tire and didn't want to take time to fix it. We only live a few blocks apart." She took a deep breath, like a child, reciting. "Anyway, I need to leave in a few minutes, I have errands this evening. But I can't find him."

"Don't worry about it. Brendon's gone for the day," Robert said casually. He willed her, for once in her life, not to ask questions.

Fat chance. Her mouth flew open like a damn baby bird's, demanding an explanation.

"He left—and didn't come back? But he said he'd ride home with me. That's not like Brendon, to go without saying anything."

"Tell her, Robert," the governor commanded. "It isn't as if we could keep it secret."

Robert sat in his favorite chair, just to the side of Sanden's desk. He motioned to Susan. "Sit down, love."

Susan pulled up a ladderback and sat on its edge. She looked from the governor to Robert, her expression concerned.

Robert made his voice gentle. "You must realize that while we're all positive Brendon had nothing whatever to do with Carter's death, especially in light of the second two killings last night—still, his frequenting a place like the Seraphim, and the publicity that's been brought on by that scandalous and cruel murder, are a tremendous embarrassment to the office of the governor."

"But . . . but . . ."

"What Robert's trying to say is that he had a talk with Brendon and suggested he take a couple of weeks off. Vacation. He's had a hell of a shock," the governor said.

"And to be frank," Robert took up the narration, "I made it clear to him that I expect him to voluntarily resign. Not right away, though. I don't want it to look as if we demanded his resignation."

"But you did?"

"In a manner of speaking."

"I know how you feel, Susan," Sanden said. "I'm not entirely sure this is the right action, myself. Brendon's been a good employee. But Robert has a point. When you work for an elected public figure, you need to keep your act reasonably clean."

Susan nodded. "I'm not criticizing, sir. I just never thought . . ." A red flush spread across her pale face.

Robert saw his chance to exit gracefully, looking like an all-around good fellow. He walked over, put his hand on Susan's shoulder, and squeezed. "Come on, love, let's get out of the governor's way. I'll buy you a drink."

For a moment he thought she was going to balk. Then Susan stood, warily. He slid a fraternal arm around the slim waist and led her out. She yielded without protest, but her body seemed rigid beneath his touch.

That had never happened before.

TV, print, and radio reporters were walking all over one another, verbally and physically, to have a go at Chief Jurgen.

Rainfinch watched alone in his cubicle, on the five-inch black-and-white set he kept for such occasions.

He grinned as the chief adroitly sidestepped a pointed question from Moriarty. The trick, Rainfinch knew, was to keep your cool and answer in a way that sounded as if you were giving good, solid information, when in reality 50 percent of what you said was so much formalized double-talk. Not lies; you were dead meat if you lied to them. But not the full truth, either.

Rainfinch's conscience, often a lot more sensitive than he would have liked, was not in the least bothered by this necessity. It was a fact of life caused by the difference in their jobs. Cops wanted to catch criminals and put them someplace where they couldn't harm society—at least for a reasonable length of time. In order to do that, it was vital to keep the criminal from knowing everything the cop knew.

Reporters . . . well, it seemed to him reporters were devoted to blabbing every morsel of information they could ferret out. And then endlessly speculating about what that morsel might or might not mean.

He grinned again and shook his head as Moriarty tried a flank attack that failed. You couldn't blame them, he supposed. It was the nature of the beast.

His telephone rang. The intercom line blinked red. He picked up the receiver. "What is it, Rosie?" Usually Rainfinch's phone rang straight through, but during the press conference he'd asked the detective bureau receptionist to run interference for him.

"You have a call—"

"Take a number, will you? I don't want to talk right now."

"Lieutenant, it's your sister."

"Put her on."

A lump of leaden apprehension gathered in his chest as Julianna said, "Abe, is that really you? When did you get to be so important? It must be easier to talk to the head of the CIA."

"Sorry. Rosie was just doing her job. I asked her to hold my calls for a few minutes."

"I wasn't criticizing. Actually, I'm impressed."

The teasing note in his sister's voice threw him off guard. "How—how is—?"

"She's better, Abe. Saying a few words, and writing notes like crazy. Her left side is partially paralyzed. The doctor says it's possible she could recover completely, but he won't promise anything. The best news is, she's out of intensive care and into a private room."

"That's great, wonderful news. Look, we've had two more killings that appear connected to the Hall case, but in a day or two I can—"

"No."

"What do you mean, no?" Surely his mother couldn't be so angry she didn't want to see him?

Julianna actually laughed. "I told her why you weren't here. I was furious with you—I guess I made that fairly clear. But she wrote me a note, the longest one she's managed. You are not to come until you've caught the killer."

"Tell her it's not exactly a one-man operation."

"Are you kidding? And destroy her illusions? She likes Governor Sanden, Abe. She voted for him before she left. She thinks he's going to be president, some day. Probably the only thing she and Dad agree on anymore. If this murder of one of his staff members is causing him trouble, she wants you to put a stop to it."

"Oh, right," Rainfinch said dryly.

Julianna chuckled again. "You have your instructions. And big brother, I think I was something of a bitch, the other day. Forgive?"

"Forget it. You had a right. You were worried."

"And about Dad. I guess it's time I grew up and faced the fact he's a selfish son of a bitch who doesn't really care about anything or anyone but the great Maestro Rainfinch."

"I'm not going to touch that one. I'm hardly an impartial judge."

"I need to go. Mom—Julia, that is—did I tell you she makes me call her Julia, now? She told me starting up a career that's been on hold for twenty-five years is hard enough without a grown daughter calling her Mom all the time. Anyway, she insisted I come away and practice a couple hours this afternoon. So I need to get back to the hospital."

"Julia." Rainfinch tasted the name, reflectively. "Well, I'll be damned." His voice became tentative. "Is there any chance . . . ?"

"That she'll play the piano again? God, it sounds like a soap opera, doesn't it? There's no way of knowing yet."

"What about you? Is your tour completely down the drain?"

"Those guys are so wonderful, Abe. They say I can join them in London, or Frankfurt—anywhere along the line. They're not taking anyone in my place, they'll limp along till I can come."

"That's great. Julianna—tell her I love her. And I'll try to live up to her confidence in my abilities."

"I'll tell her, Abe."

"Keep in touch, will you, sis?"

The press conference was over by the time his call ended. Rainfinch unplugged the midget TV, slid it back into a corner of the bookcase, and put on his khaki overcoat.

He hadn't seen or talked personally with Monk Smith since Monk's lover had been murdered. It was time to pay him a visit.

$\triangledown$

20

"NEVER LIKED HIM much, did you, Abe? I doubt you even remembered his name, he was just the fag interior decorator who lived with Monk Smith. Keyes. His name was Archie Keyes. But I expect you do know that, now."

They were sitting in the main room of the former parsonage. In better circumstances it had been warm and welcoming, with a cozy charm Rainfinch could never experience in the broad, high chambers of the home his great-grandfather built. Here the ceilings were low, with thick arches leading to a hallway on one side and dining room on the other. There was a bay window, with yards and yards of gauzy stuff draped across in artful disarray. The walls were done in a green-and-burgundy Victorian print. The fireplace was surrounded by built-in bookcases of knurly wood, finished a deep golden color.

It was the type of place, Rainfinch thought, that made you think about long winter nights, reading while the fire crackled, listening to music. Or spring days with the door open to the front garden, and hordes of tulips massed on the library table in front of the window.

On this cold and blustery day there was no fire in the hearth, and anguish hung in the air like a physical presence.

Monk's bitter words stung. They held more than a little truth.

"I didn't know Archie well. I only met him a couple of times. You cared about him, and you're my friend. That sets him apart. Beyond that, all murder victims are important to me."

Monk gave him a long look. His eyes were the kind of bleak that cops see too often, that made you want to flinch and turn away. "What a pretty little speech. A bit stiff, but quite nice. I warn you, Abe, you'd better find the person who did this. Fast. Because if I get to him first, there won't be anything left for you to arrest."

"Take it easy, Monk. Don't go blasting off in all directions like a load of Chinese firecrackers. When are you going to reopen the club?"

Monk stood and walked to the front window. He shrugged. "The Seraphim is no more, Abe. They win."

"That's not like you. Giving up."

He turned and faced Rainfinch, feet splayed, swaying slightly. "Oh, right, I'm a fighter. What the hell is there to fight for? I'm going to get out of here. I never want to go inside that damned building again." He sat, heavily. "Maybe they're right, my outraged neighbors. Maybe I committed sacrilege, brought this down on Archie and me."

"Do you believe that?"

"I don't know what I believe."

During the conversation Rainfinch had been aware of movement in the kitchen. He had supposed it was a housekeeper, or a relative. Now Frannie Da Sorta appeared with three short, fat glasses, an ice bucket, and a bottle of Kentucky sour mash. Without asking he dumped ice into the glasses, sloshed liquor over, and passed it around. Then he sat.

Rainfinch was glad to see him. He needed Monk's cooperation, and he though Frannie might side with him.

"You're right about one thing. The Seraphim seems to be a catalyst. That's why I want you to reopen, as soon after Archie's funeral as you can. I promise you, we'll have surveillance here every night."

For the first time, he saw a spark of life in Monk's eyes. "You think the killer will try again, and you'll catch him." He drank off the whiskey in long, thirsty swallows and shook his head. "That means you'd be using my customers as live bait. I won't do it."

Frannie swirled the cubes in his glass. "Think about it, Boss. If we shut down, it's kinda like lyin' on the mat for the count, without even tryin' to get on our feet. I think the lieutenant's right."

Monk poured himself another two fingers of whiskey. He glowered at Rainfinch, but answered Frannie. "How long do you think they'll tie up officers watching our place? All the killer has to do is wait until they leave."

"The killer won't know we're there at all. I don't plan on my people wearing signs saying 'I'm a cop.' "

Monk made a gesture, touching in its helplessness. "Let me think about it."

Rainfinch knew when he'd been dismissed. He put on his overcoat and gripped Monk's shoulder as he headed for the door. "I'll talk to you later."

Monk nodded.

Frannie, surprisingly quick on his feet for an old pug, beat their guest to the door, opened it, and walked outside with him.

"He'll do it, Lieutenant. He's kinda lost his bearings, right now, but Monk ain't a quitter."

Rainfinch nodded. "I know, Frannie."

On the way downtown he couldn't help thinking about the last time he'd left the former parsonage. It had been close to the same time of the evening, after his meeting with Monk and Beth Farraday. Archie Keyes had been there, hovering anxiously, offering drinks, surreptitiously wiping dust off the edge of a table with a paper napkin.

He got on my nerves. Monk saw, and remembered.

Once he managed to put that guilt out of his mind, his mother came back. Okay, she probably wasn't going to die, but a stroke . . . would she ever be able to stretch those long, graceful fingers across piano keys again? If not, what was left for her? He couldn't see her slinking back home so Martin Rainfinch could gloat.

But if she stayed in New York, what would she do? He grinned. Not sit around and mother Julianna, that was for sure. Not Julia Rainfinch's style.

Without conscious decision, he had been driving back to the station. Suddenly he wondered why. What was he doing? He had to turn it loose, to relax for a few hours. He felt a bleak loneliness, so powerful it cut to the core, like some deep sickness that might never go away. He wheeled the Ford into a sharp U-turn and headed home.

Inside the house, he picked up the phone and dialed Susan Elias.

Susan was testing the elastic in a pair of panties when the phone rang. The elastic failed, and the panties were tossed into an overflowing box of rejects.

She had declined Robert's offer of a drink when they left Max Sanden's office, which hadn't pleased him much. Then she'd stopped at the cleaner's, dashed into a market for apples and cereal, come home, and had a hot bath. After that she began a ruthless assault on her closet, stripping it bare and piling clothes on the bed, chairs, and finally the floor. Next it was the dresser's turn. Piles of sweaters, slips, panties, and brassieres were heaped haphazardly.

Susan did not consider herself a particularly neat person, an opinion heartily shared by parents, old college room-mates, and lovers. But when the larger elements of her life went awry—broken romances, career problems, trouble with friends or family—she invariably sought solace by bringing order to her living space. After all, you might not be able to make humans and events toe the mark, but you could damn sure order sweaters, slips, and hosiery around.

The phone irritated her. If one more reporter called her at home—

She didn't have to answer. There wasn't a law, for heaven's sake.

In the end she snatched it up, and when she heard Rainfinch's voice her insides vibrated slightly, as if someone had touched her with a tuning fork.

"No, I wasn't doing anything special." Mountains of tumbled clothes glared accusingly at her.

"Dinner? Well . . . I don't see why not."

"Nothing fancy. Wear something casual. After we eat—
some friends of mine are getting together. Maybe we could
drop in for a while."

He asked if she could be ready in thirty minutes. Susan
agreed, then attacked piles of clothes and burrowed like a
frenetic mole until she found a soft, faded blue cotton
sweater and her favorite old Levi's. She added a pair of
rough-side cowboy boots with walking heels. She'd already
had her long soak in the tub. A hasty brush job left her hair
rearranged but not subdued. A dab of powder across the most
prominent freckles, lipstick, and a spritz of her favorite
cologne, and she was ready.

Abe grinned when he saw her. "I like you this way. I was
afraid your interpretation of 'something casual' might be a
designer pantsuit, gold kid shoes and a half dozen chains
around your neck. You being a big-time social career girl."

Susan slid into the gray Ford police cruiser. "I can't believe
you said that. Is *my* name Rainfinch? Do *I* live in a famous
mansion? Is *my* father a symphony conductor who hobnobs
with the local jet set? I grew up on a ranch in the Osage. A
small one." The ranch was a slight fabrication. Actually, she'd
grown up the daughter of two small-town schoolteachers, and
spent her summers on her grandparents' ranch.

He held up a hand in surrender as they pulled away from
the curb, but Susan had warmed to her subject. "We're riding
in a police car, for heaven sake. I thought you'd pick me up
in a Ferrari, or at least a Jaguar."

He laughed. "Sorry to disappoint you. The only car I own
is a 1968 Morgan. Currently it doesn't have a top, so I did
you a favor and drove this. At least it's not a black-and-white;
nobody'll think you're under arrest."

Susan had never seen him laugh before. She decided he
ought to do it more often. "I guess it's okay to do this? Drive
a police car on a date?"

"I have what they call a take-home car. I'm free to use
it—but not carouse around, needless to say."

She looked at him from under lowered lids. My God, she was flirting. She thought she'd forgotten how. "We're not going to carouse?"

He shook his head. "Right now I couldn't whip up a mild revel, let alone a full-tilt carouse."

They had dinner at a small, homey place with red plastic booths, motherly waitresses, and good food. Susan was amazed at how easy he was to talk to, now that there weren't any hidden agendas. At least, not on her part. She wasn't expected to gouge information out of him. And if he had any less-than-social motives, they weren't evident.

By mutual unspoken consent, nothing was said about Carter Hall, or the Seraphim, or the second two murders. Or Maestro Rainfinch.

She did ask about his mother.

"I talked to my sister Julianna this afternoon. Things look better. They say she's out of danger. But it's too soon to know if she'll play the piano again." He made a wry face. "As my sister says, it sounds a bit like a soap opera."

Susan gave him a long look. "What a shame—things—keep you from going to be with her. I know you must want to."

He nodded. "I'd come to a decision. The hell with the Seraphim murders, let someone else worry about them. There's always plenty of business for homicide cops. Maybe not as intriguing—but I only have one mother. I intended to explain things to my major and catch a plane. In the meantime, though, Julianna told her why I wasn't there. My mother wrote a note—she's not talking much, yet—saying she didn't want to see my ugly face until I'd caught whoever killed Governor Sanden's aide. She likes your boss. Thinks he'll be president, one day."

They were hovering close to the forbidden subject, and Susan didn't want it to intrude. She asked him things about being a cop, silly things, and he began telling stories. Not the grim ones she might have expected—well, some of them were grim-funny, but mostly they were just humorous. Susan loved it.

Back in the car, pleasantly sated, they traveled in companionable silence. He hadn't told her where they were going, and she didn't ask. She was content just to sit and ride, until in a few minutes he pulled up in front of a neat, story-and-a-half frame house.

Susan was familiar with the neighborhood, an inner-city area called Mesta Park that had been built in the teens and twenties, allowed to run down in the sixties and seventies, and now was undergoing a spirited revival. Many of the people she knew who lived here were artists, writers, musicians.

"I was tempted to buy a house up in the next block," she volunteered. "The neatest brick bungalow, with a crazy art deco bathroom, all lavender, black, and green tile. But I don't know how long I'll stay in this city. I might move away, somewhere."

"You mean, to Washington?" he asked dryly, getting out of the car.

They had started up the sidewalk when the sound came, a violin, so sad and beautiful it made Susan's eyes sting. They stopped to listen. Abe took her hand and held it. She thought the music, the cold, damp night, and the enigmatic man beside her made one of those crystallized moments she would never forget. It would be tucked away somewhere in her mind for the rest of her life, to bring back and savor, more vivid than a photograph.

The music stopped, and the front door opened. A slim, clever-faced man came out on the porch, still holding the violin.

"Abe. Come inside."

Introductions were made. Their host, Eli Morse, called, "Rosa, Abe's here," and a young woman with magnificent, fiery hair appeared.

"I've just put the baby to bed—" she began, in a voice with an unmistakable Australian lilt.

"I've seen you," Susan blurted. "You're director of the children's theater, aren't you? I took my niece to see your production of *Jack and the Beanstalk*. It was great."

There were two more men in the room. One, a giant with black hair and a black beard, was sprawled on a sofa, a guitar across his lap. His name was David. The other was older, balding, with a fringe of silky, shoulder-length brown hair. He held a strange, archaic-looking instrument, a recorder.

When they had settled in and were provided with mugs of steaming spiced cider, Eli told Susan, "We're a group who specializes in American folk music. Sometimes Abe drops by when we practice."

"Yeah," Jacob, the older man, said. "Now and then he even brings his fiddle, and saws on it a little bit."

Susan turned on Abe. "*You* play the violin? I didn't—"

"Damn it, Jacob, do you have to tell everything you know?"

Jacob laughed, unrepentant. "There are worse crimes, lad."

Time slipped by, filled with music, spirited discussion of music, and laughter. Susan sat back and watched. She was enjoying herself more than she had in—oh, she couldn't remember. Sometime before her life was filled with media people, and chiefs of staff, and governors, and bids for the presidency. And, of course, murder.

A few minutes before midnight the group broke up. Eli, Rosa, and the others bid Abe Rainfinch an affectionately insulting good-bye that spoke of close friendship. Rosa asked Susan to come again.

While they had been inside the low clouds had blown away. Now it was sharp and clear. The stars had a cold glitter, and steamy vapor plumed up from Abe's mouth. Susan, chilled in her light raincoat, tried not to shiver. That would really be too much of a cliché. *Oh, dear, I'm cold* (timid feminine voice). *Here, I'll put my arm around you, that'll keep you warm* (macho masculine voice).

As they drove away Abe said, "We're only a few blocks from my house. Will you come by?" He glanced at her. "To talk. Give me credit, I have a little more finesse when I'm working up to a seduction. It's just . . . I'm so damn tired, but I won't be able to sleep."

Susan nodded. "I know what you mean. And yes, I would like to talk. I haven't been sleeping well lately, myself. The minute I sneak between the sheets the specters make a ring around my bed, and start dancing. Anything to postpone that."

"They dance for you, too, huh? I thought I had a corner on the specter market."

Susan shook her head. "Not half, my friend."

They were silent for the rest of the drive. Susan thought that any discussion of what specters were capering for whom might touch on the forbidden subject.

They pulled into the circular drive at the south side of the Charbonnet Mansion. There was a dim light in a circular tower at the southeast corner, and light streamed through the leaded glass panels of the entrance beside the port cochere where they parked.

Abe pulled a bulky old key out of his pocket and unlocked the door. Inside, a wide, high-ceilinged hall led to a staircase. To the left and right of where they stood double doors opened onto the dining room and a library. Above their heads was a cobalt enamel and crystal chandelier, and beneath their feet an old oriental runner in faded reds and blues. Susan could see that to the right of the stairs an even larger hallway intersected. This was just a side entrance.

"My God," she whispered. "You could fit my entire apartment into your foyer."

He looked at her and shrugged. "It's just a house, Susan. Built by a Cherokee horse and mule trader."

She laughed. "Horse and mule trading must have been damn profitable."

"There are certain piratical rumors about great-grandpa, but I like to think he was just a good businessman. We're going up there," he added, with a gesture toward the staircase. "I camp out on the second floor."

At the landing there was another massive hallway to the left, but he led the way directly across and into a comfortable room done in shades of green, from palest chartreuse to brilliant emerald. There were elegant antique pieces—a gilt

French curio cabinet filled with small jade objects, a delicate carved love seat in satin brocade, a porcelain and gold clock on the mantel, replete with cherubs and matching urns on either side. But there were also two massive chairs with thick down cushions beside the fireplace, and even—how prosaic could you get?—a small television set squatting sulkily on a table.

Abe took her coat and disappeared. Susan curled up in one of the fireside chairs. In a moment he was back, handing her a bottle of beer.

"Would you like a glass?"

Susan shook her head. "No, but will that thing light up?" She pointed at the open brass stove inside the fireplace.

"I was just going to tend to it." He pulled a box of kitchen matches from behind the cherub clock, struck one, and lit the gas jets, then tucked it back in its hiding place.

"Why gas? I somehow expected a roaring wood fire."

Abe settled into the other chair. "Think about it. When this house was built, wood fires were no luxury. I've been told great-grandpa's gas lights and fireplaces created quite a sensation, in their day."

The fire was warm against her face, the beer good, and the chair incredibly comfortable. Susan burrowed a little deeper.

"What was it like to grow up in a place like this? I can't even imagine. Did you have governesses, and nannies, and stuff?"

For a minute she didn't think he was going to answer. Then he said, "Why don't you pull off your boots? I'm going to. That used to be the first thing Mom did, when she came home on cold winter days. Took off her shoes and sat on her feet, in that same chair. She used to say her toes were always cold."

Susan nodded. "Mine are, too. And I will, thanks."

He raised his arms and clasped his hands behind his head. "To answer your question—I wasn't born here, you know. Mom was a student at Julliard when she met the great maestro. He'd been one of those alleged child prodigies, writing music and conducting symphony orchestras by the time he was twelve. Then he hit a burnout phase. To hear him tell it now, Julia Charbonnet, the little Indian girl from nowhere, caught him in a weak moment and married him before he had a chance to realize what was going on."

Susan made a gesture that encompassed the room. "Some little Indian girl from nowhere."

"That's the way he thought of it. And still does. The truth is he never quite lived up to what was expected of him. Being a child prodigy must be hell."

"People say he's a fine conductor. How lucky we are, to have him here."

"Yeah. But he was struggling, before we came. He seemed to have lost the ability to compose. He blamed that on marriage, and the necessity to support a family after Julianna and I were born."

"Where *were* you born?"

"In St. Louis. Then Julianna came along while we were in England, on an abortive attempt to resurrect his career there."

Susan traced the delicate filigree rosebuds on a Meissen vase with her finger. "So how did you end up here?"

"When I was seven my grandfather wrote Mom that old Maestro St. Simeon was in poor health. The symphony board wanted a second conductor. Someone younger, who could take over when they finally took the old man's baton away from him."

Susan frowned. "That sounds cold-blooded."

"It was. After Martin Rainfinch took the job and we'd been here six months, he gave them an ultimatum. Either he got the top position or we'd move on. My grandfather was a heavy contributor, and he wanted his daughter and grandchildren here, where he could watch over us, not racketing around the world. So he fixed it—but all you asked was what it was like to grow up in this house. I've given you the family history. Now it's your turn. Tell me about that ranch in the Osage."

Susan wasn't ready to talk about herself. "What's to tell? A ranch is a ranch. You know I'm acquainted with the maestro; he's at most of the big functions in the governor's mansion. I had always wondered how he ended up in his wife's hometown."

Abe gave a small, cynical chuckle. "When he could be performing before the crowned heads of Europe? At least, that's what he'd have you think. I don't want to talk about Martin Rainfinch anymore." He sighed. "And I don't really know how to answer your original question. This place was just—home. Julianna and I had good times. There were always a lot of people around. Parties. Music. There was a housekeeper, and a maid, and a yard man. But now . . . it's damn quiet. Someone comes in three days a week to clean. I sleep here. That's about it. Boy, I'm really dredging things up, tonight. You've gotten more out of me in a few hours than anyone has in the last ten years."

"I've heard for years that the state historical society wants to buy the Charbonnet Mansion. Why don't you sell?"

He finished his beer, and slid the bottle around in wet circles on the mirror-topped table beside his chair. "It would be the sensible thing. The roof leaks, the plumbing is bad, the wiring a nightmare. The state has the money to fix everything, keep the yard up, replant flower beds. I can't do that. The maestro spent most of what my mother inherited years ago. But I just can't turn it loose. Not yet."

"I know what you mean." She laughed, embarrassed. "Well, it's not quite the same thing. My grandpa died last year, and left me his home place. It's a small spread by cattlemen's standards, but I've always loved it—so many happy memories. There have been several offers to buy, and I can't imagine I'd ever want to live there. Still . . ."

He nodded. "Yeah."

Susan drifted off into her own memories, and was startled when he said, "After this whole Carter Hall thing is over—"

"Do you believe the other two deaths were related? Robert Friar thinks they were all random killings by someone who hates homosexuals."

He leaned forward, his face rigid with anger. "The governor's chief of staff needs to take care of his job and let me do mine, without his goddamned interference. You might tell him the only thing he accomplishes by dangling goodies in front of Clifford Stamps or whispering in my father's ear is to make me wonder what the hell he's covering up."

Susan felt as if she'd been slapped. Not a woman who'd gotten where she was by being meek, she fought back. "What do you mean, 'dangling goodies in front of Clifford Stamps?' I don't believe that—and you couldn't possibly know, if it were true. As for your father . . . he's your problem. I guess you'd better take me home."

He stood. "You're right." His voice was quiet, the anger drained out. "I apologize for unloading on you, I know you don't control what that ass Friar does. But while I'm on the subject, I'll say this. He's a viper, Susan. Don't trust him for a minute."

She walked over and glared up at him without flinching. "What gives you the right to say that? You don't know anything about Robert."

"I don't have to. I recognize the type."

The drive to her apartment was chilly. After he walked her to the door, though, he made an effort.

"I'm sorry I blew up. I like you a lot, Susan. Thanks for your company this evening."

"I enjoyed it," she replied truthfully. "At least, up to the part where you told me what a skunk you think my boss is."

"Your boss? Is that all?"

"Not that it's any of your business, but he's also my friend."

"Friend . . . oh, hell, Susan. You're right, it's none of my business." He took her hands and held them briefly. For a moment she thought he would say more, but he turned away and abruptly left.

Susan had forgotten the chaotic mess she'd left in her bedroom. She washed her face, brushed her teeth, and then went to work. Two hours later she crawled into bed, squinting through tears to set a clunky wind-up alarm clock that was a survivor from college days.

What the hell had happened to her world, anyway?

$\triangledown$

21

ROBERT FRIAR AND the governor had gone to the northeast-
ern part of the state and were not due back until Wednesday
evening. The trip included a highway dedication, inspection
of improvements to a small municipal airport (a new wind
sock and a barbed wire fence to keep cows off the runway),
and speeches in three high school auditoriums. Although as
press secretary Susan usually went along on such jaunts, she
had managed to avoid this one because four highway commissioners were hitching a ride in the governor's airplane;
that loaded it to capacity. Although one of the commissioners
roguishly suggested she come and sit on his lap, she had
declined as graciously as possible.

It was a quarter to six when she left the capitol building,
relieved that it hadn't been necessary to face Robert. Her
emotional self felt like a glob of overworked taffy, pulled this
way and that by Carter Hall's murder, the media, Robert,
Abe Rainfinch. . . .

"I'm not a well person," she had caught herself mumbling
several times during the day. Because if she were, she
wouldn't be so damned paranoid that Robert might discover
she'd gone out with Abe.

She could spend her free time with whomever she chose.
Robert had never come close to making any kind of commit-
ment; nor had she, for that matter. So why feel guilty?

Because she knew how the governor's chief of staff would
interpret it. Sleeping with the enemy. Metaphorically, of
course.

At least, so far.

When the two men had first met that afternoon at the governor's mansion, she'd been amazed by the instant mutual antagonism. Bringing them together had been like throwing a handful of gunpowder on an open fire. She blamed Robert, for the most part. He bragged of being a "political animal," didn't he? He'd demonstrated time after time he was capable of charming people he loathed. So why the unmistakable arrogance toward Abe? It was ridiculous. No one in the governor's office had anything to hide.

Or did they? A nagging question. She couldn't seem to get rid of it. Why had Brendon Guiste been thrown to the wolves—staked out like a goat on a tether, a sign hung around his neck inviting "Devour Me."

She was almost in her car, parked along the U-shaped drive of the west entrance, when the familiar black Lincoln limousine, driven by a spit-and-polish state trooper, glided by. She was seen. The car pulled to a stop. Robert emerged, stuck his head back inside to say a hasty word to the governor, then covered the ground between them with swift strides.

"Susan. Glad I caught you," he said warmly, squeezing her arm.

Oh, here it comes, the full Friar treatment. Wide, boyish smile, one hand smoothing back an unruly lock of hair. That special look, mischievous and admiring at the same time, that hinted at delightful secrets and made you feel the most cherished person in Robert's world.

Damn it, she'd never been cynical about those things before. Okay, amused sometimes, but not cynical. This was Abe's fault. *Damn Abe.*

"Sweetheart, I tried to call you for hours last night. The Big Max thought we ought to put out a new press release about the withdrawal of federal funding for the Spirit Cloud Dam project. We're taking some hits on that deal. I needed my favorite phrasemaker, but I couldn't find you. So I had to write it myself."

"I'm sorry."

Silence. Did he expect her to tell him where she'd been, for Christ's sake, and with whom? After an awkward moment she added, "I was out for a while. With friends."

"Well . . . I guess that's your privilege. But look, when Max and I need you, we need you. So tomorrow morning you get a pager, to take everywhere with you." He pointed a playful finger at her. "*Everywhere*. If you shower, it showers. If you go to bed, alone or not—well, you get the idea."

"Oh, really—"

"No arguments. Actually, we should have done this a long time ago. But I haven't had trouble locating you until recently. You're getting secretive on me, Elias."

"No, I—"

He gave her a quick kiss on the cheek. "Gotta run."

Susan saw that Meg, the governor's secretary, had come down and was walking toward the limousine with a sheaf of files.

"I'm going back to the mansion with Max, we have to work on some stuff tonight. So you have one more unfettered evening. Make the most of it. After that, I'll run you down wherever you are."

Susan stood dumbly beside her car, fighting anger. It wasn't unreasonable for a governor's press secretary to be expected to wear a pager. But why now? And the way Robert had put it. Like the stupid little black box was his personal spy.

It had been a long day. Maybe that was why April, Danny, and Lou were crowded in Rainfinch's office, arguing querulously about who should attend what funeral.

"Oh, no." April shook her head emphatically. "Listen, I had to endure that four-hour extravaganza they put on for Carter Hall. Everyone who'd ever known him, from his third-grade teacher to the owner of the Capital Barber Shop, felt called upon to deliver a few thousand well-chosen words. As if they thought a lifetime of personal anecdotes would cancel out the way he died. And those poor old people, his parents, frail as stick figures, sitting under the canopy at the cemetery like pitiful potentates while people paid their respects to the fallen crown prince."

"That's downright poetic, Morgen," Lou said. " 'Pitiful potentates.' Careful, you'll bring a tear to this bleary old eye."

April ignored him. "I had two guys from Projects with me, watching for known fag-bashers, neo-Nazis, anyone who looked out of place. We worked the crowds at the funeral home, the church, and the cemetery. Nothing. I don't think we're going to catch this killer in such a stupid move—hanging around the victim's funeral to gloat. Besides, unless it's someone who sticks out like the Grateful Dead at a Mormon ice-cream social—"

"Poor girl," Danny said solemnly. "Gets all the nasty jobs. Funerals and horny kitty cats." He settled his weight on a corner of Rainfinch's desk. Lou and April, in folding chairs, were wedged in the scant four feet between the front desk and the scarred gray wall.

"Granted," Danny continued, "I agree our chances of scoring at a funeral are remote. But the lieutenant here says we should cover the services for Solent and Keyes. I guess he's right. Leave no tern unstoned—all that crap. I'm just saying you should take one, and Lou and I'll sit in on the other. What's fairer than that?"

"I'll tell you what's fairer. I've already done mine. You take one, let Lou take the other, and we'll all be even."

Rainfinch decided the wrangling had gone far enough. "Okay, here's the drill, troops. Archie Keyes's services are tomorrow morning, ten-thirty, at the Hesse-Hill Funeral Home. Danny and Lou, I want you there. That'll leave plenty of time for you to get to the graveside services for Solent. Three P.M., Good Shepherd Cemetery."

Lou squinted. His face screwed into a wily expression, which made him look like a wizened old monkey.

"I'd have thought you'd want to be at the Keyes deal, Lieutenant. Monk Smith being an old buddy of yours."

Rainfinch grinned. "More like an old acquaintance, thank you. And there's no use trying to punch my guilt button. It's been gouged to the breaking point in the last few days. I'm numb."

Danny yawned and stretched. "Are we finished for tonight? I need dinner and a bed. Not necessarily alone, of course."

Lou snorted. "You're braggin', Kid Valentino. Hell, if you were half the stud you think you are, they'd be puttin' up a plaque in your honor on the lineup room bulletin board."

Rainfinch only half heard the bantering. He'd been on the verge of asking April to go with him on a visit to Maude Mae Haslip. He wanted to meet their only eyewitness, and since the photographs of car models that fit her description of the murderer's car had been rounded up and delivered by Auto Theft, now seemed a good time. He didn't want to go alone, though. A strange man knocking on the old woman's door after dark might frighten her.

But what about afterward? He and April. Together, in the evening. Should he suggest they have dinner? Would she misinterpret the offer? He stole a look at her. Beautiful, desirable. Hell, maybe he didn't trust his own motives.

To an outsider, her current attitude toward him would seem perfectly normal. She didn't avoid him, and that terrible tension in their work relationship had dissipated. He had to admit that was due mostly to the fact that he'd stopped picking on her now that they weren't sleeping together.

But April, who had never flinched or backed away from any encounter, didn't seem to look him in the eye anymore. And there was a kind of remoteness about her, as if she were only going through the motions.

Sexual attraction. Was that all it had been? Hadn't he, hadn't they both, felt more in the beginning, or was—

"—don't you agree, Lieutenant?" Danny asked.

"What? Agree to what?"

The three detectives laughed.

"You drifted away on us," Lou told him. "Have you thought of something we should know about?"

"Uh, I was just going to ask if anyone had followed up on the idea that Carter Hall might have had a love nest tucked away somewhere." *Whew. Good recovery.*

The detectives looked at each other. Lou spoke. "I guess that was my deal. Sorry, after the second two killings I just let it slip through the cracks."

"Okay. But get on it now, will you?"

"First thing. That is, when I'm not going to funerals."

"That reminds me," Danny said, "I'm due to testify tomorrow in district court on the Janie Norcross case. You remember, the teenager who was kidnapped from that amusement park last year and bludgeoned to death? The D.A. called and said if I wasn't present and ready to take the stand at eight o'clock he'd send a couple of deputy sheriffs after me."

Rainfinch sighed and rubbed his left temple. "Yes. All right. I know everyone's got other cases clamoring to be worked on, but right now we're catching so much hell on this thing. . . ."

Lou nodded morosely. "The goddamn television reporters haven't had so much fun since a tornado killed eighty people down in Little Dixie. Moriarty, that girlfriend of yours—"

"Moriarty isn't—I don't want to hear it. On second thought, though, you two win about the funerals. Your time is too important. The Projects officers can handle them alone."

There was a general murmur of approbation, then Lou gave Rainfinch a particularly shrewd look.

"Abe, you don't believe these were random killings of homosexuals, do you? You think they were personal—someone with a grudge."

Danny, with uncharacteristic seriousness, said, "If that's the case, then Carter Hall has to be the catalyst."

Rainfinch nodded. "That's how I see it. We know Dutch-boy Solent did some drunken bragging the night he was killed. Several people heard him popping off that he had information about Hall's killing, and was working with the police. As for Archie Keyes . . . his death doesn't fit the pattern of the others—gun instead of knife, no mutilation. I think he was just damned unlucky."

April looked at a spot above Rainfinch's head. "I agree with you. I think that's how it went down. The poor bastard decided to carry out the trash in the middle of the night, and stumbled onto a murder."

There was a short silence, while everyone thought it over. Finally Lou said "Okay, that means the killer was in the Seraphim, had returned there *after* he got his original victim. Why?"

Danny shifted his weight on the desk from one cheek to the other. "There could be a number of reasons. He felt safe and wanted to hear what was being said about his triumph. Or he wasn't sure he hadn't fouled up somehow and wanted to hear what was being said. That's two."

"Or he may have had more than one person on his original hit list. He felt secure enough to return for a number two and instead got tangled up with Solent and Keyes," Rainfinch suggested softly.

Lou pulled a battered pack of cigarettes out of his pocket and looked at April. She frowned. He sighed, replaced them. "Why would he go back to the same place to bag his second kill? If we're dealin' with a rational guy here, he ought to realize that ain't too smart."

Danny added his silent support to April's cigarette veto by moving the lone ashtray away from Lou. "Because he's fixated on the place, which brings us back to someone whose transistors are on overload." He looked at Rainfinch. "What do you think, Lieutenant?"

"Maybe. Partly, at least. But it could be that the Seraphim is the one place he's sure of finding his mark. Maybe our killer has a job, people he's responsible to. He can't follow his victim around all the time, hoping for a good opportunity. So he goes to the Seraphim, maybe every night, and waits patiently until he sees his chance. It's a big place, you know, and not exactly lit up like noontime on the courthouse square. What I'm getting at is that if someone didn't want to be noticed, they could manage pretty easily."

Rainfinch leaned back in his chair and was silent. He bit a knuckle. The others waited, sensing he had more to say.

"That's why I'm urging Monk Smith to reopen the club as soon as he feels able, and I have the major's okay to use as many undercover people as Projects can spare. As well as ourselves. We'll have vehicles from Projects, too, and any surveillance equipment we need. A cockroach won't sneeze in that place without our knowing it."

"All right!" Danny said.

Lou squinted. His hand crept stealthily toward the cigarette pack again. "It's a good idea. But how long do you think they'll let us tie up the manpower and equipment?"

"Let's hope for long enough. I'm not going to worry about that, yet. Right now let's talk about Carter Hall. Lou, you and Danny have handled the politicians lately. What's the consensus around the capitol about Hall? Was it generally known he was homosexual? How did people feel about him?"

Lou moved cautiously toward the ashtray as he answered. "I talked to the crusty old pols, and let the Kid here handle Yuppieville on the second floor."

"He means the governor's office," Danny explained to April.

"I don't need a damn interpreter," Lou complained. "The old-time state-house guys hated his guts. Said he was arrogant and stuck on himself, but they also admitted he was smart and a hard worker. Far as his sex life was concerned, I didn't get the idea anyone gave a damn. Unless, of course, it could have been used against him, or in some cases, against Sanden. Most of them seemed to have had their suspicions."

He turned to Danny with a look of polite inquiry. "How about you?" His index finger hooked over the lip of the ashtray. April slapped his hand, seized the ashtray, and sailed it into a wastebasket, where it disappeared with a tinny thunk. "Hell," Lou muttered.

"I don't know why you haven't thrown that smelly thing away before," April said to Rainfinch. "You just encourage him."

Danny waited to see if anything else interesting would happen. When it didn't, he said, "Sanden's staff is one bunch of nervous overachievers. I can't figure out the deal, whether they're hiding something or if it's just ordinary paranoia over all the bad press."

"And having to deal with uncouth types like homicide detectives," Lou added.

April broke in. "You can't blame them for being jittery. Those media werewolves would make the Pillsbury Doughboy paranoid."

Lou snorted. "Hell, I reckon. Damn Pillsbury Doughboy's a creampuff if I ever saw one."

April giggled. "Well, you get my point."

"You two mind if I finish my report to the lieutenant?" Danny asked. "Thank you. Lieutenant, you already know Hall's secretary idolized him. Nearly everyone else gave him high marks for brains and hard work, then made it clear they never socialized with him. But listen, when I went to see Brendon Guiste, a very nervous secretary who was in his office going through files said he was taking some time off."

"Oh, really?" Rainfinch with interested.

"I talked that gorgeous receptionist they have into taking a coffee break—"

"You mean Ettalou Percival?"

"Yeah. Those legs are hard to forget, aren't they, Lieutenant?"

"Impossible to forget."

"Anyway, she told me the office scuttlebutt is that Guiste is out for good. Fired—or will be."

"Oh-oh. Sacrifice time." April played an imaginary violin.

Rainfinch was tired of cocking his head to look up at Danny, who was still perched on the edge of his desk. He grabbed a third folding chair. "Take this and sit. You're giving me a neck cramp."

Danny obeyed, wedging April between himself and Lou.

"About Guiste. That's a development that needs attention. We'll work on him again, maybe he'll be resentful enough to throw a little dirt. Don't do anything now, I want to think over how to go about it. He loathes cops."

Lou gave him a sharp look. "You think he and Henderson might have—?"

"Frankly, I don't. But who knows? Danny, did she say who axed him? The governor, or Robert Friar?"

"Oh, Friar. Sanden doesn't dirty his hands with unpleasant personnel matters. But I expect he must have approved. Ettalou says he runs a tight ship."

"Not tight enough, if he trusts Friar."

"You really have a thing about that guy, don't you?" Lou asked.

Rainfinch did, but he didn't want to discuss it. "Okay, I think we've hashed and rehashed long enough. Why don't all of you get out of here? I want to see everyone first thing tomorrow." He saw Danny begin to protest and held up a hand. "Not you, I know you have to be in District Court— and April, will you be ready to take those photos we got from Auto Theft by the old lady's place in the morning?"

"I was planning on it. This time I'm wearing jeans."

"You mean to hell with the sharp young businesswoman image?"

"You got it."

"Okay. I want to meet Maude Mae and Duke, so maybe— but we'll cross that bridge later." He made a gesture waving them out. Chairs were folded; Danny stretched prodigiously and then put an arm around April's shoulder. "Come on, the old fart and I'll buy your dinner."

As they walked out Lou griped. "What do ya mean, the old fart and I? It's a damn good idea, but you brought it up, so you pay. When it's my idea, I'll . . ."

Rainfinch realized he'd been massaging his left temple

again. The pain had been there all day, just behind the eye socket, as if someone with a pitchfork was grimly determined to jab out his eyeball and escape.

God, what a thought. He needed sleep. It seemed like he was always thinking that and never doing it.

He opened the desk drawer and poked through paper clips, rubber bands, pencils, pennies, and odd scraps of paper until he found the small bottle of aspirin. He put two in his mouth and washed them down with warm Coke.

Through the doorway of his office he could see the Homicide squad room, dimly lit at this time of evening. As he watched, two detectives straggled out, arguing amiably. Then the room was empty except for a thin, balding man in the far corner, chewing on one of the cardboard sandwiches from a machine in the break room. Julio Angel, a bright, nervous detective with chronic stomach ulcers. Rainfinch could see he was leafing through a set of crime scene photos, over and over again.

Quiet settled around him. It was a good time to think. The phones were as nearly silent as they ever would be, Communications routed after-hours message to whomever the duty roster showed to be on call. The room outside his door, crowded with desks and chairs, its walls papered with photos, charts, drawings, and wiseass comments, was almost eerie without its complement of laughing, talking, arguing, cursing detectives.

Only the buzzards remained—buzzards of every size and shape, made of ceramic, of fuzzy fabric, of plastic. Buzzard lamps. Pristine buzzard eggs for virgin detectives, eggs with one tiny crack and an emerging beak for detectives with only one solved case to their credit.

Rainfinch looked at the motto over his own door, a banner held in a buzzard's beak: "When Your Life's Work Is Done, Ours Has Just Begun." He knew the profusion of carrion birds sometimes shocked the few civilians who penetrated this far into the detective bureau. He also knew that black humor was necessary for survival in this job made up of blood and stench and body parts, foul, viscous coffee, sleepless nights, the clutch in your gut when the phone rang, the collection of mental images, too painful to talk about, that never went away.

He pulled a blue-lined yellow tablet toward him and picked up a pencil.

Lou had been right, of course. Although every possible angle had to be explored, he was as certain Carter Hall's death was a grudge killing as if the knowledge had been revealed to him in foot-high flaming letters scrawled across the wall, by—he laughed aloud—by seraphim.

He looked up. Julio Angel was staring at him, startled by the solitary laugh. He waved at Julio, who shook his head, grinned, and went back to work.

An-hyel', Rainfinch thought. Angel, in English. He chuckled again. The world was just full of heavenly personages.

He wrote Brendon Guiste's name on the pad and put a circle around it. How to get inside? Guiste had to be angry, resentful. Maybe he didn't realize yet that he'd been permanently axed, but he must have his suspicions. He was isolated, an outcast from the job he treasured.

That just might have been a miscalculation on Robert Friar's part. Idle people have lots of time to fret about injustices. But how to get inside the circle, the shell of reticence?

There was Moriarty. He wrote her name on the pad and connected it to Guiste's with an arrow that penetrated his circle.

As far as Rainfinch knew, none of the media had sniffed out Guiste's "vacation." He could pick up the phone, alert Moriarty, then sit back and see what she could wheedle out of him.

No. He obliterated her name with a line of *X*s. The whole chattering, snapping pack would sniff out Guiste's private misery and make it public soon enough. Damned if he was going to help. There had to be another way.

Robert Friar. He knew with a certainty bordering on mysticism that Friar was a warped and dangerous man. He sighed. The world was full of warped and dangerous people, only one of whom killed Carter Hall. And Friar had been in Washington, D.C., the night Hall died. He'd been ostensibly home in bed the night of the second two killings.

Home in bed. Good idea.

He nosed his car out of the underground parking garage into sullen, blustery rain. The temperature hovered around thirty; crusts of ice were beginning to form on the asphalt. In a few minutes he pulled into the circular drive on the south side of his house. Looking up, he thought what a bleak and sinister aspect it presented, looming black and massive against the charcoal sky. Tower, dormers, roofs pitched every which way, like something Disney would create for the Wicked Witch of the West.

Inside, on a sudden whim, he went from room to room, flipping on lights. Library, gold sitting room, music room, dining room, kitchen. Second floor—bedrooms, baths, the two rooms where he existed. Third floor—ballroom, servants' bedrooms, tower. He imagined it from the outside now. One hundred and eighty-seven windows, glittering against the dark.

Before he left the third floor he checked the buckets and pans that were there to catch rainwater. All in place, none needed emptying.

Back in his own area, he locked the doors into the great hallway and went to bed. He switched off his bedside lamp, leaving one patch of darkness in the heart of all that blazing light.

On those occasions when the telephone rang while Rainfinch was sleeping he always picked it up immediately, brain cells jarred awake, heart thudding, stomach tense, ready to pull on clothes and launch himself into the night.

Now, in answer to the blaring summons, he said "Rainfinch" to the receiver, squinting at the clock. Two A.M.

"You arrogant son of a bitch." The voice was slurred, but familiar. "You shit. Stay out o' my way."

"Who is this?"

"You know goddamn well, you arrogant prick. 'S me."

Rainfinch sighed. "I'll give you five seconds to identify yourself and state your business." Even as he spoke, a terrible suspicion formed.

"Tell you somethin', maestro's son. Gov'ner's gonna have your ass on a platter. Finished. Better learn t' play a piano. Maybe Daddy'll hire you."

Now he was sure. "Clifford Stamps."

"Tee-hee," Stamps acknowledged mischievously, in a sudden, drunken change of mood.

To his utter astonishment, Rainfinch felt concern. In the police department family no one who had a drinking problem kept it a secret for very long, but Stamps's name had never been mentioned in that context. "Where are you, Clifford?"

"Tee-hee. Hee. Not gonna tell."

Like Rainfinch, Stamps drove an unmarked cruiser at all times. There was a small sad litany, known by every cop, of officers who had ruined their careers by drunken antics in police cars.

"Listen, Clifford, stay right there. I'll come take you home. But you've got to let me know where you are."

"Hah. You gonna help me? You hate my guts, stinkin' rich boy. Ha."

With terrible effort Rainfinch resisted slamming down the receiver. What kind of pressure could have caused Stamps, whose sole concession to human weakness was an occasional throbbing vein in his head, to lose control like this?

"Where are you, Clifford?" he asked again, softly.

"Hee-hee. Gotcha. I *am* home, you stinkin' shit."

That was all he needed to know. Rainfinch replaced the receiver carefully on its cradle and went back to sleep.

▽

22

N<small>UBIE</small> L<small>EE</small> E<small>STES</small> was certain about one thing. The gods
who ruled the universe had made a dreadful mistake when
they allowed crummy luck and a righteous woman to
manipulate him into a job as a sanitation worker.

Sanitation worker. Hah. Might as well say it, he was a
garbageman.

Well, he'd show this jerk town his backside soon enough,
he assured himself, hunching narrow shoulders against a
biting north wind as he tossed an umpteenth plastic trash
sack into the disgusting maw of the Beast. Nubie Lee caught
a handhold and swung himself up to ride half a block to the
next stop. The Beast groaned prodigiously as it lumbered
down the street.

The thin black man blew his nose on his sleeve. There
were tears in his eyes that weren't entirely caused by the
winter morning's chill. He slammed a fist into the Beast's
hindquarters and made a sound that was half moan, half
sob. It was so blindingly unfair for him to suffer like this.
Because Nubie Lee Estes, aka the Glitter Man, was rich.

Had been rich.

The Beast ground to a stop and he dropped to the ground
automatically, trotted from yard to yard, gathered his har-
vest, and stored it. But his mind—aah, his mind was back
where seabirds banked in salty tropical breezes, where long,
hot nights were filled with rum drinks, and dark-eyed,
satin-skinned, willing women, and fast cars, and . . .

Oh, yeah, that was Eden, that was bliss. Until he fell in

love with a sweet-assed, bible-totin' girl who had caramel eyes and exactly nine freckles across her golden, upturned nose.

"Don't you even think what I see in your eyes, man. I don't truck with no dope dealers." The first words Raylinda Sue had ever spoken to him, in that brown-sugar voice of hers. He'd been cruising in his Beemmer convertible, the sun as warm as wine on his shoulders, when he'd seen her sashaying down the street. Her cute little butt, moving so sensuously under the short white skirt, had settled his fate. He was an ass man.

He pulled to the curb and said something suave. Then he saw her face and was lost beyond redemption.

She was eighteen years old, a preacher's daughter, visiting her Auntie Cecile in Miami, Florida. When the Glitter Man confidently laid siege to her virgin temple, with flowers, the finest chocolates, and a fluffy Persian kitten wearing a diamond bracelet as a collar, Raylinda responded by hightailing it back home to the protection of her blood-and-thunder Daddy.

The Glitter Man pulled off his work gloves and blew on chapped, callused hands. He still couldn't quite believe the folly of what he'd done five months ago. Left his customers, his house, his Beemmer in the care of his best friend Ralph, and followed a naive little teenager as if he was one of those guys wearing armor and going on quests, like you saw in the movies.

Flanked by Daddy, and Mama, and Big Sister, and three brothers the size of NFL linebackers, Raylinda had said that yes, she might find it in her heart to love a sinner like the Glitter Man, if he was willing to mend his ways and revert to being Nubie Lee Estes, a hard-working, God-fearing Christian man.

A sanitation worker. A trash man. He remembered the condescending hundred-dollar tips he'd handed around the previous Christmas to trash men.

I bet they hated my guts.

Time had finally brought them around to the coffee-break point on their route, a dead-end street with one vacant house at the end, where wildly overgrown evergreens provided some concealment for an idle city truck and its resting employees. The Beast slowed to a stop with a menacing grind of its gears. Jimmy, the huge, friendly, grinning man who was Nubie Lee's partner on the route, was best friends with Lukas, the driver; he hurried toward the cab and climbed inside.

Glitter Man bent over next to the Beast to shelter himself against the wind and lit up. He was smoking part of a fine but dwindling stock of hash. The other guys knew it, and shunned him, but they wouldn't snitch off on him. They also knew about the knife he kept strapped to his right thigh.

After a few drags he felt better, felt like he could make some plans, study on what to do and work things out in his mind. He couldn't live like this any longer. And he couldn't live without that silly damn girl.

He was going back to *his* home, *his* arena, *his* place. And Raylinda was coming with him, like it or not. He'd tried it her way, existing like a piece of living, breathing manure, so he could "cleanse himself," so he could "purge the evil, sweat the sin out of his body."

He grinned. Once home, he'd lock Raylinda's sweet little ass in a room, shoot her up a couple of times, and she'd be docile as a lamb. And if those ree-tard brothers of hers followed, they'd find themselves floating face up in saltwater, waiting to feed the sharks.

There was only one problem. Rich as Glitter Man had been when he left the good life, Nubie Lee Estes didn't have a dime to his name. Ralph, his bosom friend, his main man, had behaved like any up-and-coming dealer; he'd stolen the Glitter Man's customers, his home, his drop-dead wardrobe, his suppliers—even his convertible.

"Get home. All I gotta do is get home, and I'll part that little shit's hair down to his gizzard," the Glitter Man mumbled.

But he had to have traveling money.

The first thing that came to mind, of course, was to find a supplier and sell enough stuff to get him out of this hellhole. But he hadn't survived this long by being careless. He was in strange territory, an area where California toughs were moving in. Guys whose brains were fried from using their own stuff, who ranted and rapped twenty-four hours a day about what badasses they were and what color scarves they wore. Who blasted the guts out of people for the fun of it.

He shook his head, blew his nose, and wiped what was definitely a tear off his cheek. There was no justice. No goddamn justice in the world at all.

And that was that precise moment—when the Glitter Man had been brought to the depths of shame, when a dejected Nubie Lee Estes was snuffling and kicking dead leaves with the toe of his rubber boot—that the gods woke up to their responsibilities. Divine intervention came in the form of a dull gleam a few feet beneath the black iron grid of a storm sewer. The slight, shivering man knelt on cold asphalt for a closer look. Snagged in a rotting mess of paper, leaves, and twigs, was the Glitter Man's salvation.

"Goddamit, Beth, I am *not* gonna go that pansy-boy's funeral! Won't be anybody there but a bunch of creampuffs—and us. It's not good for my image," Shadid Garber finished triumphantly.

Beth was undeterred. Shadid's blustering protests were window dressing. She would play the game, though.

"Archie Keyes was Monk Smith's lover. Monk puts a good deal of money in your pocket by leasing the Seraphim building. Therefore, we are obliged to show our moral support by attending Archie's funeral."

They were in his office, a huge room with an acre of thick desert-sand carpet between the door and an antique desk large enough to host a ping-pong tournament. Shadid sat behind this formidable piece of furniture like a malignant toad, ready to gobble up with a flick of his tongue any unfortunate visitor who displeased him.

He looked up at Beth. She stood in front of him, feet firmly planted and hands clasped behind her back, in the manner of a schoolteacher lecturing a recalcitrant student. "Will you sit the hell down?"

Beth arranged herself in one of the pair of chairs that crouched in front of Shadid's splendid desk like supplicants kneeling at the throne. They were perfect client chairs. Attractive enough not to spoil the decor, but subtly uncomfortable, so that no occupant was tempted to settle in for a long, cozy chat.

Shadid glared at her. Flick went the pink, pointed tongue. "I suppose you know Monk's threatening not to reopen the nightclub? If that faggot son of a bitch reneges on his lease I'll take everything he's got. I'll take his last cent—his last damn pair of lace panties. He'll have to float a loan to buy a cup of coffee."

Beth grinned. "You're all heart, Shadid. Monk's prostrate with grief over the death of his lover, and you're threatening to sink a fang into his jugular. Whatever will people say?"

Shadid grinned back. "People expect it of me. Everyone knows Shadid Garber's a heartless, money-grubbing sumbitch. You wouldn't want me to disappoint them."

Beth seemed to be spring-loaded. She rose from the chair, walked to a spot behind him, and gazed down into the parking lot.

"Would it be such a terrible thing if Monk shut down for good? The Seraphim's been nothing but trouble. Maybe the place *is* cursed."

The little attorney let out a strangled yelp. He swung his chair around so he could look at Beth. "What the hell are you talking about? You think I could find another tenant for that damn hulk of a building? No church group would touch it, the sanctimonious pricks, not after—*what about my money?*"

Beth shrugged and turned to face him. "Think of it as a tax write-off. You're always rooting around for ways to avoid giving the government any of your money."

When Shadid spoke again his voice had transformed into a tone few people had ever heard. "What's wrong, girl? It's not like you to back off a fight."

Beth walked back to the chair and sat. She leaned forward to avoid a spindle that gouged just below her shoulder blades.

"Have you looked at my caseload lately? I get further behind every day. And the new building. You've left all the details to me, all the wrangling with contractors and workmen—it's gotten to the point that I wake up in the middle of the night gasping for air, my heart pounding, afraid I'll miss something vital because I'm so damned tired all the time. This Seraphim mess is like a bottomless swamp with quicksand all around. I want it off my back."

Shadid emerged from his throne. He walked over and patted her shoulder awkwardly. "Honey, if I didn't think you'd slug me one, I'd say you need a man. Some piss-and-vinegar young stud, who'd put the roses back in your cheeks. How about that detective—that young Rainfinch fella?" His encouraging smile looked more like the leer of a concupiscent Buddha. "You like him. Don't try to fool your ol' Uncle Shadid."

Beth blushed furiously. "Don't be a fool, he wouldn't— you know what cops like him think of criminal lawyers. I'll worry about my own love life, thank you very much. And don't change the subject. Look, Shadid, we're moving into our new building in a few days. That neighborhood association knows we lease the Seraphim building to Monk. They already hate our guts. How pleasant will it be, when those people are our neighbors?" Beth drove home her point. "Feelings are running so high, I wouldn't be surprised if we begin having problems with vandalism."

For an instant the stocky little lawyer looked concerned, but then he brightened. "In that ritzy neighborhood? Don't be silly. Besides, I thought that's why we're letting the old Haslip dame keep her digs—public relations."

"Maude Mae can only help so much. And never kid yourself, vandals don't all live in hovels and have smelly armpits."

"Okay. Listen, honey, we'll just float a while on the damn church building and see what happens. And we'll go over your caseload together—maybe we need to hire some kid fresh out of law school to take over the penny-ante stuff. I'd even let you pick him out. Would that suit you?"

He continued in what was almost a whisper. "Damn it girl, I don't want you getting sick on me, or something. I couldn't do without you. You know that."

Beth felt a sudden sting in her eyes; to her astonishment tears brimmed. She fought for control. When she spoke her voice was husky. "I'll be okay—but I have every intention of taking you up on the offer of an assistant, so don't think you can sweet-talk me out of it later. And now you're up and moving, let's go. We'll be just in time for the funeral."

She stood, strode across the carpet desert, and opened the door. Shadid followed, arguing querulously. "Goddammit, Beth, I still don't see why *I* should—"

Abe Rainfinch woke up with a stiff neck, gritty eyes, and a mouth that tasted like goat dung. Toothpaste, eyedrops, and a long, hot shower helped his physical problems, but a restless sense of apprehension remained.

The three Seraphim murders ate at him, as if some cataclysmic destructive force had been unleashed. He had an uneasy sense that he was functioning poorly, had allowed personal problems—his mother's illness, his father's intransigence, the breakup with April, that damn Clifford Stamps and his silly, pretentious posturing—to muddle his thinking, prevent him from concentrating all his intelligence and energies on finding the killer.

As sometimes happened when he was feeling low, he sank into gloomy philosophizing about what it meant to be a cop. He knew what the public expected of its public officers. Unerring decisions to be made in a split second, strength tempered with compassion. And God help you if you let the smallest point of law, the most minute regulation, slide, because the world had an overgenerous supply of defense attorneys who delighted in portraying you as a jack-booted Nazi run amok among helpless innocents.

Yeah, well . . . the truth was cops were human beings, with wives who bitched about hours and pay; girlfriends who sulked when they were abandoned in the progress of a night on the town or a night of lust—left in the lurch when their warrior was called to duty; children who seemed bent on making the family orthodontist be able to afford a villa on Capri. His married friends complained that those same children grew up overnight while you weren't watching. While you were out on the mean streets chasing bad guys.

And then there were fathers like Martin Rainfinch, who mentioned your occupation with the same revulsion as if he'd been forced to admit his son mugged old ladies for a living.

And love affairs that went sour, and great monster houses that you couldn't afford but couldn't part with, and mothers who went far away and got sick, and sisters who blamed you for not being there. . . .

Stop that. Stop brooding like the Prince of Denmark and catch the goddamn killer.

As he passed through the detective squad room, Rainfinch stopped at April's desk. He smiled winningly and in a light, oh-by-the-way, voice asked, "When's Mitchelson due back?"

Earlier he had avoided Lou's suggestion to call April's partner in from vacation, knowing she'd smell a rodent and get her feelings hurt. But Mitch was a smart and seasoned detective. He would need that kind of help when the Seraphim surveillance began.

"Next week, I think." April was doing stuff with small, scribbled bits of paper—sorting, discarding, entering the most useful information neatly in a spiral notebook. She didn't look up. "You have the duty roster, it should say. Why?"

"The Seraphim surveillance," he explained hastily. "I wasn't sure when—and since you're his partner—I'll need him like hell when Monk reopens the club." Oh, swell. He'd stammered that out with real finesse.

To his surprise, April laughed. "Put him in drag. He'd love that."

Rainfinch grinned, thinking of Mitchelson's prominent Adam's apple, his cadaverous frame, and the constant blue shadow that seemed glued to his bony jaws.

"It would be interesting. But I think not."

"When will the Seraphim open for business again?"

"Monk has agreed to Saturday night. Reluctantly. With Frannie Da Sorta's help, I convinced him it might help find whoever did his lover."

Their moment of rapport was gone. April changed the subject abruptly. "Do you still want to go with me to call on our witness?" True to her word, she had dressed in old jeans and a cotton sweater for her visit to Maude Mae and Duke. Her hair was pulled into a no-nonsense knot at the nape of her slim neck. She leaned back in her chair and waited for an answer, arms crossed, pale face neutral.

"Yes—why don't we telephone to make sure she's home?"

"She called yesterday and told me she'd had her phone disconnected. Said she'd gotten a couple of crank calls. The truth is, Shadid Garber's firm is moving into the building very soon. Their phone system's already installed and working. I think our wily old girl has ideas about taking advantage of free telephone service."

Rainfinch chuckled. "She can get into their offices?"

April nodded. "When the area was first closed in, she worried that one of the workmen might leave a cigarette burning. So Beth Farraday gave her a key."

Rainfinch was worried about something else. "She complained of crank calls? What type? I don't like that."

"I didn't either. I questioned her pretty closely. She insisted it had to be neighborhood kids she'd run off from the construction area a time or two. Heavy breathing, no one said anything. But according to her there was rock music and chatter in the background."

"Huh. Let's get on over there; I want to talk to her myself."

"If you like." April's tone conveyed that as far as she was concerned Lieutenant Abe Rainfinch was excess baggage. She plucked her jacket from the government-issue coatrack, on which a particularly malignant buzzard perched.

"My car's closer. Why don't we take it?" Rainfinch said.

April stopped in the hallway. "Abe, let's go in separate vehicles. I want to check on a couple of things after I leave Maude Mae. It'll be more convenient if I have my own wheels."

"Sure. Of course," he said to her back, and followed her out of the squad room.

Maude Mae wasn't in her apartment. Downstairs, the detectives questioned a pair of finish carpenters who were adding embellishments to the woodwork in a lavish executive rest room.

The older carpenter, who was built roughly like a bear and had a long, gleaming black ponytail, put down his glue brush. As he began to talk, the younger, a redhead with a fiery Jesse James mustache, set to work with a nail gun. Rainfinch put a hand on Mustache's shoulder and frowned. The gun stopped.

"That nosy old bat who lives upstairs?" Ponytail asked. "Ain't seen her today. You, Luke?"

"Naw, not today. Yesterday she and her kitty—I like kitties—she and Duke left to stay overnight with a friend. Taxi picked 'em up. She told me to make sure the building was locked up good an' tight when we left."

"Did she say when she was coming back?" April smiled winningly as she asked.

The young carpenter's complexion flamed with pleasure, until it nearly matched his facial hair. "Yes, ma'am. This morning sometime."

They thanked the workmen and walked back to the front hallway, where a staircase led up to Maude Mae's apartment.

April looked at her watch. "It's almost eleven. Want to wait around a while?"

Rainfinch felt restless. "Why don't you stay? We need her to take a look at those pictures. And for God's sake, caution her again to be careful and keep her mouth shut. I'll see you back at the office."

He got in his car and started it up, still brooding about Maude Mae. The old girl shouldn't be in any danger as long as no one knew what she'd seen. But she was a solitary spinster whose only intimate companion was a cat, and the Seraphim killings were the sensation of the hour. How long would she be able to resist telling someone what she witnessed?

As if to mock, the defrocked church loomed in his line of vision. Lest he forget.

On impulse he pulled across the mouth of the alley and rolled to a stop by the front entrance, now closed and secured by a heavy chain and a businesslike padlock. It saddened him. As a neighborhood kid and later a grown man, he couldn't remember ever having seen those gates locked before.

Slowly he pulled around the corner, where the parking lot opened out from the canopied club entrance. He parked his car and walked toward the path that led to the parsonage. Archie's funeral would be in progress; Rainfinch hoped Monk hadn't been so distraught he'd left the whole place unguarded.

Almost immediately his doubt was answered. Frannie Da Sorta appeared on the path in front of him, dressed in sweatpants and an orange, gold, and black jacket that identified him as a Golden Gloves coach.

"Morning, Lieutenant."

"You didn't go to the funeral, Frannie?"

"Naw. I thought it might be a good idea to hang around here."

"A damn good idea. Had any problems?"

"Not so far. Maybe people are scared of the place."

"Could be. But I'm glad you're looking after things."

Rainfinch turned to go back to his car, and Frannie walked

companionably along with him. On a random thought, he suddenly asked, "Frannie, what did you think of Archie Keyes?"

The old fighter scratched a stubbly jaw. "He was all right, I guess. Nothin' like the boss. But they seemed to be real close."

Rainfinch didn't comment. After a short silence Frannie burst out, "I wouldn't say this to many people, Lieutenant, but you, you've known Monk a long time. It's just . . . I don't understand some things about him. He ain't—ain't swishy, like Archie was, an' a lot of those others. Some of those guys, they oughta been born with a slit between their legs instead of a cock. But Monk's a real man. So why—?"

"Why is he homosexual? I don't know, Frannie. I don't have any answers for you, and I'm damned if I'm going to worry about it. Monk's an honorable man. He's always been square with me. That's the way I see him."

Frannie nodded. "Yeah. Me too."

Back in his office Rainfinch found Lou Curran tilted back in the desk chair, reading the latest FBI Association magazine and chewing on an unlit cigar.

"Anything interesting in there?"

Lou looked up. He slammed the chair back onto four legs. "Where the hell you been?"

"Where the hell have *you* been? Get out of my chair."

"Okay, but you're not sittin' in it. You come with me. I got something to show you."

In the car, Lou explained as he drove. "You were right, by God. Carter Hall *did* have a cozy little sex nest where he took his lovers. It's off Nuevo Laredo Drive."

"The condominium complex that's so raunchy they have a dozen or so condom dispensers in the clubhouse?"

Lou grinned as he nodded. "You got it. Under our boy's high-class hide beat the heart of a wild child."

"How the hell could he take such chances? He was bound to crash and burn."

Lou nodded. He produced a paper cup and spat out the brown, viscous, chewed-up mess that had been the end of his cigar.

"Sweet heaven, that's sickening. I'll stop so you can buy some cigarettes."

Lou chuckled. "I got cigarettes. Cigars are for chawin', and I ain't getting rid of this little dude. Wait till I pull it on April. She'll be beggin' me to smoke."

As they drove up to the gates of the Spanish-style complex Rainfinch asked, "What good is this going to do? We can't get in without a court order."

Lou waved a paper at him. "Already done. Jean Houghton in the DA's office wrote it up for me and caught Judge Thomason in his chambers. He read the order, signed off on it, and here you are. Aside from that, Hall's parents gave verbal permission for us to take anything we need."

"Fast work. So all right, I'm impressed. What did you do, eat an extra bowl of Wheaties this morning?"

Lou shook his head. His narrow shoulders drooped. "I screwed up on this deal, Abe. Should have jumped onto it right away, after you first mentioned the possibility Hall could have a shack-up somewhere."

Lou Curran was too sharp a detective to appreciate a comforting lie. Rainfinch said, "Yeah. But sometimes it's not easy to know where to jump first." With a sudden, deft attack he plucked the cigar from Curran's mouth and tossed it out the window. "Now. Let's see what we've got in here," he continued, over Lou's creative and profane protest.

The casita was painted hot pink, with violent blue-green trim and an orange roof. Lou jabbed a key in the door and swung it open. Inside was a small living room with a tiny adobe-style wood fireplace in one corner. The walls were aqua, the furniture white leather. The floor was Mexican tile, and a thick sheepskin rug covered the area in front of the hearth.

"How did you find this place so fast?" Rainfinch asked.

Curran picked up a sheaf of magazines geared to the interests of male homosexuals from a table beside the sofa.

"I leaned on Guiste a little. Like you figured, Lieutenant, he's kinda lost his enthusiasm for protectin' Hall, or anyone else in the governor's office, come to that. He told me about this place readily enough when I asked. Then I went out for a fast visit to Hall's parents."

"I hope you didn't—"

Lou held up a hand. "Not to worry, Abe. I didn't so much as let out a peep about what we expected to find here. Miz Hall senior said she knew he had a place in town where he spent the night sometimes, when he worked late. He'd given them the telephone number."

"And the door key? Does it match the unidentified one on Hall's key ring?"

"Yep. The front office here let me have this one, when I came by earlier. It's identical to the one on the ring."

"Good work." Rainfinch led the way down a short hallway to the bedroom.

"Hot damn," Lou whispered. The cubicle was solid mirror, walls and ceiling; the floor sheepskin, five inches deep. A king-sized waterbed sat on a dais, an island in the sheepskin ocean. There was no other furniture.

First they checked the closet, donning plastic gloves before they opened the door. There were a couple of suits, some starched dress shirts on hangers, a topcoat, three pairs of dress shoes, and some designer house slippers that matched a plaid designer terry robe. Nothing else.

Rainfinch walked to the framework under the bed. It contained huge drawers. He opened one. It slid out smoothly, as if it were mounted on ball bearings.

Lou stood beside Rainfinch and stared into the drawer. He whistled. "The mother lode. There's enough crap in there to open a porno store."

They set to work, methodically laying aside the warehouse of exotic sexual equipment, some of which strained the imagination. Rainfinch no longer even tried to remember a time when this sort of thing had shocked him.

They were on the last drawer and had almost given up

hope of finding anything useful when Rainfinch noticed a slight bulge under the scented drawer liner. He pulled it loose to reveal several five-by-seven color photographs.

Lou shook his head. "I get more disappointed in this guy by the minute. Photos hidden under the drawer liner. How obvious can you get?"

"In all fairness, he probably didn't expect anyone to be searching for them. He just tucked the things out of sight so the wrong lover didn't happen onto them accidentally."

In the general spectrum of sex photos these were pretty tame, obviously amateur, automatic timed exposures from a tripod aimed at the bed. As Rainfinch and Curran handed them back and forth from gloved hand to gloved hand, they saw that they portrayed Hall with various love partners, all youthful.

"You'd think a clever fella like him could have rigged up a better peep show," Lou complained, squinting at the pictures.

Rainfinch gathered up three or four of the blurred prints. "Look, these could all be the same guy." He pulled out one. In it Hall's young, curly-haired lover was facing the camera, mugging with his tongue out. "This is the best face shot, but I doubt we can identify him from it. Let's take them back to the wizards in the photo lab and see what they can come up with."

Curran took the print, pulled on a pair of battered reading glasses, and scowled at the gleeful figures performing for the benefit of the camera. He shook his head. "That guy's just a kid, with the face of an ornery choirboy. Reckon he could've butchered those guys?"

Rainfinch knew it was a rhetorical question.

Maude Mae and Duke returned at half past eleven. In spite of the embarrassing harness he wore, Duke managed the part of the debonair gentleman when he spotted April, stretching his back up for petting and purring raucously as he rubbed his face against her leg.

You devil, April thought. Never try to convince me you're a sweet, innocent puss. Underneath that scrawny hide beats the heart of a randy old lech.

Maude Mae pulled him away. "Come on up, lovey," she told April. "I'll make us a nice cup of tea."

"I'd like that." April followed the jaunty old woman, who was wearing her best lavender lace dress and black hat with red and violet silk roses.

The tea was hot, fragrant, and miraculously free of cat hairs. With it they ate butter cookies filled with raspberry jam. Maude Mae had offered to make her a sandwich, but April declined.

When they'd finished eating and drinking, and Duke had been dissuaded from kneading April's thighs and was curled up in her lap asleep, she finally managed to start Maude Mae examining the glossy, vivid automobile brochures. It was a long process, with many a "My, would you look at that" and "Goodness, what a pretty color, like a jay's wing," and, after asking the price of one model and getting an approximation from April, "My stars, child, my daddy's whole farm sold for less than that."

But finally, after Duke had been roused again and was licking April's wrist with his sandpaper tongue, Maude Mae had eliminated all but two from the stack of jazzy sports cars.

"I'm sorry, April honey. I'm as sure as I'll ever be that it was one or the other of these, but I just can't decide between them."

April reached out and squeezed one of the knotted, blue-veined hands. "You did good, this is a big help. Tell you what, we'll borrow specimens of the models you chose from a car dealer, hopefully in a dark color, and bring them by for you to inspect. We'll park each of them in the alley, right where you saw the killer's car."

Maude Mae's face lit up. "Oh, yes. Could we do it after dark, so things will be kinda like they were then?"

"Yes, good idea. We'll attract less attention that way, too." April leaned close to the old woman. "Maude Mae, look me in the eye. Do you swear you haven't told a soul about being a witness to the first killing?"

Maude Mae fussed with her empty teacup. "Why honey, I promised, didn't I? Don't you worry about Duke and me."

Sure. Right, April thought as, after a protracted leave-taking, she climbed into the car. She had delivered another lecture about keeping the door locked and bolted at all times, and not letting *anyone* Maude Mae didn't know into her apartment when she was alone, ever, under any circumstances.

She also had elicited a promise that Maude Mae would have her telephone reconnected immediately. Now, before she started her engine, she pulled out a small spiral notepad and jotted a reminder to contact the phone company and ask them to expedite restoration of service. She didn't want that innocent spending one more night than was necessary alone in a vacant building without immediate access to a telephone.

Duke could take care of himself.

23

W HEN SUSAN ELIAS phoned Abe Rainfinch at five-thirty Thursday evening, he had every intention of keeping the conversation on a business-only basis.

He started out well. "Miss Elias. What can I do for you?"

" 'Miss Elias?' " she threw back at him, with an uncertain laugh. "Did I call at a bad time?"

"No, not really—Susan. What's up?"

"Well—" she hesitated, then plunged ahead. "I was going to invite you to dinner. I've made this Mexican stew that will singe your tonsils, and jalapeno cornbread, and there's an awful lot of it. But I guess you're too busy."

She sounded vulnerable and hurt.

"Not so fast. Pardon the snarl, it's been a long day. I'll come over if you promise to take the thorn out of my paw. "What time do we eat?"

At seven o'clock she answered the door dressed in a soft, creamy jumpsuit and smelling like heaven on earth. Or was it the Mexican stew? Suddenly he remembered he hadn't taken time to eat all day, except for a package of cheese crackers with peanut butter from the vending machine in Patrol's break room.

Susan must have realized that the gleam in his eye anticipated food, rather than her body or her company. She sat him down at a table laid out with fat candles in terra-cotta holders, earthenware pottery, and old silver that had the dull sheen of constant use. First she brought in a crockery pot and served the stew, which contained generous hunks of meat, vegetables, and wicked green chilis. Then came a platter of cornbread and frosted pilsner glasses of Corona, with crescents of lime on the rim.

The cornbread was tender as a love song and buttery, the stew, washed down with Corona, spicy as promised. Pure bliss. After his feeding frenzy abated they talked idly, with almost the easy familiarity of old friends.

But no, it wasn't quite that. Other hungers surfaced. He kept noticing the sheen of her wild curls, the sweet curve of her breast beneath white cashmere, the enticing hollow where ribcage curved into slender waist, encapsuled in the aura of a very sexy perfume. Her lips were full and soft, and her eyes . . . he was beginning to have feelings that were anything but platonic.

After dinner she made strong, fragrant coffee and laced it with cognac. A flamenco guitar throbbed from the stereo, and Abe recognized the musician. He leaned back on the sofa, sipped, and smiled. "Santa Fe. Have you ever seen Maria dance to that?" No need to identify the dancer further. If you'd spent time in Santa Fe, you knew.

"Have I not. Isn't she magnificent? All bone and tendon, and taut muscle—like a fine thoroughbred horse. Not a spare ounce on her."

He nodded. "The most incredibly sexy woman I can think of."

Susan laughed, and looked down on her own slim but well-curved body. "She makes me feel like a fat sow. I suppose she has breasts, but I've never noticed them. And her rear end is so hard buckshot would bounce off it. And yet you're right—she exudes sex."

Abe allowed his face to show the admiration he felt. "Fat sow isn't the phrase that comes to mind when I look at you."

Sudden color washed across her face. "Thanks for that, at least. When I called earlier you sounded irritable—I thought I might be making a nuisance of myself."

"It wasn't aimed at you. Occupational hazard, I guess. Cops can be a surly lot." Abe wondered how long it had been since he'd known another woman who blushed. Susan did it fairly often. It was refreshing.

"So can politicians," she was saying. "Only they're careful never to do it while the cameras roll."

There was a small companionable silence while they listened to music and savored the smooth fire of brandy and coffee.

"Abe—I'm almost afraid to mention this, but things seem different between us tonight. Have you noticed?"

He nodded, stifling an irresistible urge to seize her and cover her with mad kisses. "You mean we're easy together. None of the tension that was blowin' in the wind before. You forget, we did have our moments the night we went to Eli's house. And after that—until the subject of your boss came up."

"That's true."

"Let's declare tonight 'King's ex.' I like it better this way." In his mind he traced a finger from the pulse at the base of her neck down into the silken V below. She closed her eyes as he found the zipper tab and pulled, releasing bare breasts with firm, rosy nipples. She murmured with pleasure as his mouth moved from one delight to another. He picked her up and carried her to the bed, and they made love with a passion that rivaled the Spanish guitars.

"Abe, what are you thinking?"

He blinked. "What?"

"You had an odd look on your face. Reminded me a little of Uncle Ira's old billy goat. I asked what you were thinking."

Well, he couldn't tell her, but perhaps he could show—he moved closer and curved his arm around her waist. An alarm went off, loud and strident.

"Good grief, what's that? Do you come equipped with a burglar alarm, like somebody's pet Porsche?" But of course he knew, after the first shock. A beeper. A goddamned beeper. He reached for his pocket.

Susan reached for her pocket. Her face was a furious shade of red. "Mine, I'm afraid."

She shut it off. He asked if she hadn't better make her call. She said no, she wasn't a puppet on the end of a string, for gosh sake, she was entitled to a little privacy.

But the spell was broken, and they both knew it. He kissed her goodnight, thanked her for the dinner, and left.

Susan stood by a window and watched the taillights of his car dwindle and disappear, and still she stayed and stared vacantly at dead grass and the delicate tracery of bare tree branches against a moonless sky. She didn't really know Abe Rainfinch at all. How could she feel she'd lost a love, she wondered sadly, when the man had never been her lover?

Her beeper screeched again. She glanced at the number display, then threw the thing into a closet and slammed the door. And then, with a grim sense of inevitability, she walked to the telephone and dialed Robert Friar.

It wasn't until he drove to work the next morning in shame-faced winter sunlight that seemed to apologize for its long absence, that last evening's finale struck Rainfinch as some-what humorous. Not wildly funny, the kind of thing that ends up as a hilarious anecdote told over the fourth round of drinks, but at least worthy of a private, rueful chuckle.

Maybe, he thought with some regret, he and Susan were never intended to be more than acquaintances. Except, there were those fleeting moments. . . .

Someone had left a Homicide cruiser in his parking place. It was caked with serious, big-league filth that probably meant some two-bit dealer had been executed and dumped in the middle of a field, or down by the river. He drove around and parked in front of the building, nosed against the curb between two black-and-whites, and thought about the old cop's maxim: One thing about this job, business was always good.

On the way upstairs he bumped into Clifford Stamps, who nodded curtly and bustled past. It occurred to Rainfinch that Stamps had been avoiding him since the incident of the late-night drunken phone call.

"Hi, Cliff," he called jovially after the rapidly disappearing figure. "How're things going?"

Stamps didn't answer.

Moments before Brendon Guiste called, Robert Friar had finished conducting a full staff meeting in the governor's conference room. Such events were rare. Usually he met only with the command echelon and let his orders filter down to lower ranks through department heads like words from Mount Olympus that must be interpreted for common ears. He had been at his best this morning: charming, witty, egalitarian. He departed the room on a wave of spontaneous applause.

His secretary began an elaborate semaphore as he sailed past her desk, and mouthed "Brendon Guiste."

He reacted with *"No,"* made a throat-cutting motion, then flung up a hand as he changed his mind. "Wait. Put him on."

In his office he settled back in the marine-blue leather chair that was one of the tokens of his exalted rank. Six thousand dollars for a chair, and no one dared breathe a word of criticism. Of course, Big Max didn't know. Big Max's chair was standard issue from Central Purchasing.

"Brendon," he said with warmth. "Let me call you back on my private line."

When that had been accomplished, he asked in his most humanitarian tone, "What can I do for you, friend?"

Compassion was wasted. Brendon was angry. He had done a lot of thinking, he said, about his role of sacrificial lamb. He damn well didn't think it was fair.

"I don't know what you expected. You got yourself into a scrape. No one set you up." Robert's voice had chilled considerably.

"Listen, Robert, no one is more loyal to Max Sanden than I. But I've been shafted. Look at Richard Henderson—he was along that night, too, but he wasn't fired. Not even reprimanded."

"I realize that, Brendon. But you knew when you were hired onto the governor's staff what our standards were. No whiff of scandal would be tolerated here. It was spelled out to everyone."

Guiste's answer was so soft Robert had to strain to hear.

"I didn't think I'd ever do this—but hell, why not? What have I got to lose? Friar, if you don't get me reinstated, fast, I'm going to start leaking a little information about you and Carter. For all I know, *you* could have—"

"Killed him? Why would I do that? Besides, you forget, I was in Washington with Big Max."

"I'm not naive. People like you can always find someone else to do their dirty work."

"Oh, really, Brendon. This isn't the movies. It would be unwise of you to indulge in character assassination, or make wild accusations."

A bitter laugh answered the threat. "How could I possibly be worse off than I am now? And they're not wild accusations. I have proof."

"What do you mean?"

Silence.

"Proof of what? What are we talking about, here?"

The bitter laugh again. "We're talking about a certain senate page, among other things. Suppose his parents should find out—"

Screaming inside, Robert made his voice calm. "Okay, this is getting us nowhere. It looks like we have a stalemate."

Silence.

"Perhaps you could be quietly reinstated after a few weeks. Let's get together and discuss it."

"I'm on my way."

"*No.* The Big Max and I have appointments all day, and tonight we're dashing up the turnpike for a dinner with the Association of Independent Oil Men. Tomorrow—it has to be tomorrow evening. Here in my office. Make it seven-thirty."

"Tomorrow's Saturday."

"When did that ever make a difference?" Robert asked wearily. "I live in this place."

"Okay. Just the two of us? Don't try to sandbag me, Friar. I can ruin you."

"No need for threats." Robert pulled off glasses and rubbed the creases at the bridge of his nose. "I'll see you tomorrow."

He put the receiver gently back in its cradle and pushed a button on the old-fashioned intercom. "Hold my calls. And don't let anyone in here for the next thirty minutes."

He unlocked the drawer that held his stash of liquor and poured himself a liberal dose of Russian vodka.

It was time to make plans.

Beth Farraday rapped briskly on Shadid Garber's office door and entered before he had a chance to respond. At the sight of her his face settled into an expression of welcome that had an anxious quality to it.

"Come in, honey." He noticed she carried her briefcase and had a coat slung over her arm. "Where're you off to?"

"A deposition in Laney, Wells, Condon's offices, then over to our new building. You really should meet me there, Shadid. The offices are finished, except for a few last-minute touch-ups. You'd better come look, or forever hold your peace. I've scheduled the movers a week from tomorrow."

Shadid shook his head. "Can't do it. I have to be in Judge Simms's court this afternoon for a show cause hearing. But it doesn't matter. If the place suits you, it'll suit me."

"Remember you said that. Wish I'd had my tape recorder going."

Shadid stood, braced his bandy legs, and stretched. "I've been sitting too long. I'll walk you to your car."

At the door he held her coat, reaching high to settle it across her shoulders. "You're too damn thin, Beth. You on some kind of silly diet?"

She shook her head and touched his shoulder. "I've always been thin. You know that."

"Yeah. You're a worrier. Listen, honey, I meant it about hiring a grunt to take some of the load off you. What say we look over the graduating class down at the university? Or do you want someone older—with a little experience under his belt?"

"Why *his*? Can't I hire a woman? You said I could choose."

"Now Beth, goddamn it, don't tease—where the hell's your car?" He broke off, looking around the parking lot.

"In the shop. I'm driving this." She walked to a sleek black car and unlocked the door.

Shadid whistled. "That what you gave Kent for graduation? Must have cost a year's salary. You're too good to that kid, honey."

Beth shrugged. "Not really. He's the only brother I have—the only relative, for that matter."

"Yeah, and you dote on him like a mother hen. Time you cut him loose. He's a man now. Anyway, you oughta get something like this for yourself. Kiss off that bunged-up oil-burner you drive before it explodes, or the clean-air freaks put out a contract on you, whichever comes first."

Beth slid her long form into the low seat. "As a matter of fact, I might just do that. You're right about one thing, Kent doesn't appreciate my meddling in his life anymore. He's suddenly become a very independent young man." She turned the key in the ignition and stepped on the accelerator, which resulted in a satisfying roar.

Shadid stepped back. "Goddammit, girl! That's no way to treat a precision machine. Take it easy."

In answer Beth rolled up the dark-tinted window. Then she took off with another roar of the engine. She caught sight of Shadid through the rearview mirror, staring after her with his hands on his hips, a bemused look on his face.

Lou Curran spread several five-by-seven photos across Rainfinch's desk. They were enhancements of the ones taken from Carter Hall's love nest, cropped so only the faces were visible. Rainfinch studied them, one by one.

"Not bad. Who did this for you?"

"I took them over to a guy I know at the university. They've got some experiments going in computer enhancements of photographs. Damnedest thing I ever saw. We oughta have equipment like that in our photo lab."

"It's on the want list, along with a number of items our forensic chemists are wild to get their hands on. All we ever hear from the budget people is another stanza of, 'Times are Hard.' Don't get me started on that." He picked out two of the photos. "I'd say these are definitely the same person."

"Yeah. Good-lookin' kid." Lou shook his head. "Wonder why he would have got tied in with Hall?"

"That's not hard to imagine. Hall wasn't much to look at, but he was rich. And his job lent him the mystique of power."

"To each his own, my Granny said, as she kissed the purple cow."

Rainfinch gathered the prints and handed them back to Curran. "Okay, make the rounds with these, starting with Monk Smith."

"Will do," Curran said wearily. "See ya later."

On a sudden impulse Rainfinch stood and called after him. "Lou—wait. Find Danny and send him out with those. I want you to stay around here."

The wrinkles on Curran's forehead arranged themselves into a questioning look. "What gives?"

"I don't know . . . nothing. Just stay close, okay?"

"Sure. I'll go find your cousin Danny. I love giving him orders."

Rainfinch had resolutely begun work on a neglected pile of reports on other cases when a hesitant voice said, "Lieutenant?" He looked up. A sturdy young female patrol officer stood in the doorway. There were dark circles under her eyes and her uniform was slightly rumpled.

"Come in, Lindstrom. Have a seat. What have you done with Jed Duckett, locked him in a broom closet?"

She sank into a chair with an unconscious sigh.

"My beloved training officer is home in bed, I hope. I'm off duty, sir."

"So—what can I do for you?"

She leaned forward.

"Lieutenant, I brought in a black guy named Nubie Lee Estes last night. Got a call from Sweet Sue's Tavern about 2330. Nubie Lee had pulled a gun on a guy in the parking lot." Lindstrom grinned. "Not a wise move. His intended mark was six-four or so, and would probably weigh in at two-eighty. He pumps iron down at Cecil's Gym. Guy by the name of Ramona. Nubie Lee is five-five and has to jump up and down for the scale to register one-forty. Ramona took the gun away from him and was threatening to shove it where the sun don't shine when I got there."

Rainfinch nodded, smiling at the mental picture. "I know Ramona. Hispanic, an all-right guy. A few years back when I was in Projects, a drug bust turned into a real brawl. I was trying to hang onto a weasel so tripped out I couldn't faze him, it was like trying to corral a Terminator. Then this shadow loomed over me, I looked up, and there was your friend Ramona. Damned if he didn't wade in on my side. Found out later the weasel had been trying to date his girl."

Lindstrom nodded. "I personally wouldn't want to do anything that might irritate Ramona."

"But you didn't come here to exchange war stories." He glanced at the clock on his desk. "Good grief, it's almost two o'clock. You've been off duty for hours."

She flushed. "You've been busy, Lieutenant. I didn't think I should interrupt. But I wanted to tell you about the gun. It's an old .32 Owl Head. You know, the kind that breaks open at the top, and the barrel swivels forward? Duckett told me a few years back there were a lot of them floating around certain parts of town."

"Oh, yes. I got cracked over the head with an Owl Head, still have the scar to prove it. What makes this one special?"

"Estes is a sanitation worker who has delusions of grandeur. Calls himself 'Glitter Man' and insists he used to be a big shot in Miami. Anyway, he says the Owl Head was a gift from God. I asked him several times as nicely as I could to explain how and why God presented it to him, and he finally said it was lying in a pile of trash at the mouth of a storm sewer just a mile from the Seraphim—you remember, Lieutenant Rainfinch, I was first officer on the scene the night Hall was killed. Of course, Nubie Lee could be lying, but—"

"But the gun needs to be checked out." Rainfinch felt a surge of adrenaline. He stood. "Where is it now?"

"It went to ballistics this morning, sir."

"Good. You want to come along, or are you too tired?"

She followed eagerly. "Are you kidding?"

In the hall Rainfinch asked, "Does Jed Duckett know about this?"

Lindstrom managed to look demure. "I don't believe he made the connection, sir." She groaned. "That's not fair. He's coming down with a beaut of a cold, his nose and ears were so stopped up last night I don't think he heard half of what Estes said. He's a damn good training officer, even if he doesn't approve of women officers on the street."

Rainfinch nodded. "He is. Maybe you can help rearrange his prejudices."

Lindstrom snorted. "That'll be the day. I'm not holding my breath."

$\bigtriangledown$

24

"Listen, Duke. Fair is fair. If that harness was too tight you known durn well I'd buy you a new one. But I'm not wastin' money when all's wrong is you pullin' too hard and then puttin' on that pore-choked-kitty act."

Duke crouched and slashed his tail. Maude Mae squatted. "Look at me, you villain."

Duke stared at a spot above her head. His eyes dilated. He shrunk back on his haunches.

"Oh, that's an old trick, that is. Spider on the ceiling, my eye. I'm not gonna look."

She looked. Stood up, squinted, then pulled spectacles out of her shopping bag and looked again. "No spider! No nothing, you lyin' bag of fur. Now come along, I'm tired of your shilly-shallyin'."

Duke had a fine sense of timing. He could calculate the exact moment when Maude Mae's patience had been pushed to the limit. Now he yawned elaborately, stretched, and began an insolent strut toward the apartment door.

At the foot of the stairs Maude Mae stooped and ran her fingers across the lush new carpet in the entrance hall. She looked up at the sparkling chandelier. Dropping Duke's leash, she walked over and touched the fresh gold letters that decorated the mahogany entrance door into the firm offices.

"Ain't it all grand, Duke? Made the place into a palace, they have. Hoity-toity."

Duke didn't answer. He was doing some experimental scratching in a corner.

Maude Mae grabbed up the leash. "Cut that out. Don't even let it cross your mind, cat. You want to get us evicted?" Dragging the offended feline, Maude Mae opened the door and launched herself out onto the sidewalk without the loss of her purse or a single plastic or canvas shopping bag. The door banged shut behind her, and she stood to catch her breath. Her bright old eyes searched up and down the street like those of a magpie bent on adventure.

She didn't recognize the car at first. After all, she had only seen it from above and behind. But as it slid away from the curb in front of the building its sleek shape and darkened windows caught her attention. Then it braked to ease into traffic, and she saw that distinctive bright red band of light across its molded rear end.

For once, being old and farsighted wasn't a handicap. In the watery sunlight she could see that license tag clear as anything. YOY-889K. She jerked Duke back inside with a wrench that made him yowl and slammed the door behind her.

Sacks, bags, her purse, and Duke's leash fell to the floor, and she stood like an onion shucked of its outer layers. Snatching up the purse, she extracted a stubby pencil and a tiny spiral note pad. YOY-889K. There, she had it.

Duke, seizing the main chance, dashed to the nearest corner and lifted his tail. He exercised restraint. Just a discreet remarking of his territory, and no one the wiser.

In the excitement of discovery, it hadn't occurred to Maude Mae to be frightened. Now she felt a pang of apprehension, and remembered with guilt how she'd promised her and Duke's detective friend, April, that she'd have the phone reconnected. Well, she would, it just hadn't come handy yet. Trouble was, since the downstairs construction had been completed and that fancy permanent door installed, she couldn't get inside to use the lawyers' telephone. Unless— Leaving the bags on the floor, she gently tried the fancy knob on the law firm door.

It opened. She smiled with satisfaction.

* * *

April Morgen caught Rainfinch as he emerged from Ballistics, a worn but triumphant Joanne Lindstrom sailing along in his wake. He saw the momentary puzzled flicker in April's eyes as she took in Lindstrom, then ignored the patrol officer and held out a slip of paper.

"Abe, our old sweetheart just called."

"The indomitable Maude Mae?"

April glanced at Lindstrom again. She hesitated.

Rainfinch suppressed irritation. April was right to be careful, even in the office. He briefly introduced the women and explained Lindstrom had been first officer on the scene of the Hall killing. Joanne, picking up on April's hesitancy, acknowledged the introduction and turned reluctantly to Rainfinch.

"Guess I'm excess baggage, Lieutenant. Thanks for letting me tag along to Ballistics. I'll be off for a hot bath and bed." She walked away, head erect, shoulders self-consciously squared.

"What was that all about?" April asked.

"You first. What have you got there?"

She fell into step beside him. "Would you believe the license number of the killer's car?" Her tone was offhand; any detective knew that often what seemed like a major break in a case ended up leading down a mouse hole.

"Tell me about it."

April repeated Maude Mae's story. When she finished he asked, "Did she see the driver, and could the driver have realized she was watching?"

April shrugged. "She couldn't see inside the car at all, it had darkened windows. And even if she was spotted, who pays much attention to nosy old ladies? She swears she hasn't told a soul what she witnessed the night Hall got it."

"You believe her?"

April hesitated. "I don't have any reason not to. She's sharp. Surely she has sense enough not to put herself in danger by running off at the mouth. Still—"

"Still." Rainfinch had his own ideas about lonesome old ladies, their imaginations, and their ability to keep secrets, but he suspected April wouldn't welcome his views. "You know, she could want to help so badly that she saw a similar car, and jumped to conclusions."

April nodded. "Of course that's possible. In fact, I suppose it's probable."

"We'll hope for the best. Run a trace on it right away."

"Not so fast. It's your turn, Abe. Why did you and the rookie come out of Ballistics with canary feathers dripping from your mouths?"

Rainfinch allowed the exaltation to show in his voice. "A gun. Of all things, Archie Keyes was shot with an Owl Head. And we've got it."

"An *Owl Head*? That's an interesting angle—where did it come from?" April looked suspicious, as if he'd worked some sleight of hand while her back was turned.

"From the rookie. It always pays to be nice to rookies."

"Oh? And where did she—?"

"Can't explain now. I have to grab Lou, then we're off to the jail for some serious conversation with one Nubie Lee Estes, alias the Glitter Man, lately of Miami, Florida. Meanwhile, run that license number and see what you come up with. Then locate Danny Bent and get him back here. You'll probably have to page him, he's out circulating the photographs Lou and I found in Hall's passion pad. Tell him we'll all meet in my office—" he checked his watch—"a couple of hours from now."

April squeezed his arm. "Abe, we're closing in on him. I can smell it."

"Yeah. That's what the big-game hunter said just before the lion gobbled him up."

She made a face at him and started up the hall.

"April?"

She turned. "Yes."

"I like that outfit."

Her eyes widened in surprise. She looked down at the soft

gray challis dress, then said "Thank you" in a tentative voice before walking on.

Why did I have to say that? he wondered as he stuck his head in the homicide squad room to summon Lou. Why couldn't I leave well enough alone?

He knew why. The truth was, April would never be just another cop he worked with, or even a friend. Like Adam, he'd tasted the forbidden fruit.

Susan Elias and Calla Magee were going over lists of supporters to be honored with certificates naming them Admiral of the Inland Seas or Field Marshal of the Governor's Guard, or a proclamation stating that June the umpteenth was officially Joseph William Jefford III Day, when their secretary appeared at the door, bustling with importance.

"The governor wants to see you in his office immediately, Susan."

"Oh. All right. He sent for me? I'll be right there." Her best woman-in-charge-of-her-world voice disintegrated into that of a high-schooler who'd been summoned to the principal's office.

She looked at Calla. "I haven't forgotten a meeting, have I? No, of course I haven't." She gestured at the stack of honors certificates. "You know what to do with those. Carry on."

After a detour by the women's lounge to smear on lip gloss and wet her dry mouth with a fast cup of water, she walked quickly to the inner sanctum. Meg, the governor's harried secretary, looked up long enough to motion her in.

The governor was alone. That was rare. Usually when she came here Robert Friar was sprawled in his favorite chair.

Sanden smiled. "Sit down, Susan."

She did.

Big Max looked at her and sighed. He seemed tired and vulnerable.

"Is there something I can do for you, Governor?"

"Yes. Tell me what the hell's going on around here."

"I don't think I know what you mean, sir."

"Skip the sir and the governor crap, my ego doesn't need oiling at the moment. This is Max, talking to Susan." He lifted a hand and waggled it. "There are currents and eddies blowing around my staff. I can sense them, but I don't know the cause. I can't put my finger on anything, and it worries me."

"Well, of course—there's Carter. What happened to him."

"It started then. Or was that just when it became apparent? After that—until those other two poor devils were killed—you couldn't go to the head around here without falling over a half dozen media people. Then Robert insisted Brandon Guiste be sent packing, and that was another upheaval. To be frank with you, I never much liked Guiste. But he was a good worker."

Susan waited in silence. The governor seemed to be feeling his way.

Max Sanden picked up a Steuben glass bear that he used as a paperweight and examined it as if he'd never seen it before. Finally he set it aside and leaned forward with his elbows on the desk.

"We both know the people who work for me are hardened to media invasions. As for Carter and Brendon . . . it may sound callous, but they weren't the best-loved people around here." He shook his head and riveted her attention with the famous brilliant blue eyes. "I trust you, Susan; you're sharp and you're straightforward. Do we have a morale problem? Or is it something more than that?"

"I think I know what you're talking about," she answered carefully. "It's as if everyone's waiting for something else to happen. I feel it, but I don't understand myself."

He nodded, then picked up the bear again. "That's an honest answer. Okay, I won't keep you longer. If you think of something you feel I should know, come straight to me, will you? And don't mention this conversation to anyone else. Not anyone."

She stood. Not even Robert? This was something new. "Of course."

"And Susan, be careful."

Be careful? What a strange thing to say. She shivered. There was a draft in the corridor. Someone must have opened an outside window again, in spite of all the complaints from maintenance that open windows played havoc with the old building's heating system.

She hunched her shoulders and rubbed her arms. An open window. That must be it.

"Goddamnit, Abe," Lou said, "if you're gonna pace the floor, let's go where you can take five steps without hittin' the wall. You look like one o' those little rodents goin' round and round in a cage. You're makin' me dizzy."

Rainfinch laughed and sat down behind his desk. "Major Adamson told me the other day that this used to be a broom closet. I'm not sure he was kidding." He stood again. "Where the hell are Danny and April? I told her—"

"Told April what?" she asked, walking in with Danny Bent, who expertly juggled four cans of Coke. He passed them around. By the end of the day, the coffee in Homicide's big steel dispenser was so evil even the strongest stomachs quailed.

"Thanks, I needed that." Rainfinch popped the top and drank, relishing the cold liquid. He set the can down and took a deep breath.

"Okay. Maybe we're finally getting some breaks." In a few sentences he told about Nubie Lee Estes and the gun, leaving out the part where Nubie Lee insisted the Owl Head had been a gift from God. He turned to Lou. "Does that cover it?"

"Yeah. He's one scared little trash man. He'd been tryin' to sell the Owl Head inside the bar, to scrape up money for bus fare to Miami." Lou's face crinkled into what passed for a grin. "He never shoulda told us that. We contacted Miami PD, their narcotics people are real interested in talkin' to him about a few little matters."

Rainfinch nodded. "They're welcome to him. He's not our killer. His girlfriend's father is pastor at Bethel Avenue

A.M.E. They had a big tent revival going the night Solent and Keyes were killed. It lasted until after two in the morning. The reverend figured Nubie Lee had a lot of sins to repent, so he made sure his prospective son-in-law had a front-row seat and stayed in it."

"The reverend's a good man," Danny said. "We've worked together with youth groups. If he says the guy was there, he was."

"Yeah," Lou agreed. "Little guy didn't fit the profile, anyway. None of the victims were robbed, and he sure ain't a fag-basher."

"So that leaves us with his claim that he found the Owl Head in a pile of debris by a storm sewer grate. I think he's probably telling the truth. Patrol officers talked to the two men who worked the route with him yesterday, and they said he told them he'd had a sign from God. He was going back to Florida and be a big shot again, and he wasn't hauling anybody's damn trash anymore," Rainfinch summed up.

"I gather it's not registered," April said.

Lou grunted. "The Owl Head? You kiddin'? Owl Heads date back to the fifties or before. Gun registration wasn't real popular then."

"Interesting, isn't it? A gun like this is something of a rarity. Anyway, it's a dead end until we have a suspect. How about the car your old gal and her kitty spotted, Morgen?" As he asked the question, Rainfinch noted the brilliance of April's eyes. She was onto something.

She looked at Danny. "You want to tell, or shall I?"

"It's your deal. I was just along for the ride."

"Will you two wipe those possum leers off your faces and let us in on the secret?" Lou grumbled.

"The car's registered to one Kent Farraday, M.D. The address he gave was Central City Hospital, so Danny and I went there. He loosed the famous Bent animal magnetism on the lady in charge of personnel. Doctor Farraday is doing his internship at Central City." She turned to Danny. "You take it from here."

With a flourish, Danny laid two photographs on Rainfinch's desk. One was the best of the prints made from originals found in Carter Hall's passion pad. The other was a straight-on driver's license photo.

They were of the same person.

"Farraday," Rainfinch said. "Shadid Garber's law partner's name is Beth Farraday—do you suppose . . . ?"

"There's a connection?" April finished for him. "Damn betcha. He's her brother."

"She's listed in his personnel file as next of kin," Danny said.

Rainfinch gave him a sharp look. "Do the people at the hospital know why we're looking for him?"

"Of course not," April answered scornfully. "Give us some credit."

"Don't suppose he was hangin' around the hospital, all helpful like, waitin' to be picked up for questioning, was he?" Lou asked.

Danny snorted. "When has it ever been that easy, old man? I talked to his best buddy, a woman doc named Kover. They went through medical school together. She said he'd worked ER all through Christmas and New Year's and was taking a four-day weekend now to make up for it. She thinks he's out of town."

He grinned at April, who looked as wicked as her virginal coloring allowed. She was enjoying herself. Rainfinch knew the feeling.

"Morgen managed to give the impression there was a family emergency, without spelling anything out. Dr. Kover fell all over herself trying to help. She gave us Farraday's home address and phone number—he has an unlisted telephone, incidentally. She also suggested we contact his sister, Beth."

Rainfinch resisted an impulse to leap out of his chair and do something. Anything. Think first, then act. Damn, that was a hard rule to follow. He took a deep breath.

"Okay. Have you checked to see if he's at his apartment?"

"Yes, and no," Danny answered. "The car's not there. We didn't want to push it any further until we talked with you."

Rainfinch nodded. "Right. If he's out of town—did you ask Dr. Kover if she knew where he planned to go?"

"She didn't have any idea," April answered. "That was when she suggested we contact his sister. Incidentally, she mentioned that Beth Farraday gave her brother the jazzy car as a graduation present."

Rainfinch picked up the photographs. "Danny, has Monk seen these shots from Hall's place, yet?"

"Yeah. He looked hard, but finally said he couldn't recognize the guy. We showed him the other photos, too— the ones that weren't so clear. Nothing."

"So much for Hall's bedroom photography." Rainfinch gave Danny a sharp glance. "You think Monk could have been holding back?"

Danny shook his head. "I didn't get that impression. Just that he wanted badly to be able to point a finger at someone, but it was no use."

"Okay." Rainfinch picked up Farraday's driver's license photograph. "Take this out there right away—use standard photo ID procedure, since we have a suspect now. Multiple shots with similar subjects. After that, run them past Brendon Guiste. And Danny, if Monk should come up with a correct identification—tell him if he makes a move toward Farraday I'll kill him with my own hands."

He turned to April. "Get the word out to all mobile units. I want that car found, but not stopped. I want to know the minute someone spots it."

Lou, who had been uncharacteristically quiet, said, "I keep thinkin' about him bein' that gal lawyer's brother. Hell of a coincidence."

It was. The four detectives thought about it.

Finally Rainfinch said, "Shadid Garber owns the Seraphim building; Monk leases it from him. Beth Farraday seems to handle the business arrangements. If she and her brother are close, it's not surprising he'd have known about the place from the first, and frequented it. Maybe that's where he met Hall."

April nodded. "Makes sense."

"I don't guess we have enough on Farraday to get a search warrant for his apartment," Danny said.

"No," Rainfinch said. "A shaky ID on the car. The fact that he, along with a few hundred others, knew Hall and apparently had sex with him. It's not good enough. Let's see what else we can come up with, before we try that."

"We gonna talk to the sister? See if she knows where he is?" Lou asked.

"Absolutely not. If they're as close as it appears, she'd be more likely to warn him than help us. You have to remember, too, she's a criminal defense attorney."

"Yeah." Curran wore what passed for a scowl, but was actually his thoughtful look. "That breed o' cat's not famous for their helpful attitude toward cops. I wonder . . . think she knows little brother's light in the loafers?"

Rainfinch stood. The other three were on their feet instantly, as if connected to him by invisible wires.

"Lou, we need to find the major and report. Then we'll head for Farraday's apartment." He turned to Danny and April. "Let's get on with it. Stay in touch."

▽

25

Rᴀɪɴꜰɪɴᴄʜ ᴀᴡᴏᴋᴇ Sᴀᴛᴜʀᴅᴀʏ morning knowing that he'd dreamt about his mother. He couldn't remember the dream. Only a lingering mental image remained, of her hands, pale and motionless, folded in her lap.

It was dark outside. He lurched into the bathroom, brushed his teeth, and began to shave, refusing to acknowledge the fear that his sleeping mind had allowed to surface.

He'd been so relieved when Julianna called to say Julia was no longer critical, that she didn't want Abe to come. He'd scarcely thought of his mother and sister in the past twenty-four hours. Great support he'd been, in their time of need.

Well, he was a police officer. Which meant that at times he was no one's son, no one's brother, no one's lover. Good cops had the ability to shove everything—everyone—aside at times. To exist only in the chase. It was elemental, a drug to the senses, a deadly game with its own set of rules.

But you paid for it. And so did the people who loved you.

He stayed in the shower until the hot water ran cold.

Towel around his waist, he dialed Julianna's apartment, but was thwarted again by her answering machine. He hated the damned thing. It would be worth a trip to New York just to yank its support system and smash it.

He glanced at his own. Sure enough, its evil red eye was blinking. He reached for it with fingers clenched into claws.

No, better not.

It was six-forty-five by the big round clock on the detective bureau's wall when he walked through to his office. Danny

Bent, clear-eyed and immaculate, was already there, skimming computer printouts.

Rainfinch dropped sullenly into his own chair. "I don't suppose anyone found Dr. Farraday during the night?" A rhetorical question. If their prey had been spotted, Rainfinch's pager would have jumped off the bedside table with the news.

"No. He hasn't shown up at his apartment, nor has the car been located." Danny raised a quizzical eyebrow. "Are you still set against asking the sister if she knows where he is?"

Rainfinch thought it over. Finally he said, "Yes. Kent Farraday's her kid brother. From the information we have, she dotes on him."

Danny nodded. "And she's—"

"—a criminal defense attorney and Shadid Garber's partner. Maybe I'm making a mistake, but my gut feeling is still to keep her out of it."

"You're probably right." Danny held out the papers he'd been looking at when Rainfinch arrived. "Here's the schedule I worked up for surveillance on the Seraphim the next few days. You'll notice we have light coverage every night from 1800 to 2130. From then on it's the full show, inside and out, until everyone's gone home."

Rainfinch studied the plan. "Looks like you've got all bases covered. Danny, I want someone to watch Monk Smith at all times."

Bent gave him a sharp look. "Do you know something I don't?"

"No. Just a hunch. Monk's the catalyst in all of this, isn't he? No Monk, no Seraphim." He grinned. "I see you fished April's partner back in for tonight."

"Yeah. Mitchelson was a little leery of the deal, but I told him he shouldn't worry. Somehow I can't imagine even the most desperate old queen grabbing a feel of Mitch's bony tush."

"Guess not," Rainfinch agreed with regret. "But God, wouldn't I love to see that."

He thought of something else. "Last night, you called to say you'd shown Monk the driver's license photo of Kent Farraday, along with others. He picked it out and said it resembled someone he'd seen with Carter Hall. Then he said it might be Beth Farraday's brother, who's something of a regular at the bar. Is that how it went?"

Danny nodded. "Right, I didn't let him know he'd made a correct identification, just thanked him."

"How did Monk act?"

Danny shook his head in puzzlement. "Not like I expected, given the circumstances. I thought he'd come on like a raging bull—demand to know what we had on Farraday and threaten to get even for Archie Keyes's murder."

"And instead . . . ?"

"It was almost as if he didn't care. No, that's not exactly right. As if nothing matters to him anymore. He's a sleepwalker, Abe. Going through the motions. Oh, he did remember something ironic. The day Monk first looked over the building, with Shadid Garber and Beth Farraday, she told him she and her brother had attended church there when they were kids."

"That is intriguing. If Farraday's our man, it conjures up images of ritual sacrifice on the doorstep of his desecrated temple. Which reinforces my hunch Monk might be in danger."

Danny grunted. "Swell. Defense shrinks could have a field day with that."

"Did you ever locate Guiste?"

"Yeah, finally. He was pretty well sloshed, and belligerent. But Abe, he recognized the photo right away. He said Hall had busted up with Farraday several weeks ago."

"Oh? He say who broke off with whom?"

Danny nodded. "Hall ended it. Guiste said Carter Hall wasn't into sustained relationships. He always tired of his lovers quickly. According to Guiste our Doctor Farraday took the rejection pretty hard."

* * *

At four o'clock Saturday afternoon Monk Smith walked the twisted path from parsonage to church building. He unlocked the door into his office and entered.

He was alone. It was the first time he'd been inside the building since Archie's death. He flipped on the lights, passed through into the corridor, and then on to the shadowy interior of the club itself. He pulled out a chair at the house table and sat, heavily.

"Oh, Archie," he whispered. "We had such grand plans for this place. How did it come to this?"

There were things he should be doing. He tried to rouse himself, but it was no use. He heard Frannie come in. The bar lights went on. Music came from the speakers. He smiled bitterly, hearing Sondheim's "Send in the Clowns."

Footsteps crossed the dance floor; someone pulled out a chair and sat beside him. He didn't look, supposing it was Frannie.

"Monk," Melina Moriarty said, softly. "May I talk with you? Just me, no cameras, no microphones," she hastily qualified when he swung around and focused on her face.

He knew Melina. They were both active in a local musical theater group, as was Beth Farraday. In fact, Farraday and Moriarty took a good deal of kidding. The Irish twins, the Irish Mafia.

He tried a weak joke. "Sure. Where's your terrorist sister?"

"I haven't seen her in a while. That damn Garber keeps her nose to the grindstone, I guess."

"He does, but I've never heard her complain." He didn't want to talk of Beth anymore. Because that led to thoughts of her brother.

"I didn't come to talk about Beth." Melina unwittingly echoed his sentiment. She reached across the table and gripped his hand. "How are you, Monk?"

This gentle person was a different Melina than her public knew.

He shrugged. "It hurts like hell. Archie was . . ." He let the words drift.

Moriarty cut to the core of the pain. "It wasn't your fault. Some twisted weirdo—you couldn't have foreseen or prevented what happened."

Monk heard the noise level increase behind the bar, glasses rattling. He looked at Frannie, and a silent question and answer passed between them: *Do you want me to get her out of here?*

No, it's okay.

He turned back to Moriarty. "If we'd never opened this place—" He made a defeated gesture. "That's not all. Archie and I had been going through a rough patch. He'd been sick for so long. I was impatient and irritable."

"Those things happen in any relationship."

"I've been telling myself that. It doesn't help."

They sat in silence for a few minutes. Finally Monk said, "You know, someone told me once there was a medieval sect who believed the higher forms of angels, archangels and seraphim, fed on human flesh the same as people feed on cattle and sheep."

"That's a hell of a grisly idea."

"Yes."

Maude Mae and Duke stayed cooped up inside the apartment all day. It was cold and blustery outside, and Maude Mae's favorite college basketball team was playing in a televised tournament. In a weak moment, down at the Korner Koffee Shoppe where everyone in the neighborhood gathered to gossip, she had allowed herself to be baited into betting five dollars on her boys. As she explained to Duke, it had been one of those situations where you couldn't honorably refuse to put your money where your mouth was.

In the closing minutes of the game her team foiled a last-minute offensive barrage and won, 112 to 118. With cries of glee that Duke found quite excessive, she flipped off the set and bustled around, collecting hat, coat, overshoes,

Duke's harness and leash, and, horror of horrors, the sweater she had just finished knitting for him.

The most forceful expletives he could muster didn't deter her. "I made this for you, and you're gonna wear it."

Duke's head emerged from the neckhole. His ears were back and his eyes mere slits. Maude plunged her hand into one of the leg holes and brought forth a paw. One by one she extracted feet, until the indignant cat was engulfed in baby-blue yarn. His tail lashed with fury.

Maude Mae was oblivious. "I suppose we should wait till Monday, but by Jupiter, I want to see Homer eat crow right this minute."

She pulled Duke through the door and locked it. "I know you can't go inside, but we can tap on the window. He'll have to come out from behind that counter and face the music." Impatient with the cat's sullen balk, she swooped him up in her arms.

"We haven't got time for you to act like a durn fool. Homer goes off duty at six-thirty, and it's six-fifteen now."

When they stepped outside and the wind caught them, she almost changed her mind. But that, she figured, would be giving in to Duke. A body had to show that cat who was boss, now and then.

Halfway up the block a figure materialized out of the gathering dusk. She set Duke down on the sidewalk and clutched her purse against her body.

Duke stood tense, but as the figure came closer he relaxed and his tail came up in the universal cat greeting.

Maude Mae relaxed, too. She couldn't quite recognize the young man who stood before her, in the bad light and all, but since Duke vouched for him . . .

"Hello, Miss Haslip. It's an ugly evening for you and your kitty to be out. I wonder, could I impose on you? There's something I want to tell you, and I would really love a good hot cup of your mint tea."

Maude Mae squinted. She hated to tell the young man she didn't quite know who he was. "Well, I . . ."

Duke hated wind. He was hauling against the leash, determined to get back inside.

Maude Mae made up her mind. "Yes, come along, then. A nice hot cup of tea would be grand."

At six-forty-five Susan Elias knew she had to go back to the capitol and put in a few hours at her desk. She'd been there most of the day, and had counted on spending the evening at a wonderful, silly escapist movie with friends. After that they'd pig out on pizza and talk half the night. Heaven.

But Calla Magee called to say she was running a temperature of one hundred and two and had stomach cramps. Flu. It was decimating the governor's staff with such ferocity that some of the more flippant wags were calling it "Carter's revenge."

Monday there would be a spate of joint announcements of federal goodies, from the governor, the state's two U.S. senators, and seven congressmen. That way everyone got pats on the back for bringing home sugarplums. But the announcements had to be researched and written, and fact sheets prepared for Sanden on each project. Calla would ordinarily do all that, but chances were excellent Calla would be home in bed. Susan had promised to drive up and pay her parents a long-promised visit on Sunday. That left tonight.

"Don't worry about it, silly," she told Calla. "If you're sick, you're sick."

"That's such boring crap to write," Calla wailed.

"It won't be the first time I've written boring crap. Remember, I had your job not long ago."

"I'm letting you down."

"You are not letting me down. Have you talked to a doctor?"

"Yes."

"Need anything?"

"No."

"Okay. Take care of yourself. I'll check on you before I leave town in the morning."

She telephoned her friends and explained, then bundled up in jeans, boots, and her old blue sweater.

She didn't like going to the capitol at night. The damn marble floors echoed and whispered in the dim light. All outside exits were locked and secure, she reminded herself at she pulled up and stopped almost in the mouth of the west ground-floor entrance. She was ready to show her ID card to the guard who appeared at the door, but he knew her.

"Hi, Miss Elias. You just going up after something, or will you be here a while?"

"I'll be in my office three or four hours, Scott."

"Hell of a way to spend Saturday night."

Susan grinned. "I could say the same for you."

"At least I get to study on weekend duty. I take the bar exam next summer."

"That's swell. See you later." Scott was a good kid. Susan put aside the thought that he couldn't very well study and watch the TV sets that monitored hallways and entrances at the same time.

She had her own key to the massive plate-glass doors that blocked access to the governor's wing. The door relatched behind her.

Night-lights kept the place from total darkness. Susan stifled an urge to flip on all the switches as she progressed. Taxpayer's money, she reminded herself.

Inside her own lair Susan felt better. She made a foray into Calla's adjoining cubbyhole for research material and began to write.

Then she heard someone talking.

At first it seemed she must be imagining things, but after a few moments she recognized Robert's voice. He frequently came to the office at odd hours to take advantage of the WATS line.

She got up to let him know she was here. Maybe they could go for a bite to eat later. She felt a little guilty about the recent resentment she'd shown toward him. Opening the door to his office with a smile of anticipation, she was surprised to see he had someone with him.

"Oh, I'm sorry—"

Robert looked up. "Come in, love. Brendon and I are having a very interesting discussion. Since you're here you might as well join us."

Guiste turned to face her.

Then she saw the gun.

▽

26

Rainfinch tried to stifle an urge to look at the clock again. He lost. Not even eight yet. Ten minutes since the last time he'd checked.

He was in his office, catching up on overdue paperwork. He thought about Bill Tilghman, an early-day lawman who was his personal hero. He bet ol' Bill never had to while away hours reviewing and signing requisitions and studying incident reports.

He wanted to go to the Seraphim. It was too early, of course. He'd just be killing time, restless and antsy, like the rest of his troops. Surveillances were not about excitement, but boredom. If Farraday showed up, he wouldn't be apprehended. Only watched, at this point.

He threw in the towel after reading the same complicated request for new equipment four times without being able to decide whether to kick it on upstairs or send it back for clarification. Shoving it aside, he picked up his coat.

He was climbing into the Ford when Stamps grabbed his arm. He flung off the grasp and almost had the PIO on the ground before he realized who it was.

"What the hell's wrong with you, Cliff? You know better than to grab a cop like that."

He knew with a sinking feeling something was bad wrong when Stamps mouthed an agitated apology. "Rainfinch, you've got to come with me. Right now. Please."

Rainfinch threw open his car door. "Get in," he ordered. Stamps skittered to the passenger side.

"Where are we headed?" Rainfinch asked, squealing tires as they rounded the barriers of the garage labyrinth and emerged into the street.

"The capitol. For God's sake, *hurry.*"

Rainfinch wheeled around a corner, tires squealing again. He reached for the siren and light buttons under the dash. Unmarked units had red lights mounted inside the grill, in case of emergency.

Stamps grabbed his hand. *"No.* No siren."

"What the hell's going on, Cliff?"

"Robert Friar just phoned me. He was in his office. Said Brendon Guiste had come there, and started a fight with him. While we were talking Robert suddenly yelled, 'He's got a gun!' I heard a shot. A woman screamed, then the line went dead."

Rainfinch hit the main road and accelerated, weaving through light traffic. "Why did the stupid ass call *you,* instead of 911 or capitol security? Have you talked to Communications?"

"You don't understand these things, Rainfinch. Whatever happened, the governor's not going to thank us if this turns into another media event."

"Media event? What in the hell are you talking about, Cliffie? If Guiste's running around attacking people, do you think you can hush it up?" He grabbed his mike and pushed it into Stamps's hand. "Do it."

Stamps hesitated.

Rainfinch snatched the mike, gave his own identification number, and reported the incident. By this time they were only a few blocks from the capitol. He heard the call go out. Two units reported in, close by. He heard one siren, then another. Sending Stamps a look that dared him to interfere, he reached under the dash and flipped the switch. His siren joined the chorus.

His car and a black-and-white screeched up to the west basement door simultaneously. He could hear another approaching from the north. Rainfinch and the uniformed officer from the black-and-white arrived at the door together, weapons drawn.

Rainfinch yelled "Police Officers! Open up!" He knew the capitol security command post was in a room a few feet up the corridor. The officer on duty would be checking his TV monitor.

A scared-looking kid opened the door. His uniform shirt, hastily donned, was unbuttoned over a turtleneck sweater. He wasn't wearing a holster, but had grabbed his gun.

"What's wrong?" he demanded.

"Has anyone come out of here in the last few minutes?"

"No. What's—"

"Is this the only manned entrance?"

"Yes, sir. What's—"

"Could anyone get out another door without your knowledge?"

"Only someone with a key. Another officer. But I'd see them on my monitors. Except, tonight I've been studying—" he finished miserably.

"Do you have a key to the governor's wing?"

"Yes, but I'm not supposed to—"

"Get it and give it to me."

Rainfinch turned to Stamps, who was standing on his heels.

"Go back and tell communications to send any units responding to the west entrance, then stay here. Guiste is probably still inside. *Do it, Cliff!*" He took the key from the kid, then ordered, "Get yourself together and stand by." He turned to the uniformed officer. "Got your radio? Let's go."

Rainfinch led the way, running up two flights of stairs rather than waste time with the ancient elevators. The uniformed officer was a trim, well-built black man named Jed Harmony. Intelligent and quick-witted, Harmony listened as Rainfinch related what little he knew in bursts while they ran. In the background they could hear the faint wail of more sirens approaching, their noise muffled by thick stone walls. Harmony's radio crackled with voices.

The governor's wing stretched east from the main rotunda. Rainfinch had taken a west staircase. At the second floor landing he put out a hand to stop Harmony. They stood, panting and listening.

Rainfinch's thoughts were reeling. *Guiste.* Could he have been so mistaken? Henderson had given him an alibi for the night Hall was killed. And he drove a canary-yellow Cadillac, not a dark sports car.

Maybe he'd put too much faith in an old lady's eyesight and a lover's story? Could he have been so wrong?

Then it occurred to him. They had only Robert Friar's word that it was Guiste who had the gun. He remembered, too, that Cliff Stamps thought he'd heard a woman's scream. What woman?

The second floor was silent as the inside of a sound studio. Rainfinch and Harmony edged forward. They could see faint lights gleaming through the plate-glass doors into the governor's wing.

A patrol supervisor spoke through the radio, calling Harmony. Rainfinch took the radio and identified himself.

"How many men do you have?"

"Four of our officers. Two state troopers assigned to the governor have come across from the mansion—Stamps notified them before I got here. Sanden's on his way over, with his personal security man."

"Oh, swell. Ask the troopers to keep him the hell out of the way."

"They'll try," the supervisor said grimly.

"That kid on guard duty has a map of the building. As I recall there are three elevators in different locations, and God knows how many staircases. I want anybody who shows up down there searched and detained. *Anybody,* no matter who it is. Harmony and I are on our way into the governor's wing right now."

Rainfinch and Harmony sprinted the last few feet and flattened themselves on either side of the glass doors. In front of them the great open area of the rotunda curved to the north, fenced by a low railing.

"If he's in there, we're all right as long as we're on this side," Rainfinch whispered, tapping the glass. "These things are bulletproof."

Harmony nodded.

Rainfinch stuck the key in the lock and turned it. He couldn't see a damn thing inside. Slowly he pushed the door open, feeling like a gobbler at a turkey shoot.

"Don't be bashful. Come right on in."

Friar's voice. He'd know it anywhere.

"Be careful, Abe!"

Susan.

Motioning Harmony back, Rainfinch stepped through the door. As he did the overhead lights in the hallway came on, illuminating the place like a theater. At the end of the corridor, in front of the entrance to the formal reception area called the Blue Room, he could see Susan, Friar behind her. His left arm circled her waist, his right held a gun against her throat.

"Abe Rainfinch. I was hoping it would be you. Cliffie Stamps did good. Pity I won't have the chance to throw him a bone."

Rainfinch avoided looking into Susan's terrified eyes. He concentrated on Friar. "Let her go. You're a smart man, you know we won't let you out of here."

Friar laughed. He pushed Susan forward. "But of course not. Even if I could get away, where would I go? I've lost the game, but the losing will be on my own terms." He forced Susan to advance another few steps.

Rainfinch stood perfectly still, his gun aimed at the pair. Behind him he could hear voices and footsteps. "Keep everyone back," he told Harmony in a low aside.

"What are you going to do, Friar?"

"I think I'll kill this stupid bitch. You should thank me, Rainfinch. She's an absolute genius at causing trouble."

"Tell me about it."

"Gladly. I had it all planned. Here's how the story was to go. Guiste came here, started a fight. I dialed Cliffie. Guiste pulled a gun. We struggled, I got it away from him and shot him. Perfectly plausible. Then this stupid bitch walked into the middle of everything." He jammed the gun deeper into Susan's throat. She gagged.

Steady, Rainfinch warned himself. "Why did you want to kill Guiste?"

"The little toad was trying to blackmail me," Friar said jovially. "Can you imagine that?"

"How?"

"I don't mind telling you—he had photographs of Carter and me, partying with a senate page. Boy was sixteen, but I must say the little charmer was quite advanced for his age. Ah, you were hoping I killed Carter Hall, weren't you? Sorry, I had nothing to do with that. Hall was a shit, but whoever killed him started a wildfire. Or is it whomever?"

Rainfinch inched closer.

"Stop that. Be patient, I'm bringing her to you. Back up, or I may shoot her through the throat and let you watch her bleed to death."

Rainfinch inched backward, staring into Friar's eyes. What was he up to? Was he mad enough to think they'd let him get out of the building? "Get all the damn lights in this place on," he told Harmony without moving his lips.

"You'd kill Guiste for that? Couldn't you have worked something out with him?"

"I have killed him for that, haven't I?"

"Have you?" Rainfinch's back was against the glass doors. "Let her go and put down the gun, Friar. You're an influential man. You could get out of this deal with a couple of years in a psychiatric hospital."

Friar laughed. His hand came up and jerked back Susan's head. Rainfinch could see her flinch as the gun jabbed into the small of her back.

"Through the doors, Rainfinch, or maybe I'll gut-shoot her. Tell your friends to back off."

Rainfinch called instructions to Harmony and heard them relayed.

"What are you going to do, Friar?"

"You'll see. Just keep going."

Their movements took on the air of a formal procession. Through the doors. Into the hallway that circled the rotunda. Suddenly the area was flooded with light. Rainfinch blinked.

As if that were his cue—lights on, center stage, action—Friar flung Susan toward Rainfinch and sprinted for the vast open space where the rotunda rose from the first floor through to the fifth. He paused an instant to mount the low, ornate retaining wall.

Then, with a triumphant shout, he raised his arms and soared into space.

$\triangledown$

27

A<small>T</small> T<small>EN-FIFTEEN</small> R<small>AINFINCH</small> broke away from the mopping-up operation after what he had begun to think of rather callously as the Robert Friar Show.

There was a blur of rapid movement, curses, shocked faces ringing the rotunda barrier in that moment before training took over and ordered chaos began.

Susan in his arms, face distorted, body wrenched with sobs. He held her tight for a few wordless moments, but his cop's brain had moved ahead to the next problem. He released her and walked to the rotunda railing. Friar was spread-eagled on the blue tile star that was the center of the Great State Seal. Officers knelt beside him.

"Is he alive?" Rainfinch asked.

Jed Harmony looked up and shook his head. "Hit head-first and crushed his skull, Lieutenant."

Rainfinch turned back to Susan.

"It's over. You're safe, sweetheart. I need your help. Where's Guiste? Take us to him."

Her head flailing back and forth in passionate refusal. "No, no, I won't go back there. Brendon's dead. Robert shot Brendon. I can't go back there."

Forcing himself to be patient, gentle. "Just show us where he is, baby. You don't have to look. Hurry, please. He might not be dead. Maybe he needs our help."

Still sobbing, "No, no, his face is gone, he's dead, he's dead," she nevertheless clutched Rainfinch's arm and pulled him back into the governor's wing. He motioned a uniformed officer to follow.

She was right. Brendon Guiste had lost far more than the job he'd been so proud of.

Rainfinch gave over care of Susan to the young officer. The governor's wing and adjoining area where Friar had crossed to make his dive, and final stop below, were swiftly enclosed in a barrier of yellow tape by patrol officers. Not a minute too soon. Media people, who always monitored police frequencies, had begun to pour out of elevators and staircases like troops establishing a beachhead, armed with raucous questions.

He didn't see Moriarty. Apparently she did take the occasional day off.

When the horde spotted Cliff Stamps they ringed him, demanding information. Ordinarily Stamps, as public information officer, would have been in his element. Now he was ashen. He stammered and blinked. Rainfinch stayed well inside the yellow tape, safe from reporters. Stamps gave him such a look of pure misery that for once the sight of that wildly throbbing vein in the PIO's temple gave no joy at all.

Cliffie's friend, who had captivated with such sweet promises, was dead, his head cracked open on the gold-and-blue emblem that symbolized the power Friar worshipped. Painted, gilded walls surrounded him. The magnificent capitol dome soared above.

For the moment, Friar lay in state.

Rainfinch stayed until the tech people and the homicide team arrived. After briefing them he left the building, then paused to breathe deeply and savor the cold, wet sting of outside air that hit his face as he emerged from the lower level.

The governor's black limousine, parked at an angle, blocked Rainfinch's Ford. Max Sanden stood beside it, attended by two plainclothes troopers assigned to him as personal security men. Susan was with them.

Rainfinch knew one of the troopers, a tall, elegantly handsome man named Walker who always wore sunglasses. Walker held his radio against the side of his face. He listened, then relayed information to Sanden.

The few television reporters not upstairs harassing Cliff Stamps circled the governor, demanding information, a statement, a pound of flesh. Their trucks and cars were parked crazily along the drive, interspersed with police vehicles, like toys flung by some petulant child.

As Rainfinch watched, debating about how to extricate his cruiser, Susan broke down and began to sob. Someone had put a coat around her shoulders that was far too large. Her hair had curled into wet ringlets in the misty rain, making her look like a forlorn child.

Oblivious of his audience, Max Sanden enfolded her in a warm hug. Then, with great gentleness, he put her into the backseat of his limousine.

Media people closed in. An enterprising cameraman hunched over to try for a shot of Susan inside the car. Walker caught him by the scruff of the neck.

Sanden's voice rose above the clamor, angry but calm.

"Please, ladies and gentlemen. Something tragic has happened within my family—my staff. As soon as I have the facts straight, I'll talk to you. I'm going in now."

He spoke aside to the second trooper. "Take Susan to the mansion. Find out who her doctor is, and call him. I want her to stay there tonight. Tell the housekeeper. And I don't want her disturbed by anyone."

The governor, Walker by his side, entered the capitol. Reporters trailed behind like the tail of a comet. Rainfinch watched the limousine pull away, its tires crunching softly on wet pavement. Susan would be sustained and cared for, safe from intrusion.

In the sudden cessation of clamor, he retrieved his cruiser.

He began to think about Max Sanden and Susan. The governor was unmarried. He was also intelligent, powerful, and with all that, a nice guy. After tonight Rainfinch wondered if Sanden and Susan Elias could go back to being boss and employee. Or had crisis destroyed some barrier, forcing them into intimacy that would make them lovers or strangers, but never the same as before?

En route to the Seraphim, he monitored the safe frequency in use during the surveillance, so he knew Kent Farraday hadn't shown.

He opted not to pull into the parking lot, since he was driving an unmarked, but not unrecognizable, police vehicle. He found a spot on a side street and walked to the club. Since he'd originally planned to spend the evening there, he was dressed accordingly in soft, old jeans, a yellow shirt, and a navy blazer. His clothes were rumpled, but not unduly so for this time of night.

Just inside the door, he saw April's partner Mitchelson and a longhaired guy from Projects, apparently engrossed in conversation. He knew they were aware of him, but didn't make eye contact.

Rainfinch walked to one of the twin bars, where Monk stood talking to a small knot of customers. Monk saw him and nodded. Frannie Da Sorta paced restlessly behind the bar. His eyes, barely visible behind scar tissue, were wary.

Rainfinch ordered a soft drink and took it to a spot where, his back against the wall, he could watch the door, the dance floor, and Monk. Bodies clung and moved with the music, which was loud but corny and nostalgic—what was the singer's name? The one with the big nose who'd gotten his start writing advertising jingles.

April materialized beside him. She looked pointedly at her watch. "Have a hot date?"

"I suppose you could say that."

Time passed. The ice in his drink melted. His people moved, talked, came together, and parted. April drifted away, came back, drifted away again. Rainfinch stayed against his wall, watching.

The man at the sound console put on an album of music from *Camelot*. Someone sang the sweet, haunting "If Ever I Should Leave You." He looked at April.

She elbowed him in the ribs and made a subtle movement

that directed his attention toward the door. Kent Farraday had entered, arm in arm with a clever-faced older man. April was wearing a wire, but she hadn't been alerted by the troops in the parking lot. So their mark must have arrived in the other man's car.

The crowd had thinned. Farraday's friend selected a table by the dance floor. They took off their coats. Drinks were ordered. Then the older man clasped Farraday's hand and led him onto the dance floor. Rainfinch saw his UC people subtly move to surround the couple.

Rainfinch danced with April. She smelled good. Hell, she felt good.

Two dances. Three. Once he thought he saw Melina Moriarty at the bar with a group of women in airline uniforms, but decided he must be mistaken. It was late, near the one o'clock closing. Farraday seemed to be enjoying himself, absorbed in his friend. Murmuring, laughing.

"Anybody recognize the other guy?" Rainfinch asked April.

She shook her head. "If our boy's up to no good, he's a damn fine actor."

Something didn't feel right. Rainfinch released April with a squeeze of her arm and left the dance floor. He started toward Monk, who now stood alone.

Monk leaned across the bar and spoke to Frannie. Simultaneously, Rainfinch saw a drunk loose his footing and lurch against Monk's back.

Rainfinch shouted and leapt forward. He was too late. Monk cried out and clutched his side. The drunk, suddenly nimble, sprang back. He was holding a knife.

Rainfinch grabbed him and wrenched the knife hand behind his back. The assailant was thin but wiry. He struggled with the strength of passionate purpose, writhing and twisting. In this age, permeated by the constant threat of AIDS, Rainfinch did not intend to be bitten. He reached up, grabbed a handful of blond hair, and jerked.

The hair came away in his hands. Beneath it, coiled around the head like a snake, lay a fat, dark braid.

Other cops joined in, subdued the flailing figure. Rain-finch was dimly aware of white faces around them. Suddenly he heard an anguished howl. Kent Farraday pulled furiously away from restraining hands. He knelt beside the captive.

"Beth! Oh God, Beth," he sobbed.

"It's been one of those nights my ol' granny woulda called a toad-stompin' side-slappin' jubilee," Curran said.

He and Danny were huddled over a table in Patrol's break room. They had it mostly to themselves, since it was four o'clock in the morning.

"We should have suspected Beth Farraday all along," Danny said. "Instead we zeroed in on her brother and let her blindside us."

Lou grunted. "Blindside Monk Smith, you mean. As for suspectin' her—women don't do that kinda killin'. Except when they do."

"Abe talked to Frannie Da Sorta at the hospital. Monk's going to be all right. The knife glanced off a rib and was deflected upward. It didn't hit any vital organs. They'll keep him in the hospital twenty-four hours for observation, though." Danny walked to the bank of brightly lit food and drink dispensing machines, put money in a slot, and retrieved a bag of potato chips.

"He has Abe to thank he didn't get punctured good and final. Everyone else was concentratin' on the doc. Course, if I'd been inside, instead o' freezing my ass in the parking lot—"

"Yeah, yeah, old man. Too bad it didn't freeze some of the vinegar out of you."

"Vinegar don't freeze. Abe and Morgen know we're up here?" Lou helped himself to Danny's potato chips. "I'd sure love to hear what that Farraday gal had to say. If anything."

"Yeah. Shadid Garber sure showed up fast, didn't he?"

"Doc Farraday called him," Danny answered. "I don't think Abe would have let her talk without representation, anyway, considering who we're dealing with. Give Garber the slightest technicality to hang his hat on, and we wouldn't have a prayer in court—" He broke off at the sound of voices. "Here they are."

Rainfinch felt weary and sad. At the same time he was exhilarated, relieved, so driven by adrenaline that it seemed he would never be able to unwind. Entering the break room behind April, he pulled up a chair, sat backward on it, and snagged the last of Danny's potato chips.

"She say anything at all?" Lou asked.

Rainfinch nodded. "The whole nine yards. Shadid couldn't shut her up."

April brought cans of orange juice to the table, gave one to Rainfinch, and sat. "He'll go for an insanity plea. After he tried every trick in his bag and still couldn't keep her from talking, Garber requested we video the confession. She went on and on. It was the most utterly pathetic thing—"

"What did she say?" Danny asked.

Rainfinch began the story. "Let's see—okay, to begin with, at the time Carter Hall broke off with her brother, Kent was living with Beth. The doc was pretty upset and admitted to his sister for the first time that he was homosexual."

"She took that pretty hard?" Lou asked.

Rainfinch nodded. "She'd practically raised Kent. Their parents were killed in a car wreck when he was a kid. She put him through medical school. She sacrificed a lot, and in return, her brother had to be perfect."

"But he wasn't," Danny said. "Wonder why she didn't take it out on him?"

"She adored him," April explained. "I guess her brain went on overload, she became irrational. It seemed to her that if she could eliminate Carter Hall, it would somehow erase the whole incident. Her brother would be perfect and whole again."

"Kent had moved into his own apartment by then," Rainfinch said. "He told her in no uncertain terms that being homosexual wasn't something you turned on and off like a faucet. Of course, he had no idea she'd carved up his ex-lover."

"She bought him the fancy car as a graduation present. The night she lured Hall into the alley and worked him over, she had Kent's car because she'd borrowed it. Hers was in the shop."

"She's had it all this time?" Danny asked sharply.

"It's still parked in the underground garage behind her condo. She got her car back yesterday morning, but Kent hadn't picked his up yet. He's been staying with the guy who brought him to the Seraphim."

Danny had more questions. "Okay, she got away with slicing up Hall, or appeared to have. Why'd she go back the night she killed Solent and Keyes—I assume she'd been impersonating a gay male?"

"Sure. Otherwise she'd never have been able to lure Hall or Solent outside. She'd gone back to get Monk—I had a hunch about that, and I was right. But once inside she heard Solent popping off. The poor old fool was drunk. She lured him in the bushes and really did a job on him."

"Then we were right about Keyes?" Lou asked.

Rainfinch drained the last of his orange juice. Without asking, April got him another from the machine. He thanked her and pulled the tab off the top.

"Yes, we were right about Keyes. He was carrying out trash, and stumbled onto the killing. So she shot him."

"What about that ol' Owl Head?" Lou asked. "She say where she got that?"

"Shadid had given it to her. It's a neat old gun, you know, a curiosity. I'm sure he'd picked it up from one of his clients."

"Why did she knife Monk inside the club, with everyone watching? Why didn't she wait, and try to ambush him?" Danny wanted to know.

April took the question. "She sensed we were closing in on her. She wanted Monk, bad. All her hatred focused on him—he was the one who turned her former church, her place of refuge, into a gay bar. In her mind, Monk had corrupted her brother. So he had to die."

Danny wadded up the potato chip sack and sailed it into a trash can. "I think it's a sad thing," he said angrily, as if he expected the others to disagree with him. "We see so many bad guys that are pure mean. A woman like that— she's worked so hard, and everything turned to shit."

"You still can't go killin' off the people who make you mad," Lou reminded him.

"I know, but—"

"If I were a betting man," Rainfinch said, "I'd lay money she'll wind up in a mental hospital for a few years, then they'll turn her loose. With a bulldog like Garber in her corner she'll get a fair shake, and more."

April poked Rainfinch in the chest with a trim, manicured fingernail. "Enough about Beth Farraday. We want to know what the hell happened out at the capitol. I heard two people are dead, and the governor's involved, and your friend Susan Elias."

"God, that seems like days ago." He drained his second drink can. "Okay, I'll give you the straight story, but you have to prime me with another orange juice."

"Done." April fed the machine again and returned with Rainfinch's liquid bribe. He told them about Friar and Guiste.

"Whew," Lou exclaimed. "Life among the rich and famous. Ain't that a lick?"

"What incredible coincidence, all these things happening the same night." Danny shook his head in disbelief.

"Yes, and no," Rainfinch qualified. "I'm no psychiatrist, but from the day I met Robert Friar I had a guy feeling there was something screwy—something not right about him. Still, I didn't see him responsible for what happened to Carter Hall. He was in Washington, D.C. It was impossible for him to come home, kill Hall, and get back to his hotel by the time our Cliffie called him. I know, because I checked. He could have hired a hit man—maybe. But in that case he certainly wouldn't have wanted it done in a way that could ruin his golden goose."

"That's true," April agreed.

"Hall's death, and the way it happened, set wheels in motion that eventually brought Friar down. His first mistake was firing Brendon Guiste, who apparently had the goods on him about a liaison with an underage senate page. So he decided to kill Guiste. Might have pulled that off, too, if Elias didn't burst in on them."

"Kinda scary, ain't it, to think he was top hand to a man who might be president some day," Lou commented.

"I like to think he would have slipped up, sooner or later. But he was a damn bright man. It's possible he might have gone for years without anyone catching on to him, if he hadn't been caught up in the prop wash of Hall's death."

April produced a prodigious yawn. "I'm out of this place. I'm going to sleep straight through until Monday morning."

Danny and Lou agreed that was an excellent idea, and left with her.

Rainfinch was still restless. He decided to go by the hospital and look in on Monk.

Emergency medics had rushed Monk Smith to the ER at Central City Hospital. A logical choice, since it was close to the Seraphim. But as Rainfinch parked in one of the spaces reserved for police vehicles, he thought about the irony. At least Kent Farraday had been off duty, and hadn't been presented with the task of patching up his sister's victim.

Rainfinch identified himself and showed his badge to a woman in admitting. She didn't have the paperwork yet, but after a couple of phone calls she told him Monk was in a private room, seventh floor east.

On seven he checked in with the floor nurse, a fiftyish brunette with a kind, tired face.

"Rough night?"

"Bad enough. We're always understaffed. When I was a child all little girls wanted to grow up and be nurses. Now they want to be doctors. Or nuclear physicists, or astronauts. But the world still needs nurses."

Rainfinch tried to think of something encouraging to say. "Well, it's five-thirty. You'll be off duty in an hour and a half, then it'll be someone else's problem."

She smiled. "Scant comfort, but I appreciate the effort. Your Mr. Smith is in 738."

In 738 the lights were dim. Monk lay with his head slightly elevated. Frannie Da Sorta sat by his right hand, looking belligerent and uncomfortable. There was a woman seated on the other side of the bed. She looked up.

Moriarty.

"What are you doing here?" Rainfinch asked angrily. "Where's your camera man, hiding in the bathroom?"

"Cheap shot, Abe. I do have a personal life. Monk's a friend."

"Sorry. I didn't realize you knew each other."

Her eyes softened. She moved to a chair farther from the bed, and gestured to the one she had vacated. "Sit. I'll overlook the nasty crack, you're just tired and cranky."

Rainfinch smiled ruefully. "You make me sound like a small boy with an indulgent mother."

"You come here to fight with Melina or visit me?" Monk asked.

Rainfinch sat, and looked at him. The big man seemed to have shrunk. His face was lined and flaccid. Only his eyes seemed alive. Rainfinch thought he saw a tiny spark of humor there, and he took comfort in that.

"It shouldn't have happened, Monk. I meant to stay close, watch you every minute. But when Doc Farraday came in I got sidetracked, like everyone else."

"It's my fault," Frannie burst in passionately. I shoulda—"

"Will you both please shut up?" Monk asked. "It's no one's fault. Not even Beth's, God help her."

"That's certainly charitable of you," Rainfinch said.

"Not really. I'm not a martyr, I don't like being stabbed any better than the next guy. But I'm going to live. And I can't help thinking how hurt and desperate Beth must have been, to spin out of control like that."

Rainfinch glanced across the bed at Frannie. He could tell by the old prizefighter's face that he didn't share Monk's attitude toward Beth Farraday.

"I hope they lock her up and lose the key," he gritted.

Monk looked concerned. "That's not likely, is it, Abe?"

"Probably not, with Shadid Garber defending her." Rainfinch hesitated, then continued gently, "You do realize she killed Archie, as well as Hall and Solent."

Monk's mouth pulled out of shape momentarily as he worked for control. "I assumed it must be so, Abe."

It was time for a change of subject. "What are you going to do when you get out of here, Monk?"

"My kind neighbors in the historical preservation society will be delighted to know the Seraphim will never reopen. Aside from that . . . I really don't know. But I'm like an alley cat, I'll land on my feet."

"I wasn't going to mention this, yet—but hell, why not," Moriarty broke in. "Our musical theater group—that's where Monk and Beth and I met, Abe—is doing so well, they're thinking about hiring a professional director. If Monk wants the job, I bet it would be his."

Rainfinch burst out laughing. "Or you'll crucify the board of directors with some well-aimed TV interviews?"

Moriarty looked at him, clear-eyed and guileless. "I would never do such a thing," she said.

Maude Mae Haslip sat up in bed with a sigh and switched on her beside lamp. It was three in the morning. She looked at Duke, a puddle of yellow sunk into the flowered down comforter. He had rolled away from the light and burrowed his head, without a moment's break in his snore. Maude Mae watched him in envy. She longed for a cup of tea, but knew the caffeine would destroy any chance of sleep.

And thinking of tea, she remembered the young man who had invited himself up the evening before, and then, as Maude Mae struggled with Duke and the new key to her building's entrance, simply vanished.

As she'd peered up and down the street, grousing under
her breath about the manners of the young, that fat turd of
a lawyer who was Beth Farraday's partner had stepped out
of his Lincoln Continental and told her if she couldn't
unlock the door to get out of the way and let him do it. After
they got inside he'd made it clear that she and Duke needn't
expect to use the law firm's telephone anymore, either.
Durned old cheapskate.

Well, she'd get round him. All she had to do was latch on
to Beth Farraday and tell her what the problem was. Maude
Mae saw clear enough that the girl was the one who ran
things. She could bend the old buzzard like a pretzel, when
she wanted to.

And thinking of Beth Farraday, it dawned on her why the
rude young man had seemed familiar. He had the look of the
girl lawyer about him.

"Bet's he's a relative," she said to Duke, who continued
to snore obliviously. "We'll ask her if she has a brother, cat,
next time we see her."

Dawn was breaking when Rainfinch finally made it home.
Or it would have been, if the eastern horizon hadn't been
blanketed by a businesslike bank of storm clouds.

Sitting on the edge of his bed to pull off shoes and socks, he
thought he'd talk to Major Adamson on Monday and request
a two-week leave, then make airline reservations. He had some
fences to mend with a couple of women in New York City.

And after that, when he got back . . . a boyhood dream
had surfaced and been weaving in and out of his conscious
mind for some time now. Lieutenant Abe Rainfinch intended to take flying lessons. And one day, not too far off,
he'd buy an interest in the neat little Cessna 152 that
belonged to a friend of his, an OSBI agent.

Holding the two thoughts—a visit with Julia and Julianna
and the small brown-and-white airplane—like talismans, he
sat in his unlit room and watched the storm clouds gather.